ARCANE TRANSPORTER

BLIND SPOT

JAMI GRAY

Cover Art: Deranged Doctor Design, www.derangeddoctordesign.com
Publisher: Celtic Moon Press First edition, 2023
ISBN: 978-1-948884-71-6 (ebook) ISBN: 978-1-948884-72-3 (print)

SIGN UP FOR FREE READS FROM JAMI!

Join Jami's newsletter to be the first to hear about new releases, free books, special prices and other nifty events.

Sign up at: https://www.subscribepage.com/jami-gray-books

WHAT READERS SAY...

About Arcane Transporter:
"Taking a refreshing approach to fantasy magic, this fast-paced, economical thriller is told from a highly likable perspective." —Red Adept Editing

About PSY-IV Teams:
"This story is an emotional roller coaster, from betrayal, anger, fear, love..." —InD'tale Magazine

About the Kyn Kronicles:
"...a fantastic paranormal action novel is quite possibly the best book I've read this year. I could not put it down, and had to exercise serious self-control to keep from staying up all night to finish it." —The Romance Reviews

About Fate's Vultures:
"...if you like your characters with a bit more bite, with secrets, with hidden agendas, and all those sorts of things, and your worlds are a far more deadlier place, then this is for you." —Archaeolibrarian

ALSO BY JAMI GRAY

ARCANE WONDERLAND

Last Call

Bitter Spirits

Rune & Tonic

ARCANE TRANSPORTER

Ignition Point (*Prequel Novella*)

Grave Cargo

Risky Goods

Lethal Contents

Collision Course

Blind Spot

Terminal Drift

THE KYN KRONICLES

Shadow's Edge

Shadow's Soul

Shadow's Moon

Shadow's Curse

Shadow's Dream

Shadow's Fall

Tangled in Shadows (*Short Story Collection*)

FATE'S VULTURES

Lying in Ruins

Beg for Mercy

Caught in the Aftermath

Fear the Reaper

PSY-IV TEAMS

Hunted by the Past

Touched by Fate

Marked by Obsession

Fractured by Deceit

Linked by Deception

BOX SETS

PSY-IV Teams Box Set I (Books 1-3)

The Collapse: Fate's Vultures (Books 1-4)

The Kyn Kronicles Box Set (Books 1-6)

Arcane Transporter Box Set I (Books 1-3)

Arcane Transporter Box Set II (Books 4-6)

ACKNOWLEDGMENTS

This series has been such a fun ride and I couldn't do it without you my dear readers. So thank you for coming back for another round with Rory and Zev.

My endless love and gratitude to my Knight and Knights-in-Training - Ben, Ian, and Brendan.

Special shout out to my besties - Ang, Diane, and Camille - for being living examples of kick-ass women no matter what speed bumps you hit.

Hugs to all!

Jami

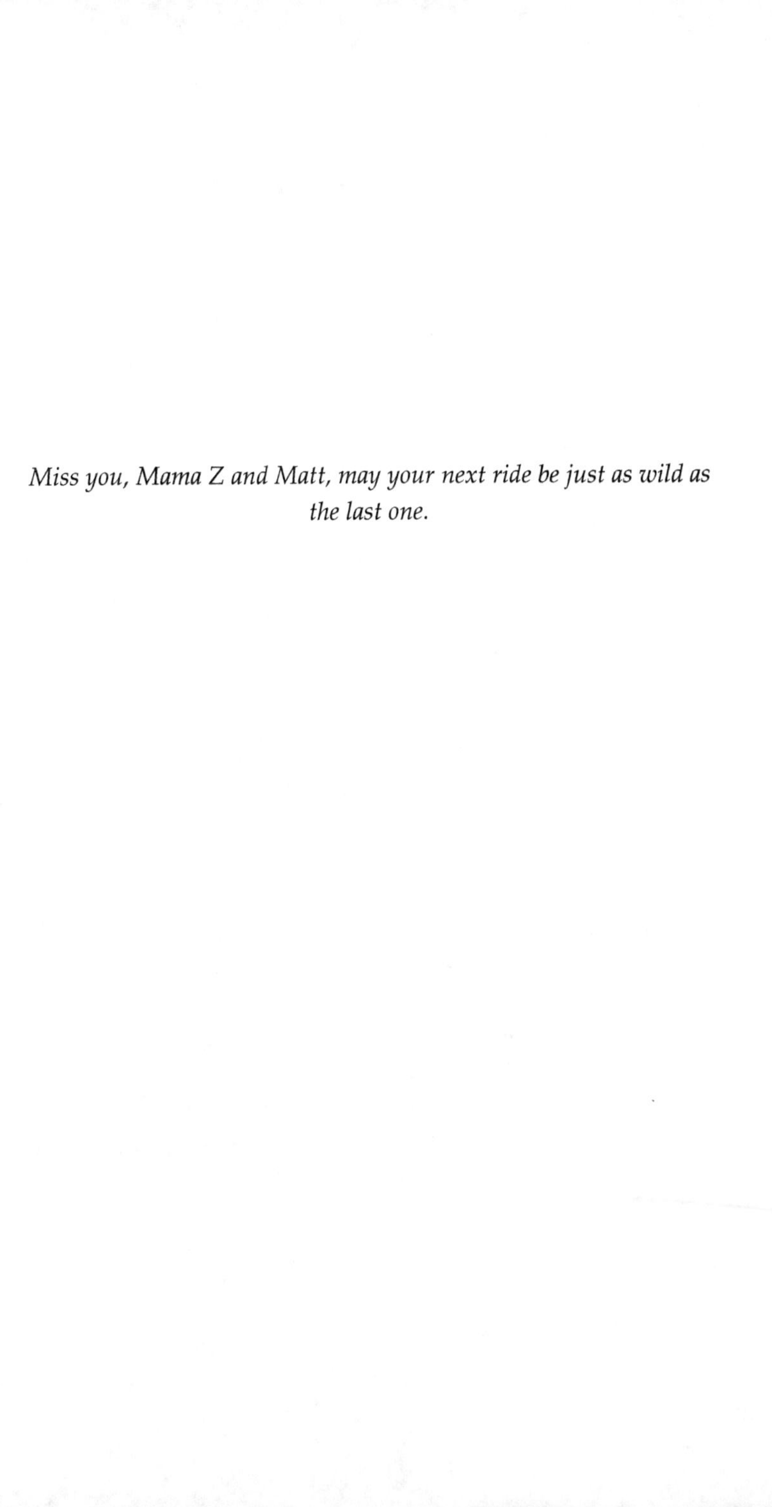

Miss you, Mama Z and Matt, may your next ride be just as wild as the last one.

ONE

A PLAYFUL BREEZE twirled through a cloudless blue sky, tumbled over the immaculate green grass, and ruffled the collection of black skirts and dress slacks before drifting away to leave another crisp November afternoon in its wake. Unfortunately, it couldn't ease the pall of grief that blanketed those gathered around the private family plot situated in the middle of the memorial gardens and surrounded by a thick hedge, a nod to the illusion of privacy. The somber priest's attempt to provide comfort to the mourners was accompanied by sporadic soft trills and chirps from winged watchers who hid among the orange and yellow leaves that still clung to the branches of the nearby trees.

But comfort was nowhere to be found. Not for those gathered to pay their last respects to Maximiliano Vasquez, scion of a beloved Arcane Family, and definitely not for the tall, raven-haired woman sitting painfully still. One hand was fisted in her lap. The other was held in a white-knuckled grip of a gray-haired, haggard-faced man who cradled a smaller, sobbing woman to his side. Christina Velasquez, Arcane Council member, watched from behind her oversized sunglasses as her beloved nephew's casket was slowly lowered, her face an emotionless mask. For those who didn't know her, the mask could easily be believed to be hiding the same grief riding Max's parents.

But I knew the councilwoman, and it wasn't grief hiding under that thin façade but an ice-cold anger. Hiding behind my own dark lenses, I studied the crowd from my spot off to the side and noticed echoes of that same emotion lingering in a few other faces as well. My gaze drifted over my great-aunt Sabella's carefully composed features and tight shoulders, only to land on the dark-haired man at her side. Sunlight glinted off another set of dark lenses, but his were unable to disguise his intimidating glower, which added an arrogant edge to his aristocratic face. Of course, Emilio Cordova had reasons for that arrogance, as did my great-aunt. Both were the heads of their respective Families and staunch supporters of Councilwoman Velasquez, personally and politically.

As for me, I wasn't there as one of Max's closest and dearest or Christina's lackey. I was there as Sabella's driver and doing my best to remain as unobtrusive as possible. If I could have gotten away with it, I would have waited for her at the car, but she'd insisted I accompany her to the graveside. I only gave in once she promised not to make me sit next to her.

My reticence had nothing to do with attending a funeral of someone I barely knew. Saying goodbye could take many forms, and if this was how Max's loved ones found their peace, more power to them. My reluctance stemmed from what would be construed by the other attendees if I took a seat next to the notorious matriarch who led one of the original, inherently powerful Arcane Families. The last thing I wanted anyone thinking was that I intended to walk in Sabella's gilded footsteps.

Thanks, but no.

Even if DNA was a harsh bitch to dodge, I had my own path to forge. Granted, it was still more of an unpaved access road, but given time and deep-seated stubbornness, I would make sure it was *my* legacy that filled me with pride. Not a birthright that was colored by fear and fawning sycophants.

That didn't lessen the curious glances sent my way every time I stepped out with her. Like right now. The weight of them was an itch against my skin, but thanks to recent practice, instead of scratching at the invisible judgment, I let my attention drift over the collection of Max's friends and family then beyond the questionable privacy offered by the hedge border.

Located in an older neighborhood of Phoenix, the memorial gardens had offered space for community members until the population outpaced the available plots. Now, the only way to claim a spot here was if your family had planned decades in advance, and Max's family had called the valley home for a very long time. That didn't mean the somber gardens didn't get their fair share of visitors, but gatherings like this were a one-off.

In fact, I clocked a couple sitting quietly on a bench near a gurgling fountain that was surrounded by an artful combination of flowers, rocks, and urn-filled niches. Beyond them, off among the rows of flat headstones, another person knelt and set aside a fresh bouquet of bright flowers before carefully removing the dried-out blooms.

Off to the side, another semiprivate garden housed a miniature mausoleum. A shadow detached from the narrow doorway. After a heartbeat, then two, the figure resolved into a man. A shiver rippled down my spine, and I had no idea why. Nothing about him should have triggered such unease. He was too far away to make out much other than that he was of average height and build, and his hair was covered by a hat that shadowed his face.

Our gazes seemed to connect, and my breath caught for a long indeterminable moment. Only when he turned and strolled away did I remember to exhale. I watched him walk away, his shoulders straight, his head up, and his hands in his pockets, as he disappeared behind a hedged wall.

Chills peppered my arms. *Who the hell was that?*

I nearly jumped out of my skin when fingers curled around my arm.

"Rory, are you okay?" Sabella's question was quiet, in keeping with our surroundings.

I blinked and looked around to see that the mourners were slowly leaving the graveside. I managed a small smile as I covered her fingers with mine and gave them a comforting squeeze. "I'm good."

Sabella was no one's fool. Her sharp hazel eyes narrowed as she turned toward where the mysterious man had disappeared and stared for a long moment before turning back to me. "Who was that?"

My shoulders rose and fell, shrugging off my disquiet and her question. "I don't know. Someone visiting a family member, I'm guessing."

A frown tugged the edges of her mouth down, but before she could ask anything more, we were interrupted.

"Sabella, are you heading over to the Vasquezes'?" asked the dark-haired woman who was using Emilio's arm to maintain her balance as she navigated the grass with her thin-spiked heels.

I wasn't sure she really needed Emilio's help since I couldn't remember ever seeing Maribel Ortiz wear shoes with heels shorter than three inches.

"Yes," Sabella answered then waited until the couple came to a stop at our side. I must have sighed, because she flicked me an amused glance and patted my arm. "Don't worry. I won't stay long."

"Stay as long as you want," I said. "I can wait for you at the car."

"Actually, you can't." There was a gentle snap to her response, though not enough to stop me from opening my mouth to argue that as her driver, my place was behind the wheel, not mingling with people I didn't know. Before I could start, though, she cut me off. "Your presence was specifically requested, Rory."

Hmm, that didn't sound ominous at all. "By?"

"Mateo and Olivia."

Ugh. More council members meant there was no polite route for refusal. I set my teeth. "Fine, I'll go in with you."

Now that she had gotten her way, Sabella was all gracious smiles. "Good." She turned back to Emilio and Mari, who were watching our exchange with ill-concealed amusement. "Will you two be there as well?"

Emilio inclined his dark head. "Yes, but like you, we weren't planning on staying long."

"I bet Locke gets to stay with the car," I muttered under my breath, earning a poorly disguised chuckle from Locke, who stood behind Emilio, and a frown from Sabella.

Emilio shook his head but continued as if I hadn't commented. "Unfortunately, we have a dinner engagement we were unable to reschedule." Whatever he saw on Sabella's face had him quickly adding, "A business dinner, Sabella."

"That's one way to phrase it," Mari drawled. "I'd call it a bloodless come-to-Jesus conversation with over-priced chicken and asparagus."

I raised an eyebrow in silent query to the curvy lawyer.

"Emilio might have to play nice, but since my only concern is the Cordova Family's interests, I don't have to," she explained.

Ahh, that explained the anticipatory glint in her dark eyes. "Who are you taking a bite out of now, Mari?"

She shot me a grin that flashed white teeth. "Salient Tech out of California, and it's not that big a bite, just a nip or two to remind them why they want to keep their fingers out of Emilio's pies."

A nip or two would mean they would leave the table with

bloodied nubs. I didn't envy anyone who went up against Mari. She might look cute and cuddly, but she was all shark when it came to her clients. That was why she earned big bucks from Emilio and was worth every hard-earned penny I gave her.

"I'm sure Emilio's pies will be in good hands." Heat hit my cheeks as I realized how that sounded. I didn't need Locke's amused snort to reinforce my embarrassment. I shot him a narrow-eyed look before apologizing to Emilio. "Sorry."

His lips quirked. "I have to agree—my pies are quite safe in Mari's hands."

Gods save me from male amusement. Speaking of which... "Have you heard from Zev today?"

Emilio's attention sharpened. "Not today, but when we spoke yesterday, he indicated he might be out of pocket for a couple of days."

"So the lead panned out?"

"He didn't share details, but it sounded like it," Emilio said.

"That's good," I murmured. And it was.

Zev Aslanov did double duty as Emilio's right-hand man and my other half. Dark, dangerous, cynical, and ruthless, he made my head hurt and my heart smile, which strangely made him perfect for me. We'd been together just shy of a year, and during that time, we'd navigated mad scientists, dead bodies, jealous exes, misunderstandings, lost memories, and mercenaries intent on taking out one or both of us. Yet somehow, we were still together. I still wasn't sure how a small fish like me who swam in the shallows of the Arcane's elite had managed to gain and keep the attention of one of the biggest predators out there, but that was my life now. As the Cordova Family Arbiter tasked with dispensing both justice and vengeance for his Family, he was feared almost as much as he was respected. That was why he'd spent the last week or so hunting the one behind Max's death and why Locke was shadowing Emilio.

"It would be nice if he could bring us a name," Sabella added, her attention focused on the dispersing mourners behind Emilio and Mari.

"Or better yet, a body." Emilio's tone was dark. "And it doesn't have to have a pulse."

Yep, Christina wasn't the only one stewing about the wizard who called himself the Heretic Key. The high-level Key crawled in the depths of the dark web, offering nearly untraceable death curses for a hefty price. Numerous victims who were tied to prominent Arcane families had been lain at his feet, but the Council Hunters, including Zev, had spent years chasing shadows with no success. After the Heretic's latest strike, Zev was more determined than ever to drag the Heretic out of the darkness and into the unforgiving light.

Mari leaned deeper into Emilio in silent warning as a small group of mourners passed by, a couple exchanging nods of acknowledgment with Sabella and Emilio. Others were soon to follow, so our little pack also turned and began making our way to where the cars were parked. I let Emilio, Sabella, and Mari lead the way as I fell in with Locke.

The subtle press of power from the crowd slowly swallowing us woke my own power, and it slid smoothly into place, holding back the press of magic. I didn't bother reining in my Prism, not when the discomfort of being surrounded by various unfamiliar magic users kept the primitive part of me on edge. That feeling wasn't helped by the unmistakable amount of sidelong glances coming my way. Besides, an innate defensive ability wasn't worth much if it didn't kick in at a whisper of potential threat.

"You okay?" Locke's question was low enough to stay between us.

"Yeah, just hate being an object of curiosity."

"Cut 'em some slack, Rory," the air mage teased. "It's not every day they get to be up close to a unicorn."

I shot him a frown before letting my face smooth back out. "Unicorn?"

"Would you rather I call you a dark horse?" He continued to poke at me. "You come out of nowhere, play a part in taking down not one but two Families, catch the eye of the one Arbiter everyone goes out of their way to avoid, and then Sabella publicly claims you as family. But the absolute topper? You come out as a Prism. Did you really think your presence wouldn't cause a ripple?"

"A ripple, I could deal with, but it's been months since Sabella's revelation."

Ahead of us, Mari, Emilio, and Sabella came to a stop as they spoke with a couple of people. Locke and I stopped short, giving them privacy. I angled to face Locke, putting my back to those moving through the gardens.

Locke tucked his hands into his pockets but kept his attention on the crowd. "Maybe that ripple would have disappeared if you moved in their circles on a more regular basis."

"Yeah, no thank you." I fell quiet as a group passed behind us. When they were out of earshot, I said, "Besides, you'd think they'd've moved on to other things by now."

The humor faded, leaving his voice serious. "Like Max's death?"

At my faux pas, heat spread under my cheeks. "That didn't come out right."

A muscle jumped in Locke's jaw as he continued to watch the mourners leave, and seeing that telling tic, it hit me.

"You knew him." It wasn't a question.

His gaze dropped to me, and even though I couldn't see his eyes behind his sunglasses, I could feel the weight of his gaze. "Yeah, I did. Him and Devon both."

Yeah, I'd really put my foot in my mouth. I dared to reach

out to squeeze his arm gently in a feeble attempt at comfort. "I'm sorry. Neither one deserved any of this." Not the young, handsome, successful Max or his bubbly, brand-new fiancée who hadn't survived the wreck that cost the couple everything. All because of a jealous, petty asshole who couldn't find his spine if it was handed to him.

"No, they didn't," he agreed in a hard voice. When our trio resumed its trek, Locke waved me forward, ending the conversation.

We were silent until we reached the parking lot, where cars were now lined up at the entrance as they waited for the officer who was holding back traffic.

Emilio stopped with Mari on one side and Sabella on the other as Locke and I came up. "Where are you parked?"

I tipped my head over to the right. "Over there. You?"

"We're over here." Locke waved toward the front of the lot. "Do you want us to walk you over?"

I shook my head. "No, thanks." I took in the faint lines of tension around Sabella's lips and the slight slump to her shoulders. If I hadn't known her so well, I would never have noticed the tiny tells. "Why don't you wait here with them, and I'll bring the car around."

Emilio had obviously picked up the same signs, because he was quick to jump in. "That sounds like a great idea. Come on, Sabella, you and Mari can sit at the bench over there while we wait."

Thankfully, my aunt didn't fuss, so I looked to Locke, who dipped his chin in reassurance that he would keep an eye on things. Reassured she was in good hands, I strode toward where I'd left the car. I waited until there was enough distance between me and the others before I blew out a long, hard breath. Today was turning out to be harder than expected. Hopefully, Sabella meant what she'd said, and we wouldn't be staying long.

TWO

I FOLLOWED Emilio's Maybach through an impressive set of wrought-iron gates set in a thick wall of adobe that guarded the private domain of the Velasquez estate situated on Camelback Mountain. All of it—the house, the land, and the ride up—was impressive, but that was to be expected from this particular part of the Valley. Here, privacy was highly coveted, and those who called it home had no problems affording it. I glanced at the rearview mirror, checking on the unusually quiet Sabella in the back seat. Normally, we would pass the time chatting, but today, she was clearly preoccupied. Her head was turned toward the window, but since it had been that way for a bit and her expression remained strained, I didn't think the passing scenery was holding her enthralled.

To combat the resulting bout of low-level anxiety her unusual behavior triggered, I decided to disturb the silence with a casual "You never told me how your trip went."

Her attention shifted from the window to me as she mentally returned to the present. "It went," she responded, her tone a little too casual.

"And?"

Yeah, I was pushing, but if I couldn't take advantage of being her niece and treading where others feared, what was the point? Besides, we weren't going anywhere. The line of cars had created a stop-and-go conga line crawl up the long, winding drive. Something had clearly happened while she was away, and whatever that was, it wasn't good. It couldn't have been if the visible signs of strain and thinned patience were any indications. Even her distracted state was worrisome. My great-aunt did not ruffle easily. I knew enough about her history to know that both life and her position in the top strata of Arcane society had created a ruthless woman who knew what she wanted, tolerated little, and demanded much. Hell, she'd been kidnapped, held captive under a curse, almost died, and still managed to handle the chaos with an envious aplomb.

"And?" she repeated.

"You rescheduled your flight home." I dared a glance back then added, "Twice."

Her sigh drifted through the plush confines of the Bentley, a new acquisition after she'd decided she was done utilizing the Arcane Guild's inventory of vehicles. As her personal driver and a Transporter who was endlessly fascinated by anything with an engine and wheels, I was slightly in lust with the sleek, sexy beast. The interior was so lush that when she shifted her weight, the leather gave a soft murmur of compliance. "It was a minor inconvenience."

Her brush-off wasn't going to fly with me. "Minor wouldn't keep you in Italy as long as it did." There was one thing that might, though. Sabella was ruthless when it came to family, and two of her three grown children lived in Europe with their own offspring. "Is your family okay?"

Her soft chuckle was dry. "You're very good at hitting the bull's-eye, dearest."

So definitely a family thing. That didn't bode well, considering Sabella's position, politically and magically, was such that only the suicidally inclined dared to cross her. The last time her family was targeted, my grandmother, Sabella's twin sister, was killed, then my father was taken out. Eventually, my mother had been forced to take me and run when Sabella's enemies turned their attention to us. It had taken years, but by the time Sabella finished exacting her retribution for both deaths, an entire Family line had been eradicated, my mother was dead, and I was a ward of the state.

My grip on the leather-wrapped steering wheel tightened, and it gave a muffled creak in protest. "Who's coming after you now?"

She made a tsk of admonishment. "Insightful you may be, but you're eternally pessimistic."

"Realistic," I shot back. "How bad is it?"

"It's truly nothing," she said, a hint of her typical arrogance reappearing. "My son had most of it in hand by the time I arrived. I simply helped him tidy up. Unfortunately, it took a little longer than expected, so my daughter decided to lend a hand. When we were done, I choose to extend my stay as I enjoy playing the doting *grandmaman* to my little treasures, and there was no rush for my return. That changed, of course, when the news came about Max and Devon..." True grief darkened her words.

Her explanation rang true, but I wasn't a Seeker, so a well-concealed lie could slide right by me, and I would never know. My great-aunt had no qualms about shading the truth if it ultimately served her needs, even with those close to her. But it didn't address the worrisome demeanor that haunted her, and being the pessimist she'd named me earlier, my anxiety didn't abate. I dared another mirror check as we'd stopped yet again, with the top of the drive in sight, and asked, "Are you okay?"

She caught my gaze in the narrow mirror, and her lips curved, softening the lines. "I'm fine, Rory." She leaned forward and gave my shoulder a gentle squeeze before settling back. "I'm just a bit worn from the funeral and flights and such."

Maybe she was, maybe she wasn't, but clearly, she wasn't ready to share. "Then we're definitely keeping this visit short."

In front of us, Emilio's car reached the top of the drive and turned off to the left, revealing a stunning entryway that rivaled a luxury hotel. I followed him into a paved section half filled with cars and pulled into a spot next to him. I shut down the Bentley and undid my belt before I twisted in my seat so I could see Sabella. "What do I need to know about Mateo and Olivia's request?"

Sabella was pulling out a lipstick from her clutch and touching up her lips, and somehow, she still managed to answer. "The impression I received was they simply had a job for you, one that required your particular skill set."

Since I was nearly impervious to most magical attacks, that wasn't ominous. Not at all. I had a fleeting wish that Zev was home and not out on a hunt. Generally, his presence served to remind the council members to mind their manners around me. Sabella could do the same, but she was more likely to sit back and let me flounder in what she considered a learning moment. Even though she was partially right, I still considered maintaining my professionalism in the face of entitled arrogance a pain in my ass.

She paused in the midst of putting away her lip color. "Wipe that expression off your face, Rory. What have I told you?"

"You've gifted me many pearls," I shot back. "Which nugget of wisdom are you referring to?"

She dropped the lipstick into her clutch, snapped it shut, and caught my gaze. "Are you a threat or a tool?"

Right now, I was feeling all sorts of sympathy for tools. "What's with the constant tests?" I groused and shifted to get out of the car.

Her hand moved so fast, I had no way of avoiding it. Her fingers caught my chin and held it in a gentle but implacable grip that matched the steely-eyed gaze boring into mine. "Consider it a compliment, not an insult. If they didn't think you could handle yourself, you'd just be another lackey." She studied me for a moment, green sparking in the hazel depths of her eyes. "Remember who you are, girl." The press of her fingers against my jaw was inescapable. "Tool or threat?"

"Threat," I gritted out, because it was the truth. I was more Sabella's niece than I was comfortable admitting, no matter how hard I tried to keep that part of me tucked out of sight.

Her red lips curved up into a pleased smile, and she let me go. "Good." She moved back and raised a brow. "Then let's go offer our condolences to the family, shall we?"

⸝⸝⸝⸝⸝⸝⸝⸝⸝⸝⸝⸝⸝⸝⸝⸝⸝⸝⸝⸝⸝⸝⸝⸝⸝⸝

Bodies moved through the impressive space, the murmur of voices dulled by the somber air. I stood off to the side of the large open entertaining space filled with friends and family of the Vasquezes and did my best not to fidget. With this many magic users in one confined area, it was hard to avoid the near-electric edge of arcane energy that drifted through the room. That underlying hum of power read like a low-level threat to my magic and spiked my anxiety, which meant my Prism was in full play, shielding me from unseen threats, real or perceived.

I had lost sight of Emilio, Mari, and Locke about ten minutes after we hit the door, when someone had called Emilio's name. Last time I saw the trio, they were headed toward the back of the house that presumably opened to the patio. Since Sabella was my responsibility, I stayed at her back and left Locke to his charges.

Sabella stood off to my right with Olivia and Mateo, quietly conversing about shared acquaintances. I was still waiting to hear what the two council members wanted from me, and based off how many times the three were interrupted by other guests, I was betting I would be waiting a bit longer.

Mateo and Olivia appeared to be attending as each other's plus one, which made me wonder if Mateo's reputation as one of the Arcane's most notorious bachelors was more hype than reality. Younger than Olivia by a good fifteen plus years, he epitomized the whole tall, dark, and dangerous thing, which played well in the media. Unlike Zev, who carried the same edge, Mateo was colder and much more ruthless. That was probably why he had no issue holding a council seat despite being in his early thirties.

Olivia, on the other hand, was the picture of cool elegance, from her blond hair artfully streaked with silver to the toes of her red-soled stilettos. She reminded me a lot of Sabella, not because they were close in age and mannerisms but because that demeanor hid a well-honed ruthlessness shared by everyone on the Council. When I first met her, I'd mistaken her graciousness for gentleness, but after months of interactions, I knew she could smile sweetly even as she left you bleeding at her feet.

Right now, all three were talking in low voices to Max's father and another older man I didn't recognize. There were no smiles to be had among any of them, just a lot of tense shoulders, clenched jaws, and sharp head shakes.

Keeping the group at the edge of my attention, I scanned those nearby and recognized a younger couple talking with Max's mother. Perry Robbins and Rebecca Tsosie. Both were close friends of Max and Devon. So close that Perry was to be

Max's best man and Rebecca, Devon's maid of honor. Perry leaned down to Max's mother's shorter form as he ran a hand through his hair, the dirty-blond strands mussed by previous passes. Dark-haired Rebecca, tucked at his side, reached up to smooth it back in place. Her gaze drifted over the gathering, collided with mine, and widened in recognition. Then she offered a small, sad smile in silent greeting.

I tilted my head in return and continued to study the room. There were other faces I recognized, like Kent Summers, another close friend of Max's, and Dr. Arturo Garcia, the Cordova Family healer. And they weren't the only blasts from my recent past. I could've sworn I caught a glimpse of the Muse, Shelby Quinn, a memory mage who had helped Zev reclaim his memories from a curse, over by the photo display earlier. But other than a few silent exchanges of acknowledgment and the occasional speculative glance from the curious, I was left alone.

Sabella broke away and began to head my way, so I met her halfway. When we got close, she said, "Come along," then headed toward a hall on our left.

With no other choice, I trailed along. Halfway down, she opened a door and disappeared inside. I followed her into a well-appointed home office, stopped just inside with my hand holding the door open, and checked behind us. No one followed, so I asked, "Do you want the door open or closed?"

"Leave it open," she said as she settled into one of two plush club chairs facing the cherrywood desk. "Olivia and Mateo should be here momentarily."

I moved farther into the room, and with anticipation riding my ass and keeping me on my feet, I wandered alongside the floor-to-ceiling bookcases that took up the far wall, checking out the titles and framed photos.

After a few moments, Sabella chided, "Child, settle."

"Can't," I muttered, even as I went to the masculine desk that faced her chair and leaned my butt against the edge. I gripped the edge, my fingers tapping restlessly against the underside as she watched me with clear amusement. Reading her unasked question in her raised eyebrow, a trick I wished I could pull off, I explained, "Talking business at a memorial is just…" I shuddered in distaste.

Sabella did that thing the older generation had down to an art—an exasperated head shake as if the youngster in front of them were just a tad bit dense. "Business is business, regardless of the event, darling."

"And with everyone occupied with the reason we're gathered, they won't note us stepping away for a moment," a new voice said.

I straightened abruptly, my attention on the couple joining us. I nodded to Olivia. "Councilwoman Johanson." Then I greeted the man behind her, who closed the office door. "Councilman Medina."

Olivia waved away my manners. "Olivia, please, Rory." She settled into the chair next to Sabella then shot me a look from under startling dark lashes. "You don't mind, do you?"

Not sure if she was asking about using my first name or requesting this discussion, I shook my head.

"Good." She smoothed down the heather-gray skirt as she angled her long legs and tucked one pointed toe behind her ankle. Her gaze shifted to the man who had unerringly found the crystal-cut decanter and matching glasses sitting off to the side on a marble-topped wet bar. "Mateo, would you pour me one as well?"

"Of course." He looked to Sabella and raised a squat glass filled with a couple of inches of warm amber liquid. "Sabella?"

"No thank you," she said.

He looked to me, I shook my head, and he turned to finish pouring. He brought Olivia's drink to her and handed it over. Then he moved around the two women and came to stand near me at the desk.

My muscles locked in an instinctive reaction to his nearness, and I fought the urge to put more space between us.

A cynical amusement lit his dark eyes. I didn't care. The last time I saw him, he'd forced me to reveal that I was a Prism. Zev had called Mateo's magical attack a test, I'd called it an assault, then we'd agreed to disagree.

"Rory"—Mateo's voice carried an echo of the ruthlessness that had led him to be one of the youngest sitting Council members—"how are you?"

I swallowed back a defensive growl and managed a polite "Good, thank you."

His lips curved, revealing a flash of white teeth as he lifted his glass to sip his drink.

"We won't take up much of your time," Olivia said. "First, thank you for accommodating us. I'm sure you're aware that Zev has been tracking the Heretic at our request."

I nodded.

"While we are confident that he'll return with quarry in hand soon, Zev's hunt has muddied some dark waters." She drummed her fingers against the leather armrest, but her gaze remained on me. "Have you heard of Court Stones?"

Sabella sucked in a quiet breath but didn't interrupt.

I slogged through my memory banks, hoping to dredge up an answer, but no such luck. "It doesn't sound familiar."

"Unsurprising," she said. "Most consider them nothing more than a myth, and until very recently, they would've been correct."

"Olivia, they were destroyed." There was a wealth of warning in Sabella's voice. "We were there."

"We were," Olivia agreed. "But we missed one."

"How?"

Olivia's shoulders rose and fell in a graceful shrug. "I don't know, Bella, but we did."

"If," Mateo cut in, an acerbic edge to his voice, "we are to believe Aslanov's source."

Before I could let loose my automatic defense of Zev, Olivia chided, "Zev is no one's fool, Mateo. If he says it's authentic, then I'm inclined to believe him." She turned back to me and resumed her story. "Court Stones was a pretty name given to an ugly magic. Like many magical artifacts, the origin stories vary, but all agree that the stones' creation was accidental. Their power, however, was another story."

Picking up on the use of the plural, I asked, "Stones? As in more than one?"

Unperturbed by my interruption, she nodded. "Seven, to be specific. Each carried some level of influencing magic."

"As in, if you had one, you could make someone do what you want?"

"No," Mateo answered. "As in, if you were a highly skilled Charmer and controlled one of the stronger stones, you could make an unsuspecting mage of lesser power do your bidding, and they'd never remember doing so."

"And if you were a fire mage and claimed one," Sabella said, picking up the explanation, "you could make someone believe they were burning to death without leaving a mark on their body."

Okay, the puppet thing was scary enough, but that last one? I suppressed a shiver. "So basically, the stones control other mages?"

The three powerhouses exchanged a round of looks before Olivia said, "A little oversimplified, but accurate."

"And if someone managed to get their hands on all seven of them?" I pushed, even knowing the forthcoming answer wasn't good. "What then?"

Mateo set his now-empty glass on the desk, the crystal hitting the wood with a solid thunk, and looked at me. A darkness moved through his grim expression. "Whatever you're imagining, double it, and you still wouldn't come close to the nightmare that would result."

"Which is why the Council decided to destroy them." Sabella's voice was sharp enough to cut.

"And why they were deliberately kept apart." Olivia's tone, in stark contrast, was gentle. "Not that it stopped mages from searching for them."

It didn't take a genius to fill in the blanks. "Let me guess—those hunts left a trail of bodies."

"Worse," Sabella said as Mateo muttered something I didn't catch.

I frowned as my gaze bounced between them. "Worse?"

"Some victims were left breathing, but their minds and power were shattered."

It took a few seconds for Mateo's statement to sink in—partially because it was bit out in a near growl and partially because the concept was so hard to grasp. The darkness from earlier had settled deep into his features, leaving a wrathful being in its wake.

A story lived there. But I wasn't stupid enough to ask for it.

Olivia picked up the tale. "Years ago, the Council handpicked a unit of Scouts and Hunters to recover the stones. As each stone was brought back, it was destroyed. Once all seven had been reduced to dust, the matter was considered closed and the threat removed."

Read, the Council wiped out any mage that had anything to do with the stones. It seemed to be a favored reaction from the ruling Arcane body.

Not privy to my cynical commentary, Olivia finally got to the point. "However, it seems one survived, and the Heretic is keen on acquiring it."

"And with Zev breathing down his neck," Mateo said, "the *cabrón* can't risk exposing himself to take possession. Which is where you come in."

It didn't take a genius to put two and two together, and the answer wasn't unexpected. I had outed myself to the

Council when I stepped between Zev and a pissed-off water mage who happened to be another Arbiter. When I survived and the water mage didn't, the Council demanded answers about my uncanny ability to remain breathing. I gave them, making the sitting power part of a select group who knew my not-so-secretive secret. "You want me to pick up this stone and play bait."

THREE

MATEO'S SMILE was all teeth. "If it really is a missing Court Stone, you are uniquely equipped to destroy it."

"No." The sharp denial came from Sabella, and we all turned toward her voice. Her hands were fisted on the arms of her chair, and the tendons in her neck stood out in stark relief as she visibly held herself in check. "She is not playing bait."

At her fierce reprimand, something deep inside me loosened the tiniest bit. I kept my mouth shut as I was in no rush to accept the role they were offering. Call me silly, but deliberately putting myself in the Heretic's path did not fill me with joy, especially since escaping his vindictive magic the first time had been a close call.

Tempt fate by repeating the experience? Yeah, no thank you.

"Bella..." Olivia leaned forward, reaching out to cover Sabella's fist, but my great-aunt wasn't having it.

"No, Olivia." She jerked her hand away from the councilwoman and shook her head. "Just because she's a Prism doesn't mean she's immune to the stone's influence."

The man next to me crossed his arms over his chest, and his gaze was hard. "No one is, Sabella." There was a grim cast to his face when he added, "But she, more than anyone else, has a better chance of surviving its destruction."

The arrogant assumption made me sneer. Silent though it was, he still caught it.

A mocking light eased the hard edge in his dark eyes as he raised a brow. "You disagree?"

"I think your expectations are a bit unrealistic." *And archaic and stupid.* I didn't share that part, knowing it wasn't smart to tug this particular tiger's tail, but... *Had they learned nothing from history?*

Decades before, the Families managed to nearly wipe out an entire class of mages when they shoved Prisms in front of their precious heirs to act as magical shields. When those human buffers managed to derail assassination after assassination attempt, they were suddenly viewed as a challenge to be bested, and a free-for-all ensued. Unfortunately, no matter how good a Prism was at repelling magical attacks, eventually someone or something would succeed.

When the remaining Prisms realized they were being systematically exterminated, they took themselves out of the game. In their effort to avoid detection, they'd hidden their abilities so well, it left their descendants clueless. It didn't help when the Arcane Council went one step further and eliminated the Prisms' existence from the pages of history. Between the two, the next generation of Prisms were left unprepared for their heritage and what it entailed.

Obviously, the Council had learned nothing from that catastrophe, because it appeared the current powers that be were hell-bent on repeating the experience. Starting with me.

"Unrealistic?" Mateo pressed.

"Being a Prism doesn't guarantee I'll survive a magical attack."

I'd learned that the hard way. Growing up, I had no idea what to call my strange immunity to magic—not until I heard the term *Prism* and started a concentrated search. Even then, I didn't have a clue until I crossed paths with Zev and Sabella reentered my life. Between the two of them, I'd been getting an accelerated course in what it meant to be a dual mage as both a Prism and a Transporter.

"Perhaps not, but your chances are higher than the majority, no?" It wasn't really a question, not with that tone, but he wasn't done. With a honed ease, he slid an unexpected blade of betrayal deep. "According to Aslanov's report, you've already managed to slip the Heretic's noose."

"Only because I wasn't the focus of the Heretic's curse." I managed to utter the words without revealing the chaos created by the realization that Zev was telling tales of a sort to the Council.

"Still, you're here and breathing," Mateo pointed out with cold logic I couldn't argue against. "Which is more than the majority of his targets can say."

He wasn't wrong. The Heretic had wreaked havoc among the Arcane for years as an assassin for hire through the dark web. He'd built his reputation by taking out members of various Families for a hefty price tag. He was a prime example of what happened when a highly skilled Key who specialized in creating lethal curses gave in to greed and turned to the dark side. As my best friend and roommate, Lena, aptly pointed out, for someone who could unravel complex hexes, creating nearly undetectable ones wasn't a stretch. And she would know, considering she was one of the top Keys for the Arcane Guild and made a healthy living undoing nasty hexes by even nastier mages.

That included the curse created by the Heretic that had led to Max's and Devon's deaths. While they hadn't escaped his expertise, Mateo was correct in saying that I was another story. Zev and Lena attributed it to me being a Prism. Personally, I thought it was because I wasn't the actual target, just collateral damage. Either way, I wasn't keen about tempting fate again, but I had a feeling I wasn't going to get a choice—not even with Sabella doing her best to defend me. I couldn't even throw Lena under the bus because she was out of town on a Guild case.

"You can't ask this of her." Icy barbs coated Sabella's statement as she protested, determined to get her way.

Anxiety sank cruel claws into my spine as I took in Olivia's mulishly set jaw, Mateo's ruthless study, and Sabella's poorly hidden worry. A niggling realization snuck in, and my fingers dug into the underside of the desk's edge until they hurt.

Fuck me.

"Actually, they can." When that bought me everyone's attention, I was grateful I was able to keep my voice level. "My contract with the Council is very explicit. They can contract for any job that falls under my skill set, including high-risk assignments, so long as there is a reasonable expectation of a successful completion." Mari, my lawyer and, dare I say, friend, warned that the language skirted the line with the definition of "reasonable," but we both agreed anything that touched the Council could carry a high degree of danger. It was the nature of their interactions, which also allowed me to charge above-market fees for my services, a financial lure that even I wasn't immune to. But it was just more proof of the old adage, "If it's too good to be true, it probably is."

Besides, the Council could, and probably would, find another loophole if they decided it was in their best interests. Therefore, Mari and I decided to leave that clause in because it gave me a sliver of control in a shitty situation. My gut whispered that Mateo and Olivia would have no problem enforcing the clause in ways I wouldn't like, especially in a case that directly impacted one of the sitting members of the Council.

I uncurled my death grip on the desk's edge and ignored

the prickling sensation nipping at my fingertips as blood rushed back in. "Logic states that as a Prism, I'm less likely to fall prey to influencing magic. Therefore, he's correct—I'm actually the best person for this." I nearly choked on the admission as I held Mateo's disconcerting gaze. It took effort, but I broke the tense connection by turning to Olivia. "And by this, I'm assuming you want me to deliver whatever it is that will destroy the stone, right?"

Even though a hint of discomfiture flitted across Olivia's patrician features, it did nothing to ease the unrelenting edge of pragmatism. "That's correct."

Sabella's lips thinned as she pressed them tightly, and her eyes flashed in warning as her temper rose to the surface. Her reaction was so out of character, I knew that whatever had happened overseas had left its mark, leaving her overly protective of those she considered hers, which meant her reactions would be unpredictable. Not a good combination at the best of times, and this was far from the best of times.

I pushed off the desk and crouched next to her before she could erupt. I covered the white knuckles gripping the armrest and squeezed gently. "Remember, it's my choice." My voice was low, keeping the words between us.

She studied me for a long moment. Whatever she saw eased her worries enough to lighten her grip and lessen the lines around her mouth and eyes. "Threat." It wasn't a question but a reminder.

"Always," I swore.

Finally, she dipped her head in acquiescence.

Decision made, I rose, straightened my shoulders, and faced the Council members. "What, exactly, do you have planned?"

By the time Mateo and Olivia finished their succinct explanation, it was my turn to battle back my frustration over being stuck in a corner with no way out. It was a stupidly simple plan, which was why it might actually work. The Council would be sending in an Arcane appraiser driven by their Transporter to authenticate the rumored Court Stone currently in the possession of a reclusive Sibyl. What the Sibyl didn't know was the appraiser would use a complex spell that would render the stone unusable. Of course, it wasn't that simple, because the cast could cause unexpected magical reactions.

"Wait," I said, cutting Olivia off after she shared the identity of the stone's guardian. "Are you talking about the Blessed Amrita?"

"Yes," Olivia confirmed. "You know her?"

I shook my head, wondering why the Council would leave a fabled artifact with a rumored shyster. "Know? Nope, but I've heard rumors."

"Such as?" Mateo asked.

I went for the least offensive one I could recall. "That while she claims her magic is the result of being touched by the divine, she's actually a Charmer with a grifter's bent."

There was no change in Mateo's expression, and his voice was hard to read when he asked, "Do you not believe in the divine magics?"

To offend or not to offend? I picked my words carefully. "I don't disbelieve that there is a higher power out there that would be inclined to offer its blessing on those mages that exemplify its attributes."

"But?" he prompted despite my delicate tiptoeing.

Hell with it. "But from what I've heard, Amrita isn't always on the side of divinity."

Cynical amusement played across his features. "That sounds as if you think such beings would follow the same moral code as mere mortals."

Okay, I really didn't want to get into a philosophical debate regarding personal ideology with the councilman, because it was likely to end badly. "How about I admit to not wanting to presume to understand the complexities that would dictate such a being's decisions and leave it at that?"

His droll humor escaped in a soft chuckle. "And I would be happy to continue this discussion at another place and time, perhaps when things are not quite so"—it was his turn to choose his words—"ambiguous."

Ambiguous was a good description.

I wasn't the only one ready to switch gears, because Sabella chose to redirect the conversation to its original course. "I'm surprised you found someone who could authenticate the Court Stones." She looked to Olivia. "Last I heard, Millie Perreault had retired and left London for Paris, and she's the only one I can think of that would be up to the task."

Olivia slid a glance at Mateo from under her lashes as she tugged at her skirt, ostensibly straightening it. "Yes, well…"

Her flustered response made me brace. *What fresh hell is heading my way now?*

Olivia straightened her spine and cleared her throat. "Rory will be accompanied by Piper McMillan."

Not missing the woman's discomfort, Sabella drummed her polished nails in a deliberate staccato on the chair's arm. "Who does this Piper work for?"

It was Mateo who answered. "Me."

Sabella's fingers froze in midmotion as she pinned him with an unblinking stare. "When did the Medina Family acquire an antiquity expert?"

"No one said she was an antiquity expert." The only sign of Mateo's discomfort was the minute shift of muscles as his shoulders twitched. "Piper's not there to authenticate the stone. That will be Rory's role."

I blinked, not quite following. "Wait, what?"

Sabella's eyes narrowed. "Explain." The one-word demand oozed silky menace.

A flash of irritation sparked in Mateo's dark gaze before it was doused. Clearly, he wasn't a fan of being reprimanded.

Welcome to my world, buddy.

"Authenticating the stone is not the goal. Drawing out the Heretic is," he said. "And to that end, we simply need Piper to convince Amrita that she can sense the stone's power. In reality, it's Rory's sensitivity to magic that will let Piper know if Amrita is trying to con us and, by extension, the Heretic."

Deeply irked, I demanded, "Run that by me again."

"As a Prism, you're sensitive to magic, are you not?"

He really had the arrogant ass part down pat, but I couldn't deny the obvious. "Somewhat, yeah."

He nodded as if my reluctant admission were a solid confirmation. "Then, as Amrita's is highly likely to test the Council's appraiser as she's not happy about our request to relinquish the stone, you can let Piper know if the stone is a legit magical threat."

"Great," I groused. "So on top of playing bait and getting myself out of this mess, I've got another body to protect?"

"Actually, Piper can take care of herself," Olivia said. "In fact, that's part of the reason she was chosen to accompany you."

Part of? Understanding, when it came, left me a bit irked. "She's there to take out the Heretic."

"Should he decide to appear, yes," Mateo confirmed.

"Do you not trust Zev to take care of him?"

"I have no qualms with Aslanov's ability to see this through." Mateo side-stepped my question with agility. "But Piper has served my family for years, and should the opportunity present itself, it is best if there is a back-up solution in place."

"Is she a Hunter or a Sentinel?" Hunters specialized in investigations, while Sentinels were all about personal security. PI or bodyguard, the distinction would tell me just how dangerous the Council considered the situation. If it was up to me, I would request one of each, and maybe the assassin skills of a Blade if that was an option. I didn't think it was.

"Sentinel," Mateo said.

"And this Sentinel is going to trigger this spell and destroy the stone right under Amrita's nose?"

He held my gaze with his, and there was no mistaking the core of ruthlessness at his center. "Yes, and you'll make sure the two of you walk away from the assignment."

Wow, wish I had his optimism.

A tiny whisper of cynicism wondered if, when it came down to it, the Sentinel's true assignment was not just the stone's destruction but an assessment of my skills as another tool in the Council's arsenal. Probably. Either way, I wasn't sure how to feel about it—insulted or comforted. Right now, I was leaning toward insulted. "And if Amrita is a Sibyl in truth? Wouldn't she see this whole situation coming?"

This time, it was Olivia who answered. "As you indicated, there is a high level of doubt about the validity of her supposed ability to foresee things."

That wasn't the reassurance Olivia obviously thought it was, because I was still worried. I didn't know much about those afflicted with foresight, but I did know that the future depended on numerous factors and could be a capricious beast, but it only took one true seeing to screw everything up. "But if she 'divines,'"—I used finger quotes—"our real intent, doesn't that upend your plan?"

"No." Mateo's response was solid. "Because the Council is sincere in its need to assess the stone's validity, and that is what Amrita has been informed."

Clearly, I wasn't going to logic my way out of this, so I shut my mouth as the next few minutes passed in heated back-and-forth between Sabella and the Council members. I kept out of target range. The longer the argument waged, the more insulted I became at the Council's insistence that I needed a babysitter. Still, I could recognize a losing argument when I heard it. Mateo and Olivia were determined to partner me with one of their own.

When Sabella realized the same, the "discussion" concluded, and I fumed as Mateo guided Olivia out of the office. As soon as they were out of earshot, I muttered, "A freakin' babysitter? Seriously?"

"Enough," Sabella snapped as she bent to reclaim her clutch, which she had set on the floor by her chair. When she straightened, she glared at me. "I may not like their approach, but there is no doubt something must be done. I trust you can do the job and then let this Piper person do hers."

The urge to whine like a sulky five-year-old was hard to suppress, but I managed. "Fine, but she better stay out of my way."

"You do understand that your job is to ensure you both come back alive?" she shot back. "I expect you to complete that assignment." She started toward the door, leaving me to follow.

I stayed at her side. Truthfully, part of me was actually grateful for Mateo's insistence on having a Sentinel at my back, but I was irked at being manipulated into the position in the first place and not quite ready to let go of my grudge. Reaching the doorway first, I checked the hall and found it empty. I turned as Sabella joined me. "And to be Mateo's eyes and ears."

"Most likely, yes." She didn't disagree, but she pivoted and blocked my way forward, bringing me to a halt in front of her. "However, I have faith in your ability to be discreet." Her gaze held mine. "And you will be discreet, won't you?"

A little offended, I stiffened and bit out, "Of course."

"Good." She moved away and started out the door. "It

comforts me to know that Mateo's people don't make it a habit to fail his orders."

"Yippee," I muttered as we made our way down the hall, then I felt heat hit my cheeks when she shot me a look of reprimand. "I'm happy to let them do their job, so long as they don't interfere with mine," I said, this time without the attitude but completely serious. "However, if it comes down to me or them, I'll be choosing me."

My aunt's smile was disturbingly beatific. "Good."

FOUR

"DO YOU KNOW A PIPER MCMILLAN?" I asked Lena later that night after trying and failing to connect with Zev. He wasn't answering my calls or texts, which wasn't unusual when he was on a hunt. Understanding the nature of his job didn't erase the pinch of resentment and worry his lack of response created.

My roommate paused in her quest to demolish the last of the raspberry sherbet, spoon still in her mouth, as she thought about my question. It wasn't long before she pulled the spoon free and asked, "Isn't she a Sentinel for the Medina Family?"

"That would be the one," I confirmed before returning to my home pedicure. With my heel braced against the edge of the barstool, I added another layer of electric-blue polish to my toes.

"Like *know* know her, no," she said. "But she's got a solid reputation with the Guild."

Sentinels were a tight clan, so hearing that was actually reassuring. Especially when the best of the best came from the Western Division of the Arcane Guild training ground. And that wasn't true of only the Guild-trained Sentinels, but all those magic wielders who earned their stripes with the world-renowned mercenary storehouse. I would know since I was once a Guild employee. But since Sentinels willingly put their lives on the line for their clients, most skirted the edge of crazy, even though they could demand sky-high fees. There was something to be said about being overly committed to a job. Hopefully, Piper wouldn't have to go the extra mile with me tomorrow.

"Good to know." I edged a smear of blue off the top of my big toe and replaced the polish brush back in its bottle on the counter.

Lena shifted on the seat nearby and tilted her head, causing the messy knot of auburn to inch closer to imminent unraveling. "Why are you asking about Piper?"

I carefully moved my foot down to the rung on the stool between us. "Because she's going to be coming with me on a run."

"A run? Why would you need…" She didn't finish her question as the answer hit her. She frowned, and her voice sharpened. "The Council is sending you out as bait for the Heretic, aren't they?"

Normally, I wouldn't get into the details of my assignment, but this wasn't just my best friend—she was also my inside source to dealing with Keys. And her knowledge could be what allowed me to survive playing reluctant bait for a psycho Key.

"In a roundabout way," I admitted reluctantly, knowing she wouldn't like the idea. Hell, I didn't like the idea.

"Explain," she demanded, pointing her empty spoon at me.

I gave her a short recap of what happened at the funeral, and sure enough, she was not happy about my Council-appointed role. "This is exactly what I warned you about, Rory."

I stifled my sigh. *Here comes the "I told you so."*

She got up and stalked around the island to yank open the

freezer, toss in the sherbet, and slam the door closed. She spun back around and all but threw the spoon into the sink. Then she started in. "They're going to get you killed."

I squashed the cynical voice that agreed and strove to keep my tone casual. "And it's my job to make sure that is not how things end."

"I get that part, but Piper doesn't work for you." She braced her hands on the counter's edge and leaned in. "It would've been better if they let Sabella hire someone to cover you. At least that way, their priorities would be in order."

Again, it was difficult not to agree. "I think Piper's the Council's version of appeasing Sabella's wrath." My attempt to pacify her with logic didn't appear to be working, so I admitted, "If Sabella had her way, I wouldn't be going."

Never one to be coy, Lena got straight to the point. "So why are you?"

I gave her the only answer I could—the truth. "Contract clause."

She shook her head, pushed back off the counter, and blew out a breath. A mix of worry and exasperation washed through her expression, but she kept her thoughts to herself. Instead, she switched tracks. "What did Zev have to say about it?"

It was my turn to be blunt. "As much as I love the man, he doesn't determine which jobs I take."

She grimaced. "That's not what I meant."

"Then what did you mean?"

"I just figured that considering the Council's request and who it involves, you would've reached out to talk things through. He is hunting the Heretic, right?" Lena knew most of the details surrounding the Heretic's latest misadventures since she'd been instrumental in identifying the curse I'd picked up from Max and Devon.

"Yeah." I looked away and carefully tightened the top to the nail polish bottle.

"So what was his take on this? Did he have anything that might help you?"

I shrugged without looking up.

At my nonanswer, her voice sharpened. "Rory?"

"What?"

"You have talked to him, right?"

"I tried, but he's not picking up."

"And you're worried," my ever-perceptive friend guessed.

"Hard not to be." I stopped fiddling with the nail polish and met her gaze. "I know he can handle himself, but according to Mateo, he's hot on the Heretic's heels, which is how I got roped into this."

Her hand circled in a "keep going" motion as she rounded the island and settled on the barstool next to me.

"Zev identified the package as the Heretic's next target," I explained.

She twisted the seat until we were facing each other. As close as we were, I couldn't miss the real worry in her eyes or the heavy reservation in her. "I don't like this."

If she knew the details, she would like it even less. "I'm not a huge fan either." It was an admission I wouldn't dare make to another. "But we both know that refusing the Council isn't wise."

She sat back and folded her arms, her mouth set in lines of frustration. "Yeah, well, I'm not the one that signed their bloody contract."

Instead of being offended, I chose to be amused, because I knew the sarcasm was based in love. "It's business."

"It's foolish," she snapped back. "But then again, you're nothing if not stubborn."

I raised my brows and drawled, "Hello, pot. Meet kettle."

"Whatever," she muttered.

When she fell quiet, I started tidying up the residue from my pedicure activities. I was about to get up and put things back in my bathroom when she spoke.

"Can you make sure Zev is on standby, just in case?"

With a heavy sigh, I settled back into my seat. "I think that's a moot question, babe, especially as he's not answering his phone."

"What about sending him a text—or hey, here's a thought —leave him a message?"

I shook my head. "Without knowing where he's at on his hunt, the last thing I want to do is screw whatever operation he has going on by dividing his attention."

Like a dog with a bone, she didn't let go. "So you'd rather blindside him by just showing up?"

Reluctantly, I had to admit she had a valid point, but it didn't change the situation. "He has his job, and I have mine." When she looked as if she would argue further, I cut her off. "Look, I don't like it either, but he and I knew something like this would eventually happen." *Just not this soon, but...* "I'll keep trying to reach him, but whether or not I get through, he and I will deal."

"Fine," she snapped, not at all appeased. "But you need your own backup."

It was clear to see where she was heading, but just like with Zev, I couldn't exactly drag my best friend along on a job. "Nope, uh-huh, you can't come with."

Instead of the expected argument, she clamped her mouth shut and studied me, clearly plotting. Sure enough, she asked, "Are you using a Guild vehicle?"

Not sure where she was going with this, I shook my head hesitantly. "No, a Council one."

"Hmm."

Okay, that didn't bode well. "What?"

When a mysterious smile curved her lips, alarms started going off. "Lena." I used her name as a warning.

She ignored it, her smile gaining a sharpness echoed in her eyes. "Since you're determined to play bait for the Heretic, no one could fault you for having a safety net."

Maybe, maybe not. It was my turn to narrow my eyes. "What kind of safety net?"

"The Evan kind."

At the mention of her significant other, who happened to be both an electro mage and a hacker extraordinaire, a picture started coming into focus, and I shook my head. "No, uh-uh, Lena. It's one thing for Evan to hack into the GPS of a Guild vehicle, a whole other fiasco to hack a Council vehicle."

She blew off my concern. "Please, they'd never know he was there."

A part of me wanted to jump all over her offer, but the practical side was justifiably leery. Evan was damn good at what he did, and if it had been any other run, I wouldn't have even hesitated because, at worst, he would get a reprimand and maybe a note from HR in his file. But when it came to the Council, the potential consequences made even me shudder. "No, it's too risky."

But Lena wasn't one to give up. "So is going in alone."

"I'm not alone."

She reached out so quick, I didn't have time to avoid her. Her fingers curled around my wrist and squeezed gently. "Rory, I love you, but for once in your life, don't be so stubborn. The Heretic almost took you out, and he wasn't even gunning for you, so let me have this." Her gaze held mine, equal parts determined and pleading.

"Lena," I started, unsure how to reassure her and hold my course.

Her gaze flicked to the charm on the necklace I wore, a gift from Sabella. Then her eyes came back to mine, a determined glint replacing her agitation. "If you're not comfortable with him tracking the car, we'll use the charm. That way, if something goes wrong, you'll know someone's coming."

As much as it sucked, her concern was valid. Over the last year, my life had been unpredictable at best and chaotic at worst, and there had been a few hairy situations where it had been a close call on whether or not I would keep breathing. I'd only made it through because she, Evan, or Zev had been there. The fact that I couldn't reach Zev concerned me more than I wanted to admit. This whole situation worried me more than I wanted to admit. Things never ended well for bait, and the fact that the Council was quick to throw me out into the bloody water was exactly why I'd tried to stay off their radar for so long. I wasn't blind to the fact that the Council had one goal—to stop the Heretic, no matter the collateral damage incurred.

Letting Evan track me through the charm didn't violate any part of my contracts, and besides, I had the right to protect myself however I felt necessary. *Right?*

"Fine." I gave in, and the knot in my stomach eased just a bit. "We'll use the charm."

She squeezed my wrist then let me go. "Thank you."

I reached up to undo the chain that held the charm in place. "Make sure whatever you two do can't be picked up by another Key." The chain came loose, and I let it pool into my palm.

She held out her hand. "Please, as if I'd ever be that sloppy."

I let the necklace spill into her hand. "I have to leave by five. Will that give you enough time?"

She closed her fist around the necklace and rose from her chair. "More than." She grabbed her phone, hit the screen, and put it to her ear. When Evan answered, she said, "Hey, gorgeous, I need your help with something," then headed to her bedroom.

I watched her go then turned back to my silent phone lying on the counter. I couldn't help but wish that Zev had picked up, because being able to talk this through with him would have helped calm my nerves. I could try again but decided against it. My reluctance was twofold. I was a professional with a reputation to uphold. Just as Zev didn't ask my permission to hunt, I didn't need his to do my job. Whether I got through or not, at this point, there was no changing the fact that I was heading straight into trouble. I knew Zev well enough to know he would not be happy with me. Then again, I wasn't exactly thrilled about him chasing down the psycho curse-slinger, either, so that made us even.

Right?

Sighing at the derisive mental snicker echoing in my head, I collected my nail polish and did the awkward shuffle to my room as I tried to keep my toes from touching the floor. Sleep was going to be hard to find, but I would do my best because gods knew, tomorrow was coming whether I was ready or not.

FIVE

THE NEXT MORNING, the predawn darkness still cloaked the sky, even though my phone showed six o'clock. I steered my precious 1968 Mustang Fastback through pools of overhead lights and into the asphalt lot that matched the address Mateo had given me the evening before. Ahead, a warehouse dominated the far side, its gray coloring a lighter hue against the early-morning shadows. It was boring and unimaginative, just another bland manufacturing structure in an equally bland industrial park. The only sign that something important lay behind the metal walls was the sharp-eyed guard sitting under one of the overhead lights, watching me get closer. He sat in some mutant cross between an ATV and golf cart with the word *security* in aggressive black letters across the short nose. Well, him and the low, warning prickle of an active ward that nipped at my skin as the tires rolled over the invisible boundary.

Mr. Security put his vehicular aberration in gear as I got closer. I tracked the guard's path as I pulled into a spot marked ACP-3, my mind automatically assessing what was trying to pass as a vehicle. The roll cage was high and somewhat narrow, which wouldn't really help if he took a sharp turn. The short engine compartment equaled electric power, which might allow it to be quick off the mark, but in the end, his electric would be no match for the horses nestled under my hood.

The comical image that popped into my head made me grin as I shut down my baby. I nudged my amusement back and shoved open the door as that bastardized cart rolled closer. By the time I locked my car and headed toward the nearby door, I was readjusting my assessment of the guard and his ride from minimal to possible PITA, because the irritating press of magic was gaining weight.

Hmm, seems someone has power.

I had my hand on the cool metal of the doorknob, ready to pull it open when the security cart came to a near-silent halt. *Yep, definitely electric.* Even from a few feet away, the bite of magic grew sharper. I let go of the handle and angled to face the guard as he exited the cart, making it rock with his movements.

Now, why would they need to magically reinforce that weird little cart?

It was uncomfortable being caught between the warding magic of the warehouse at my back and the power surrounding the guard and his ride. Mr. Security was doing his best to look intimidating. It might have worked if I wasn't used to dealing with much more dangerous types. I donned my professional half smile honed through years of practice and endured the itch of magic licking around my ankles and then creeping higher, searching for an opening to exploit. Thanks to my Prism, it couldn't find a grip, but that did make me curious as to what he expected to accomplish. I considered poking him back.

No teasing the guard, Rory. Tone polite, I said, "Morning."

"Morning," he returned as he stopped with a good five feet between us, one hand gripping his equipment belt, his other white-knuckling a heavy flashlight. Thankfully, he didn't do the whole light-in-the-face thing. Instead, there was a hint of belligerent arrogance when he asked, "Are you aware that this is private property?"

I considered a smart-ass comeback, but I tugged my professionalism closer and veiled my irritation in cool civility. "I am. However, I'm here at Mr. Medina's request to meet an associate."

He frowned and took a step forward. Behind me, hinges groaned softly in warning as the door at my back started to open. I stepped aside to avoid being hit and kept the security guard in view as the metal door swung wide.

"Good, you're right on time." A woman stepped out to join us. Roughly my height, she held open the door with one hand, the morning light glinting off the silver bracelet at her wrist, and dismissed the guard with a negligent blink. "It's fine, Rob. I've got this."

Since I was watching the guy, I didn't miss the flare of anger her casual dismissal created, but despite jutting out his jaw, he didn't say a word. He jerked his head in an awkward nod and pivoted on a heel to stomp back to his souped-up golf-cart-slash-ATV-wannabe. Once seated, he yanked the wheel to the left and zipped off on an irked midlevel hum.

"It's just not the same," I muttered to myself as I watched him putter away, amused by the incongruous scene.

"Nope," said the woman, whom I was betting was Piper. "Can't beat the deafening growl of a revving engine when you want to leave in a snit."

Since I was thinking the same thing, it made me believe she and I would get along just fine. I waited until the electric cart disappeared around the far corner of the warehouse before I turned to her. "Piper McMillan?"

"That's me," she said, her eyes bright with amusement. She tilted her head, the short strands of her pixie cut shifting with the movement. "And you're Rory Costas, my ride."

"So it appears."

Her amusement deepened as she waved me inside. "Come check out our ride. Maybe it'll sooth that temper you've got simmering."

A little disconcerted at being read so easily, I tried to excuse it. "I'm a little caffeine deprived."

I moved past her, and magic scraped over my senses. It was something I noted that often happened when dealing with high-powered mages. That meant this woman was a force to be reckoned with. That was okay, because I was too. I stepped over the threshold into the cavernous space. Lights illuminated a small collection of vehicles that filled the main space.

She followed at my heels, dragging the door closed behind her. Humor edged her voice as she said, "That, I can help with." When I stopped, she came up beside me and motioned over to a small, enclosed office. "There's a fresh pot inside."

"Then I appreciate the assist."

She moved into the small area cordoned off from the main space as I looked over my options. I tagged an everyday sedan, three bikes that might rival Zev's beloved Harley, a sporty street racer, a paneled van, two more compacts that could easily blend in the city, a truck that looked like it should be parked next to a dusty field somewhere, and the star of the group—a performance BMW with a silvery shine.

My Transporter heart let out a purr of possessiveness. I raised my voice so Piper could hear me. "Tell me we get to take the M5."

"Will it make you less pissed off at Matt?" she called back.

Unable to resist, I walked closer to the sedan. "Maybe."

Her laugh was contagious. "Then, yes, we get to take that."

"Nice." With just over six hundred horsepower with a lowered sport suspension, it would make the drive fun. Even better, the ceramic brakes meant if I had to stop, I would stop, not slide to a halt. I brushed my hand over the hood's smooth finish, and the innate connection a Transporter forged with a vehicle slid smoothly into place, like petting a sleek predatory cat. I gave her another long stroke along the driver's-side doorframe, feeling that inexplicable sentience I could never properly explain to a non-Transporter. This girl was eager to hit the road.

"Here."

I turned to find Piper holding out a travel mug. I took it with a murmur of thanks and blew across the top of it but didn't sip. "So…"

"Don't worry." She lifted her cup to her mouth, her gaze flicking to the cup then back up to me. "It's not poisoned."

My lip quirked at the obvious dare, and without breaking eye contact, I sipped the coffee. I couldn't help my appreciative hum as notes of caramel and chocolate hit my tastebuds. "Good stuff."

"Of course it is," she drawled as she leaned against the BMW. She used her free hand to motion down her curves. "As if I'd sully this fine piece with anything less than awesome."

At that, a laugh broke free. *Yeah, she and I are going to get along fine.* "So how's this going to go down?"

"Well, first, we get to navigate some pretty questionable directions. Then, if we actually find this place, you and I are going to make it hard for anyone watching to resist temptation. Of course, while we're playing our parts, I'll be making sure you and I come back in one piece. If I'm really lucky, I might even get to bust a move or two."

I couldn't help the snort at her choice of words. "Bust a move? Seriously?"

"What?" Her question was suspiciously innocent and accompanied by a wide-eyed puzzlement, which might have been believable if there hadn't been a wicked light behind it. "Bust a move, kick some ass—it's all the same."

"If you say so." Piper might get off on seeing action, but

over the last year or so, I'd learned to brace for whatever reality threw my way. It was one of the main drivers that had led me to accept Lena's tracking charm. I brushed my fingers over the warm pendant at my throat, taking comfort from the responding tingle of active magic. Piper caught the seemingly absent movement, so I tried for casual as I dropped my hand back to the BMW and lifted my coffee. "So what do you mean by 'if we find this place'?" I took a sip of the steaming brew.

Resigned irritation replaced Piper's amusement. "The Blessed Amrita is a tad rabid when it comes to her privacy and her treasures, so although the directions are seemingly straightforward, there are rumors that looks are deceiving."

Sounded about right to me. Amrita might come across as a wack-a-doodle, but she was a cunning wack-a-doodle. Then again, most charlatans were. "Maybe we'll luck out since she knows we're coming."

Piper didn't look convinced. "Maybe, but I'm thinking we won't."

It didn't take a genius to read between the lines. "She's not happy about our visit." When Piper winced, I figured that was an understatement, which made me wonder. "How did the Council get her to agree to an appraisal?"

Something too fast flashed through Piper's expression before she veiled it. "Mateo can be quite convincing when he needs to be."

"I bet," I muttered then took another sip from my cup. I lowered it and eyed the Sentinel, my voice gaining a layer of steel as I laid it out. "So basically, we're going to invade a high-level Charmer's territory, critique her shiny, pretty Arcane object, hope we don't set her off before we turn her shiny treasure into a dud, all so we can lure the murdering Key out from under his rock."

Piper lifted her cup in a mock toast. "That about covers it."

"Swear to the gods, the Council really needs to rethink

their PR." The inherent arrogance of the Arcane Council was one of those things that never changed, and that wasn't a good thing.

"Perhaps it's something you can note on their customer satisfaction survey when we're done," Piper suggested blithely.

I snorted. "Yeah, don't think it'll change anything."

"Probably not," Piper agreed cheerfully. "But for now, you and I have a job to do."

I inclined my head. "True, so let's go see how close to divinity Amrita truly is, shall we?" I straightened and took another sip for the road.

Piper's eyebrows rose as she pondered my statement, but her tone was serious. "You don't think she's the real thing." She dug a hand into her pocket, and when it came out, it held a key fob. She made a move as if to toss it.

I lifted my empty hand to catch, and it flew through the air. "What I believe is beside the point. What I know is that we'll be finding out soon enough."

Three and a half hours later, I slowed the BMW to a stop on what could have easily been mistaken for a game trail instead of a road, my knuckles pressing white against my skin as I gripped the leather steering wheel.

Piper, her apparent patience stretched to a breaking point, asked, "What now?"

Normally, I would never risk a car like that on such a surface, but Amrita's reach was apparently quite long—something I learned when we were about halfway down a weathered, two-lane asphalt road that appeared to end in the middle of a sparsely tree-clad track of land blocked by a forest service gate that had seen better days. After Piper shattered the lock and shoved the creaky gate open, I drove through. As

I passed over the cattle guard, the surface under the tires altered, but visually, nothing changed. It was my first undeniable clue that Amrita was far from pleased about our impending visit.

The second lay before us, invisible to human eyes, but instead of explaining that it was the BMW that was reluctant to tackle whatever lay ahead, I said, "I don't know, but my gut is screaming."

"Right," Piper muttered as she whipped off her seat belt and shoved the passenger door open. "I'm done being nice." She got out of the car before I could issue a warning and stomped around to the trunk. She rapped her knuckles against the metal in demand.

I popped the release and split my attention between the unseen threat in front of me and the pissed-off Sentinel behind me. That low-level hesitancy emanating from the car didn't ease off, nor did it spike. A glance behind me showed the raised trunk was blocking my view. Whatever Piper was up to didn't take long, because within moments, she was slamming the trunk down.

I released my belt, shoved open the door, and met her as she came up the driver's side with what looked like a gun barrel in one hand and a narrow metal rod in the other. The power that crawled off the objects raised the hair along my arms, and I eyed them warily. "What the hell is that?"

"This"—she hefted the matte-black barrel etched with copper-colored runes to expose a rectangular housing with an optic set on top—"is a disrupter."

I followed her as she continued around me and toward the front of the car. "That doesn't sound good."

"It won't be for whatever Amrita crafted." There was a hint of malicious satisfaction in Piper's voice.

Instead of asking more questions, I stopped at the hood and watched as Piper rested the barrel on one shoulder while she snapped out the narrow rod with a flick of her other wrist. There was a pop of magic, and the rod turned into a three-part stand, with two backward-facing legs and an upright center piece. Piper did something, and when she stepped back, the disrupter was mounted on top, aimed toward the horizon.

She walked back toward me. "You might want to get in until I finish this."

Not needing to be asked twice, I got back in the car and shut the door. In front of me, Piper's hands wove a pattern in the air, sunlight glinting off her bracelet. Power sparked, and the pressure around me took on painful weight as the magic dug down to scrape against my bones. The pain registered briefly, then my Prism took exception, thickening until the world around me took a step back, leaving me alone inside my protective shell. Instinct had me keeping the Prism in check as it yanked against my will, as if it wanted to squash the threatening power out. I didn't need the magic extinguished. I just needed a bit of breathing room from whatever Piper was invoking.

Calling forth magic differed from mage to mage. Some had elaborate rituals, others used complex runes and power circles, and still others just pulled it forth from an internal source without warning. Piper appeared to be one of the latter because a rush of power filled the air, then with a wave of a hand, she directed it toward the disrupter. The copper-colored runes flared to life, burning with an unearthly amber color. The pressure in the air broke with an almost painful crack, and the scene in front of me wavered for a long, breathless moment before shattering like a windowpane. As the pieces fell away, a new image appeared like a developing photograph.

SIX

THE PICTURE CAME TOGETHER, slowly at first, then faster and faster. Towering trees, a paved road, and at the far end, an imposing metal gate complete with intimidating spikes. By the time the last piece of the illusion drifted away, I was out of the car and standing next to Piper, my mouth open in shock.

"Holy hell," I breathed. "How did…" Words failed me, and I resorted to waving my hand toward the weapon.

"Magic," Piper said as she moved toward the disrupter and began dismantling it.

"Smartass," I snapped as the power in the air dissipated. My Prism thinned in response, not disappearing completely but backing off now that there was no active threat.

"Better than a dumbass," she shot back as she did another wrist flick, returning the tripod to its previous baton state.

Can't argue that. I got back on track. "Amrita must be a hell of a Charmer to pull this off."

Illusion mages came in three varieties: Charmers, Mirages, and Nightmares. Nightmares liked to torment people with their deepest fears, while Mirages could cloak people and things from sight, rendering them invisible. That was a handy trick unless someone bumped into the invisible person or the cloaked object, which would raise obvious questions. Charmers were my least favorite because they played with minds. They could create illusions realistic enough to interact with the physical world, like reshaping a road to discourage visitors.

Piper carried both items back to the trunk. "Hence the disrupter."

I followed and stopped at the driver's side to duck in and release the trunk. When I straightened, I said, "I thought the goal was not to aggravate her?"

Piper closed the trunk and brushed off her hands as she went around to the passenger side. She opened her door and faced me over the roof of the car. "When Mateo gave me this assignment, I did my research, because, hello"—she motioned to herself—"Sentinel. Based off what I found, it was safe to assume Amrita would skirt the line of what she could do to discourage the Council's representative. Therefore, I decided to make sure that I could level the playing field if necessary."

I looked down the road then back to Piper. "You got anything up your sleeve for making sure she doesn't twist our minds into pretzels when we arrive?"

"Nope," Piper said with a cheerfulness I was coming to expect from her, then she got in the car and closed the door behind her.

"Great." I got into the driver's seat and closed my door. Guess it would be up to me to make sure Piper and I got out of this sane. *Speaking of which…* "The spell the Council gave you, how are you going to set it without being caught?"

She lifted her arm and twisted it, making the silver bracelet dance.

I eyed the pretty object. "Seriously? It's in that?"

"Yep." She dropped her arm and pulled her seat belt into place. "Once I have the stone in hand and you confirm it's legit, a little abracadabra and mission accomplished."

Unless, of course, that abracadabra blew up in our faces. "I don't think Amrita is just going to stand idly by after you break her toy."

"Probably not," she said with the same obnoxiously cheerful tone she'd had earlier. "So I hope you're as good as Matt thinks you are."

Me too. Instead of saying that out loud, I started the car.

Conversation was nonexistent as I drove down the road. Worried about unseen threats, I kept my speed cautious and my senses peeled for anything. A breeze slipped through the surrounding trees, making leaves dance under the late-morning sunlight. Thankfully, nothing jumped out of the foliage or popped up in the middle of the road. However, our slow speed had one benefit—giving me a glimpse of something that couldn't possibly be real. I slowed even more, craning my neck as I tried to make it out. "Did you see that?"

Piper shifted in her seat and leaned forward to see out the side windows. "Was that...? Stop!" Her command was accompanied by her hand gripping my arm.

I hit the brakes.

"Holy crap," Piper muttered as her hand moved from my arm to the driver seat's headrest to brace her weight as she leaned even farther in. "Is that a house?"

I undid my seat belt then twisted to get a better look. "How did they get that up there?" I swore I could feel Piper's mouth open to answer. "Don't say magic."

She huffed out a laugh, but her weight shifted as she got a better angle, then she pointed. "There, see it? I think those are cables holding it in place."

I rolled down the window and stuck my head out. The playful breeze blew my hair over my face. I caught the wayward strands and tucked them back behind my ear. The rustling foliage did its peek-a-boo dance, and sure enough, sunlight shimmered off a series of thick cables that anchored a reflective box structure high in thick branches. "Did they build it out of glass?"

"I think so."

"Wild," I murmured, marveling at the unusual treehouse that sat nearly invisible among the trees. It made me wonder about the home's residents and why they felt the need to hide in the branches. I retreated inside and hit the switch to raise the window. "You don't think that's Amrita's place, do you?" I redid my seat belt.

"No." Piper drew back and resettled in her seat. "I'm betting it belongs to one of her people."

"She has 'people'?" I waited until she had her seat belt in place before I put the car in gear once more.

"More like rabid followers." She sounded disgusted. "They call themselves the Blessed."

"Original." *Not.* "Are they going to be an issue?" I felt more than saw Piper's shrug.

"Who knows?"

Her lack of concern was irritating. "Would've been nice to know earlier."

"Why?"

I glanced at Piper. "Seriously?" I turned my attention back to the road. "We're getting ready to confront a beloved cult leader and demand she all but hand over a powerful Arcane artifact, and you don't think it would've been important to share that our odds weren't two against one but who knows how many against two?"

"I bet your glass is perpetually half empty, isn't it?"

"Yeah, because people keep drinking the Kool-Aid," I shot back. "Come on, Piper, even you have to admit, no matter how good a plan is, the minute rabid believers jump aboard, everything goes off the rails."

"First," she said with an unsettling calm, "most of her followers are Traditionalists, so the threat level is negligible."

"Most, but not all," I pointed out, frustration making my

voice sharp. "All it takes is one mage to get in a lucky strike." And non–magic users weren't exactly without their own threat.

"Which is why you're here."

Her unperturbed response set my teeth on edge. Up until the last few months, I'd kept my ability hidden from everyone. All those years of successful subterfuge had disappeared in a blink when I exposed myself to the Council, but that didn't mean I was used to having it bandied about so nonchalantly. Gritting my teeth to keep back a growl of frustration, I squeezed out, "I'm not invincible."

The epitome of composure, she said, "No, you're not, but all I need is that split-second grace to ensure both of us walk away."

A taut silence filled the car for a long moment as aggravation battled with curiosity.

Before either could emerge triumphant, she leaned forward a bit and pointed off to the passenger side. "Look, there's another one."

I angled to see and spotted what looked like a gigantic tumbleweed tangled in the branches. "That's a house?"

"Yep," she said, her attention never leaving the weird structure. "There's a set of stairs on the back side."

Great, we were driving through someone's bizarre version of a treehouse community. With my luck, we were going to be ambushed by a bunch of furry, pint-sized, warrior teddy bears armed with walking sticks and bows and arrows.

And my land speeder doesn't have four-wheel drive.

The road curved a bit, and through an unexpected break in the tree line, I spotted a series of half-dome shapes that were too symmetrical to be natural. "We've got more." I motioned toward the earthen dwellings. "Over there."

Piper followed my direction, peering through the windows. "Is it wrong to want to go over and ask for a tour?"

"No." I finally gave in to my curiosity. "How would you do it?"

She had no trouble following my question. "You mean, getting us out if we're attacked en masse?"

I nodded.

Instead of answering, she lifted her hand, palm up.

A whisper of power had my Prism snapping solid, and I hit the brakes, barely feeling the seat belt bite into my chest at the abrupt stop. Piper's bland expression didn't change as she, too, jerked against her belt's hold. Above her palm, a flame of blueish-white erupted, forming into a lethal throwing blade that hovered in place.

"What the hell is that?" Every instinct screamed to get away, but I was frozen in horrified fascination.

"This"—Piper's unmarred fingers danced, and the burning blade slowly rotated—"is a combination of both fire and energy." The shape blurred and reformed into a lethal-looking dart.

"Dual mage?"

"In a sense." She fisted her hand, and the dart disappeared, leaving no trace of its existence. She twisted her wrist and flicked a finger.

I jumped when a flicker of icy blue burst to life just above my white-knuckle grip on the steering wheel. Instinct had me jerking back before my mind registered that there was no heat, no press of power, nothing that emanated a sense of threat. Watching the dancing flame, I risked reaching out to brush at it. My fingers went through it with no visible impact. I looked at Piper. "Is it real?"

"It can be," she murmured, power flickering deep in her eyes, adding an echoing tint of the same icy-blue glow to her hazel eyes, turning them almost copper. "If I want it to."

The unearthly blue fire gained an azure depth edged in bronze at its heart, and I knew if I tried touching it now, it would do its best to eat through my Prism. "Fire mage."

"Close." The flame winked out, and Piper's glowing gaze returned to their previous hazel as she resettled into her previous persona. "They call us Salamanders. We're actually considered a subset of the fire mages."

Images of the mythical fire lizard swam through my brain, but nothing else rose to the surface. "I don't think I've heard of that."

"No surprise; we're few and far between." She paused then added, "Kind of like Prisms."

A familiar simmering resentment lay under Piper's comment and left me collecting the shards of my shattered preconceived notions. *Why didn't I put the pieces together earlier?*

The answer wasn't comfortable, but it made a grim sort of sense. Prisms couldn't have been the only specialized power that threatened the powers that be and had paid for it by being nearly extinguished. "Did you always know?"

"I did," she answered. "My family made sure our legacy wasn't lost, because a Salamander tends to make an appearance every couple of generations."

Curious and a tiny bit envious, I asked, "Do you mind if I ask how you learned to handle it?" It was a nosy question, sure, but I had a feeling if Piper didn't want to answer, she would let me know.

"I always showed an affinity for fire, but the ability to shape it into a physical or incorporeal object didn't hit until my early teens. That's when my grandmother's brother decided to train me."

"Good that you had that."

"Yeah," she agreed softly. "How about you?"

I could feel my lips curve upward, but not with enjoyment. "I grew up in the foster care system, knowing I was going to end up behind the wheel for the Guild, so I wasn't aware I had anything else until I got into it with an older kid and my Prism kicked in."

"The kid," she said when I fell quiet. "What happened to him?"

I winced at the memories. "He was a fire mage, but luckily, all he lost was his eyebrows. After that, I had to do some digging to figure out what was going on." There was another piece, but there was no reason to bring up Alvin, the schizophrenic homeless man who was the first to give me an actual name for my ability. "It wasn't until I reconnected with Sabella that she was able to fill in the blanks."

"Better late than never, I guess." There was a quiet understanding in Piper's voice.

"Yeah." She wasn't wrong. "So if Amrita and her minions hit us as a group, you can level the field?"

"As long as you can hold them at bay for a few seconds, we should be good."

"Good to know." The road took another lazy curve, and I followed. When it straightened once more, I let out a low whistle. "I'm betting the Blessed Amrita doesn't get a funky treehouse."

Piper leaned forward and peered through the windshield at the daunting stone wall broken only by a wrought iron gate that loomed ahead. "Real or illusion?"

"I don't know." I slowed the car as we got closer. "But we're about to find out."

SEVEN

I BROUGHT the car to a stop in front of the ominous gate. Despite the fact that the gate was made of thick bars of wrought iron, there was no way to make out what lay beyond it. A strange warping haze hovered on the other side, indicating more illusions were at play. When Piper unsnapped her seat belt and reached for the door, I knew I wasn't the only one making that assumption.

I grabbed her arm before she could open the door. "No."

Hand still on the door, she turned and frowned. "Why not?"

I let her go and used my head to indicate the intercom and keypad positioned off to the side. "We're being watched. You haul out your pet disrupter, I don't think whoever's playing Peeping Tom will give you enough time to put it together."

She didn't look at what I'd flagged, knowing what that would reveal to our watchers. Instead, she let go of the door, relaxed back in her seat for a brief moment, then casually bent forward as if collecting something from the floorboards. The move effectively kept her face out of the spotlight. "Your ability, does it allow you to see through illusions?"

It was an astute question, which served as a reminder to

not underestimate the strategic warrior next to me. I considered my answer as I studied what lay beyond the thick metal bars. "Not exactly." I let that part of me that sensed active magic unfurl. "But it will give us a heads-up."

Lines of power flickered to life in my mind's eye, revealing a thick web of power that wove between the gate's bars like a smoke screen. It was so complex, it was dizzying. On some instinctual level, I understood that getting through it would take both skill and time, neither of which were currently available.

Piper didn't push it. "Then we proceed as if nothing is real." She straightened, her expression coolly composed, exposing nothing.

Since that echoed my personal plan, I simply nodded and dropped one hand to hover over the window control on my door. I could hold my strange double vision open for an extended period of time, but the cost would be a debilitating headache. Not willing to risk such a weakness, I nudged the mental door almost completely closed, leaving it open just enough that only a whisper of warning would be needed to throw it wide. I rubbed a knuckle over my brow and asked, "Shall we?"

She gave a barely-there nod.

I powered down the window then reached through to press the button next to the intercom.

A buzz sounded, and a few long seconds passed before there was a click followed by an abrupt "Yes?"

"Ms. Costas and Ms. McMillan to see the Blessed Amrita."

The intercom remained silent. For a long, tense moment, I wondered if we would have no choice but to pull out the disrupter, but then a subtle hum sounded, and the metal gate slowly began to roll back. No further direction came from the intercom, so I raised my window and put the car into gear. As we inched into the murky veil of illusion that curtained the surroundings, it swirled in a dizzying dance. The strange disruption slowly parted directly in front of us, revealing an unobstructed road.

"That's not fog," Piper murmured.

"Nope." I kept the BMW's speed down as we crept along the drive. I spared a glance out the rearview and noted that the gate had disappeared in the haze behind us. We were definitely being herded forward. "I don't like this."

"Neither do I," Piper said, an edge of hardness in her voice.

The road curved, and as we rounded the bend, the haze disappeared as if a switch had been thrown.

I blinked at what sat before us. "Piper, are you seeing this?"

"Uh-huh," the Sentinel sounded as stunned as I felt. "How is that even standing?"

"Magic?" That earned me a slight slap on my shoulder. "Ow!"

"Baby," she murmured without looking away from the weirdly constructed house.

"Bully," I shot back even as I glided to a stop. "But I was being serious. Look at it."

We both stared. Amrita's house could've been pulled from Dr. Seuss's rhyming stories of my childhood. "'From there to here, from here to there, funny things are everywhere!'" I repeated from memory. With nowhere left to go, I put the BMW into park and shut off the engine.

"Right?" Piper leaned forward and craned her neck, a necessary angle to capture whatever it was that rose up through the trees. "It's like someone tried to build a bunch of different houses and then set them on top of each other in a twisted version of Jenga."

She wasn't wrong. Unlike the strange treehouse-like structures we'd seen before, this did not try to blend in any way. The house, if it could be called that, had five levels. The bottom level was long, its siding a mix of shingles, bricks, and wood broken up by a headache-inducing collection of square, round, and diamond-shaped windows that couldn't have found a straight line if given a ruler.

Sitting above that in an irritating discordance was the second floor—a thin and narrow level with the same unexplained mix of architectural choices. Symmetrical square windows lined the third level, narrow strips of brick dividing the evenly spaced panes, the roofline so thin as to be nonexistent.

The fourth was a precariously perched cupola straight out of the Victorian era set dead center, while the final and fifth level was a neo-Gothic spire that belonged on a European church. Not much, if any, of the overall structure belonged anywhere near the Coconino National Forest, much less pieced together like this incongruous creation.

Yet there it stood, in all its demented glory.

"Maybe it's an illusion?" I asked with a carefully hopeful note as I continued to stare in horrified fascination, wondering if a stiff wind would send it tumbling down. The thought of walking inside that disaster waiting to happen had goosebumps breaking out over my arms.

"Guess we'll find out soon enough." Piper shoved open her door and stepped out.

I did the same on the other side and came around to follow her toward the short set of steps that led to a veranda. Wary curiosity urged me to nudge my mental door wider to be sure what we saw was real, but before I could choose to do so, the front door, which was set awkwardly off to the side and out of reach of the sun, swung open. Piper and I both came to a stop.

"It's rude, you know," said the tall, broad-shouldered figure standing in its shadowed entry. "To gawk like that."

"Apologies," Piper said, even as she moved to take the lead. "I was stunned by its imaginative aura." She inclined her torso in an abbreviated bow. "The Blessed Amrita, thank you for receiving me." She straightened, and her shoulders went back, her chin tipped up, while a hint of snootiness entered her voice. "Piper McMillan, Antiquarian of Arcane Artifacts."

Somehow, I managed not to laugh at the overblown introduction. *Try saying that three times fast.* Instead, I held my position a couple feet behind Piper, doing my best to be invisible.

Unappeased, Amrita moved out of the doorway and into the sun's reach, illuminating her disapproving frown. As first impressions went, hers was a doozy. Her hair was completely covered by a rainbow scarf wrapped around her head and tied off in a tail at the back. Sunlight sparked off the rhinestones adorning her green cat-eyeglasses. Despite those flares of boho fashion, the rest of her outfit was right out of a high-end woman's shop. She propped a hand on her hip. Her manicured nails were tipped in the same emerald green as the cuffs of her V-neck silk blouse, which was rolled just above a collection of leather and beads wrapped around her wrist. She inclined her head enough to have the scarf's colorful tail slither over her shoulder. The pose was as deliberate as the cultivated class-meets-mystic outfit, right down to the green pointed-toe heels peeking out from under the high-waisted, tailored black slacks.

She stopped at the top of the stairs and stared over the top rim of her glasses. "You're the Council's antiquities expert?" She gave Piper a deliberate once-over before straightening. She resettled her glasses and folded her arms. "Aren't you a little young for such an auspicious position?"

"Age isn't everything," Piper replied, completely unruffled. "However, I've worked with the Council for a number of years, and they've yet to have an issue with my work."

"So you say." Amrita's attention moved beyond Piper and landed on me. "And you are?"

"Ms. McMillan's driver," I said.

That had Amrita looking back at Piper with a poorly concealed sneer. "You require a driver?"

Piper's smile disappeared, her face falling into cold, arrogant lines that slapped Amrita's condescension back into place. "My time is valuable," she said, her implication that the other woman was wasting it coming through loud and clear, "and with the demands of my responsibilities, it's imperative to get work done when and where I can."

Amrita sniffed, unfolded her arms, and waved with overexaggerated courtesy toward the door. "As I wouldn't want to inconvenience you, shall we appease the Council's curiosity?"

Piper motioned toward the entryway. "After you."

Color seeped under the other woman's cheeks, but instead of continuing the pissing contest, she spun on one thin, spiked heel and strode into the house of weirdness.

Piper's shoulders shifted as if shrugging off the irritation of dealing with the touchy Sibyl.

I came up to her side and kept my voice between us. "Making friends already, Ms. McMillan?"

"Matt is so going to owe me," she muttered under her breath without looking at me as she regathered her mask. "Ready?"

No. "Shouldn't that be my question?"

The smile that broke over Piper's face skated perilously close to feral. "Let's do this."

Unlike me, who was wary about what we were walking into, the Sentinel was clearly confident in her ability or jonesing for an adrenaline fix. Either way, I let Piper start out ahead of me. I loosened the hold on my Prism then nudged my mental door a little wider. The tactic was risky as hell, but it made me feel better. Piper might be there to watch my back, but I wasn't the type not to reciprocate. We went up the stairs, and I let my power slowly expand until it covered both of us.

That proved to be the right decision, because as soon as we stepped across the threshold, the door swung closed behind us with a disconcerting slam. A brief image of being locked in a cage flashed across my mind. Magic prowled around my Prism's edges, searching for an opening. It felt like a prickly weight of inexorable demand against my magical skin. It didn't hurt exactly, but it wasn't comfortable. That wasn't the worst of it, though. There was something… off about the magic. I couldn't pinpoint exactly what, but whatever it was left a nasty smear over my shield. Thankfully, my Prism was just as disgusted as me and managed to slough off the clingy remnants. I suppressed a shiver.

We were in an entry that didn't match the first story's outside dimensions. Two snarling stone Chinese lion statues guarded a sweeping staircase to our left. Across from us on the opposite side, four different doors broke up the wall, each one painted a different color—blue, red, green, and black. To our right was a closed set of white double doors with oiled-bronze lion door knockers.

Our host opened the green door and continued through without looking back. "Come along."

We walked over the large, thick rug, our steps muffled as we crossed through the unusual foyer and followed her into a short hall that led deeper into the house.

The click-snap of her heels was getting farther away, but her voice remained clear. "We can chat in the sitting room."

In comparison, the only sound Piper made was the slight shift of her clothing as she strode after Amrita. I brought up the rear as tendrils of tension curled around my spine and settled at the base of my skull. Lighted niches, all of them filled, decorated the hall. Some held what appeared to be sculptures, others crystals, and one a yellowed human skull covered in runes that made my Prism shiver and my steps speed up as I passed it. Finally, we escaped the hallway of unsettling objects and joined Amrita in her sitting room.

Our hostess settled in at a round table made of a dark wood that was polished to a shine and surrounded by high-backed upholstered chairs. "Please, take a seat."

Piper took the chair closest to the hall on Amrita's left. I decided that, as a mere driver, I could stand off to the side, so I picked a spot that would let me grab Piper if shit hit the fan but also allowed her to keep me in sight so we could maintain our charade.

Amrita tapped her nails against the chair's arm as she considered Piper. Her words were startling in their bluntness. "I am not inclined to turn over my property to the Council, Ms. McMillan."

This was not starting off well. A whisper of warning brushed my mind, but focused on the potential threat in front of me, I didn't have time to chase it down.

Piper's expression didn't change, and her tone remained bland. "They are aware."

"And yet they still sent you." The statement was made in such a way as to imply that the Sibyl was unimpressed by Piper's supposed status.

Equally arrogant, Piper inclined her head.

"Curious."

"How so?"

"As an antiquity expert, I'm sure you're aware of what happened to the other Court Stones."

Piper said nothing, and I realized it was because Amrita hadn't asked a question.

"Why should I allow this divine artifact to be assessed by those who likely seek to destroy it?"

"We could go with the politic because they are Council," Piper blithely returned.

Amrita was unmoved. "I answer to a higher power."

"And I answer to the Council."

Amrita's lips compressed into a tight line. Color seeped under her cheekbones as her fingers tightened to the point of bloodlessness on her armrest. "The Council is blinded by mundane concerns and their need to prove their strength by destroying things they can't comprehend. That they believe they can erase such a sacred relic is tantamount to blasphemy."

"The Council is not interested in taking your object from you. They simply want to verify its authenticity." A hint of pity washed through Piper's face, and her voice held a patronizing note when she pointed out, "Surely, you understand their concerns? The origin of the Court Stones is clearly documented. There is nothing that marks them as holy relics, but they are considered quite powerful, and in the wrong hands, that power can be detrimental to Arcane society. The Council's tenet is to protect their people, and this assessment will go a long way to assure them, if it's authentic, it's in the right hands."

Watching Amrita, I saw the flicker of fury at the multiple implied insults Piper managed to couch in politic terms before her haughty mask reasserted itself. "Propaganda spread by the Council to denigrate the most Holy cannot negate the sacredness of this object. As one touched by the divinities' love, it is my duty to protect their stone."

"And it is my responsibility to ensure you comply with the Council's wishes," Piper returned in a coldly inflexible voice. "I'm sure you're aware that additional verification of the stone's legitimacy will only enhance your standing with your followers."

A silent standoff ensued as the two women eyed each other, and I wondered how long it would take for Amrita to buckle. Considering her open disdain of the Council, we might be here a while. As if summoned by that realization, my earlier hint of wariness made a return, bits and pieces drifting together to form a disturbing picture.

Not only was Amrita a skilled con artist who clearly believed her own hype, but her arrogance bordered on dangerously entitled when it came to the stone. So why would she allow a Council underling inside her home without some sort of protection in place?

She wouldn't.

Instinct whispered, and with a conscious shift of focus, I let my recently acquired power quirk roam unhindered. The room lit up with an overpowering mix of magical echoes visible only to me. My Prism was lit in silvery white and shaped into the hard edges of diamond's refractive surface. A shimmer of burning blue mixed with metallic copper wavered around Piper like a desert mirage as she sat unknowingly protected inside my shield.

It wasn't easy to pick out specific signatures, not with magic all but clouding the air, but something unseen sat in the center of the table, emitting a pulse of power. Strangely, that wasn't what held my attention, though. That was focused on what unfurled from Amrita. A weird mix of olive green with flecks of sickly yellow and disturbing embers of red that ignited every primitive instinct I owned. The oversized, hideous wings fluttered around her, but there wasn't an angelic feather in sight.

Divinity, my ass.

I recognized that noxious mix and strengthened the barrier between us and it, grateful I hadn't ignored my gut.

Demonic.

As the silence between Piper and Amrita stretched tighter and tighter, I dared to check the room for other signs of what we were dealing with. The room was saturated in magic, most likely because what we sat in was an illusion. I tried my best to see beyond the nightmarish strands, but studying those signatures left me fighting the urge to hurl. With no other choice but to endure, I shifted my focus to my Prism, thickening the protection, and prayed it would be enough.

The tension between Amrita and Piper broke, thankfully not how I anticipated.

Amrita pushed up from her chair, ending the silent battle between her and Piper. "I hope verification is your true intent." She brushed her hands over her hips and said with cool hauteur, "If not, then the Council can reap the consequences of their arrogance."

"If the stone proves to be what you claim"—Piper slowly rose to her feet, clearly unintimidated by the implied threat—"I'll be sure to share your warning with the Council."

Amrita's smile was just this side of evil. Sly and condescending, it left me tense. "Then let's not waste any of your time, hmm?" She snapped her fingers, and a green flame erupted from the center of the table. It burned eye-searingly bright and reached upward at least a foot before it died away to reveal the object of the hour.

EIGHT

IN THE TABLE'S CENTER, surrounded by the dying embers of Amrita's showy reveal, sat an unpolished, palm-sized stone of chalky gray with pale streaks of almost-luminescent green that seemed to be lit from within.

"You appear to be disappointed, Ms. McMillan," Amrita said with a bit of a sneer.

"Disappointed?" Piper continued to study the object. "No, just surprised."

Amrita's eyebrows rose to haughty heights. "You expected a polished jewel?"

"Truthfully, I wasn't sure what to expect." Piper started to reach out as if to touch it.

I shifted, clasping my hands behind my back, the movement a silent warning.

The hand she'd lifted smoothly changed direction. "But a raw crystal? Yes, that would make sense." She glided her fingertips along the edge of the table as she rounded it, the silver bracelet visible but inert. She continued her silent perusal until she was standing on the opposite end of the table. She lifted her gaze to Amrita, who was watching her closely. A little too closely. "May I?"

The air around the Sibyl shivered, causing the lines of power to undulate, but she simply murmured, "Of course."

Piper slowly reached out. I nudged my Prism into an invisible gauntlet that covered her hand, the bracelet, and her arm to up past her elbow. I wasn't taking any chances. Piper's fingers brushed the crystal, and it was only me who saw the resulting spark as the two dueling magics met.

Yeah, Amrita had something in place, all right.

Piper tipped the Court Stone into her palm, and the sparks turned into dark, tiny spikes that bit against the impermeable surface of my power.

Amrita leaned forward a fraction of an inch, and I tensed as those barbs started to gnaw at my Prism. It didn't hurt exactly, but it was far from comfortable. Not about to let on that I was aware of Amrita's nasty little spell, I clenched my jaw and flexed my fingers behind my back as that discomfort increased.

Piper drew the stone closer without any ill effects, and Amrita frowned, clearly not expecting the nonreaction. The Sentinel angled the stone she held between her thumb and forefinger, using the light seeping through the windows to inspect it. To my supernatural eye, power glinted like supernova fireflies among its duller cousins of dust motes.

Unaware of the play of light, Piper continued her examination, murmuring to herself about inclusions and Briolette cuts, all the while inching closer to me. When she was close, she thrust the stone toward me. "Look, see how it catches the light?"

The question wasn't as innocuous as it sounded. On the drive up, she and I had agreed the easiest way to exchange information in front of the Sibyl was to use a single word— *gorgeous*—to indicate authenticity. Anything else, and Piper would know the stone wasn't real.

Taking my cue, I played the fascinated bystander and

closed the distance between us, careful to keep my hands away from the crystal. The foul pressure against my Prism deepened, but I hadn't spent the last handful of months letting Zev run my ass ragged as he pushed me to my magical limits for nothing. He and I both knew mastering my abilities was critical to my survival.

As a latecomer to my Prism magic, I was at a distinct disadvantage. Most mages learned early on how to balance their power's techniques, both offensively and defensively, as they honed their magic. While my defensive technique was instinctual, my offensive skills had required serious practice, and Zev was a hard-ass drill sergeant.

However, in this moment, I appreciated his tyrannical-teacher approach. To determine if the stone was real would require a delicate touch, especially since I had to maneuver around whatever spell Amrita had wrapped around it. For any other mage, the task might have been close to impossible since it would be like threading a needle while navigating a minefield, blindfolded.

However, Prisms had a unique quirk—or maybe it was just me—and I had the ability to "see" magical traces. Not that it always helped. Sometimes, the echoes of power were so confusing they blurred together. Or, as in this case, the magical trails were wound around the stone in a densely gnarled, pulsating layer. Panic threatened as I tried to find some path through the ugly knot. If I'd had Lena's skill as a Key, I could be subtle, but if I wanted to disable it, I would have to use the magical equivalent of scissors to saw through the cords. Something warned me that could cause everything to blow up in my face. Literally.

All of this ran through my head in mere moments as Piper prattled on, filling my silence. With no time to waste, I made my decision and wove a hair-thin tendril of my Prism through the strands until I could reach the stone at the center.

It was like an Arcane version of the child's game Operation, except if I touched the edges here, Piper and I would receive much more than an easily brushed-off shock. Reinforcing the shield around us both, I braced and cleared the last malignant layer. With a flex of will, I traced that other sense over the uncut stone with a featherlight touch. What came back was… nothing.

"It's stunning. That's for sure," I murmured.

The barest flicker of acknowledgment was Piper's only sign of surprise as she drew the stone back. "Yes, I suppose it is." She turned, replaced it on the table, then straightened. "However"—she looked directly at Amrita, and her voice was harder than a diamond—"it's also a fake."

Instead of feigning insulted shock, Amrita gave an insolently slow clap, her lips curved into a smile that lacked anything close to amusement. "Very good."

Piper shook her head as if dealing with a wayward teen. "A test, really?"

Not at all embarrassed at being called out, the Sibyl sat back. "You expected differently?"

It was Piper's turn to do the shark smile, but hers was much sharper. "No, but I'm not here to play games."

"Neither am I, Ms. McMillan," the older woman said with a slide of silky menace. "I'd be a poor steward if I simply handed over the real relic to a Council minion."

Unruffled by the implied threat, insult, or whatever, Piper sighed and folded her arms over her chest. "I'm unsure of what else can be said or done to reassure you."

Amrita cocked her head, an anticipatory gleam igniting behind her cat-eyed lenses, and I had a feeling Piper had stepped right into Amrita's sticky web. "Is that an offer?"

"Depends on your proposal."

"In that case…" Amrita's expression was all kinds of pleased.

The hair on my neck rose in warning. I reinforced my

Prism just as a whisper of power shivered through the room. The air behind Amrita's chair wavered, and in that plane that allowed me to see magic, the sickly yellow shimmer parted to reveal a man. Of average height, his shoulders military straight, his short hair paired with a craggy clean-shaven face, he was on the older side of forty. There was nothing about his physical appearance to inspire caution, but the dull glow of power surrounding him like a smudged aura had me worried because he was in no way a Traditionalist. He was a mage.

Next to me, Piper, clearly picking up on the invisible threat, emanated a fine tension of coiled readiness, but her tone remained unruffled. "And you are?"

The man didn't move or change expression. He simply stood there, a mute sentry at Amrita's side, his gaze locked on Piper.

It was Amrita who answered, "Caleb." She didn't make us ask for more. "He's one of my acolytes."

Acolyte? More like Renfield.

Taking in the baleful light simmering in his gaze and the taint of demonic influence he shared with the Sibyl, I preferred my label over Amrita's, and that was before fine threads erupted from him to slither toward Piper.

With no way or time to warn her, I stepped forward, partially covering Piper as I prepared to intercept those tendrils. My sudden, seemingly erratic movement drew everyone's attention, including Caleb's. More importantly, those phantom threads, colored a murky orange, halted to hover expectantly a few inches from me.

I locked down my relief at the momentary reprieve. "Ms. McMillan, I don't—"

She held up a hand, cutting me off, her attention aimed at Caleb. "And why have you invited Caleb to this meeting?" Piper asked Amrita without looking away from the silent man.

"To ensure the Council's intentions, of course," the Sibyl replied. "All you have to do is answer his questions."

Piper raised her brows. "A Truth Seeker?"

"Of a sort." The other woman slid around the question. "After years of humble service, he was granted the ability to divine an individual's intent by the most Holy."

Piper studied Caleb for a long moment as she appeared to consider Amrita's explanation.

The silence stretched until Amrita added, "A simple request to put my mind at rest, Ms. McMillan, nothing more."

Piper gave her a slow nod then looked at me and tilted her head in a silent request to step aside. Jaw tight, I moved to the side. She passed by me, her steps measured, and retook her seat across from Amrita. I had no idea if her reluctance was real or not. I knew which it would be if I were the one sitting in that chair. Left with no other recourse, I repositioned until I could stand within touching distance of the Sentinel and clasped my hands behind my back as I rechecked my Prism to make sure there were no openings to exploit. Then I settled in to endure a three-way battle of wills—Caleb's, Piper's, and mine.

Time to see how good Zev's training really was.

Construing Piper's acquiescence as permission, Caleb took a step back from the table just as a ripple ran through the yellow-green mix of Amrita's magical wings. I was unsurprised when another high-backed chair popped into existence. The Sibyl really liked her illusions. Her acolyte pulled it out, took a seat, and folded his hands on the table's top, his gaze never shifting from Piper.

Undaunted, the Sentinel stared back, her face placid and her gaze sharp. It was only me who got to witness that icy shimmer that was her power thicken and darken into a metallic flame. Her reaction smoothed out some of my jagged edges.

Caleb cut to the chase. "Why are you here?"

The haunting cadence to his voice was at complete odds to everything else about the man. It was like the sirens of old, urging people to listen closely or else they would miss something important. The contradiction was so stark, my wariness spiked. That mesmerizing tone twined around the magical tendrils from earlier, reawakening them. Like frenzied snakes, Caleb's corrupted magic struck at the protective edges of my Prism. Each time the two powers clashed, an incandescent strike of lightning erupted. Anger bolstered my determination as I held back his two-pronged attack.

Caleb frowned, and that slight change of expression acted like a warning klaxon. Somehow, he was able to sense that he wasn't able to influence Piper.

Mind racing, I pictured a thin but impenetrable bodysuit wrapped around Piper and myself instead of the broader protective circle. The ability to craft such distinctive defenses had taken weeks of relentless work with Zev and, surprisingly, Sabella to master. Those hours of endless practice were now paying off as Caleb's power slithered closer, curled around Piper's ankles, and then coiled up her calf. Paranoid I was going to miss something that would leave not just me but also Piper vulnerable, I kept my mental eye on it. If it went any higher, I would be forced to reveal myself by reacting offensively.

Blind to what was happening, Piper shifted in her seat to cross her legs. Her move stretched the tendrils. I had a moment of hope that it would snap the threads, but no such luck. They held fast, but at least they stopped their advance and now simply clung to her, their orangish color oscillating between a pale haze to murky smudge and back.

Piper regarded Caleb for another heartbeat then answered, "As I told the Blessed Amrita, to authenticate the stone."

The threads darkened toward umber, and the lines in Caleb's brow eased. That beautiful voice sounded again, making all sorts of false promises. "You are working at the Council's behest?"

"Yes." Piper's lips curved into a mocking smile. "At Mateo Medina's request, if you want to be specific."

The snaking threads pulsed but remained closer to brown than orange. I took that as a positive sign when Caleb's only reaction was to ask his next question. "What does the Council plan to do with our artifact?"

I noted the possessive and, judging by the haughty edge that accompanied her answer, so did Piper. "I am not privy to the Council's decisions."

At her answer, I held my breath waiting for Caleb's power to call her a liar. When the color resettled, though, I realized that his pompous phrasing allowed Piper to skirt whatever cues he used to discern truth from lie by skating over specifics to give him a version of the truth. A very broad version of the truth. Sneaky and smart, it was also a dangerous game, as evidenced when Caleb's magic picked up a few flecks of orange.

Next to him, Amrita lifted one finger. Heeding the silent cue, he moved to his next question. "How did you pass the Blessed's tests?"

Piper's gaze shifted to Amrita. "Preparation and skill."

Even though she didn't indicate whose preparation and skill had thwarted Amrita's illusion, the older woman's attention still came to me.

Like the pet he was, her acolyte followed her movements with an eerie mimicry. More threads shot forward, this time toward me. I locked my muscles as they coiled around my ankles, and despite my Prism's protection, I had to fight back my reactionary shiver. I kept my attention on the two mages across from us.

"And, you, why are you here?"

Holding that baleful gaze, I took my cue from Piper. "Per my contract with the Council, I serve as Ms. McMillan's driver." On the edge of my vision, I caught a flash of orange and barely refrained from wincing.

Caleb made a soft hum, his gaze sharpening with predatory anticipation. He leaned in to whisper into Amrita's ear as she continued to study me.

When he straightened to his previous position, Amrita asked, "And what other services has the Council requested from you?"

Clearly, I wasn't as good at this game as Piper. Either that, or Caleb was smarter than I gave him credit for. I glanced at the man sitting at her side, turned back to Amrita, and said bluntly, "I'm a Transporter."

"A Transporter," she repeated, clearly unconvinced. She drummed her nails against the chair's arm as she considered me. With no warning, her magic whipped out and split into a two-tailed whip that coiled around my neck so suddenly, I had no chance to react. Thankfully, Piper, unable to see what I saw, had no idea what was happening and continued to watch Amrita even as the second tail curled around her neck.

Amrita's magic flared, and thanks to my innate protection, I felt only an uncomfortable pressure. When neither I nor Piper reacted outwardly, speculation filled her eyes. "Interesting."

She pushed up from her chair and glided around the table, Caleb trailing in her wake. As she drew closer, the pressure around my neck became a slow, relentless squeeze.

For the first time, Piper frowned. She lifted her hand, clearly reaching for her neck, but she stopped before she could touch it, her hand fisting. With her attention narrowed on Amrita, she lowered her hand to the table then pushed to her feet.

Amrita waved a hand at Piper, a silent indication for Caleb to keep an eye on her as she continued to stalk me. I mentally dug my heels in and held my Prism steady, determined to outlast her. When it came to magic, especially will-based magic, it was generally the most stubborn mage who won out. Stubborn was my middle name. I pivoted as the Sibyl approached, staying between her and Piper, my spine ramrod stiff and anger simmering in my veins. Behind me, I felt Piper move closer.

Amrita came to a stop, leaving only a few feet between us as she studied us both. "How are you still standing?"

Inside the walls of my Prism, Piper's magic flexed as she did something I couldn't see. Not sure what she was up to but willing to give her whatever help I could, I readjusted my shield so she could do whatever it was she was planning. A throb started at the base of my skull, an initial warning that I was overextending.

Piper moved until she stood in front of me and faced the other woman. "Did you think the Council would send me in unprotected?"

Busy keeping Piper and myself from being strangled, I nearly missed the flash of light behind Amrita and Caleb's squeaky gasp that followed.

Amrita spun around, only to come face-to-face with a narrow blade of flame hovering a hair's breadth from her lashes. A visible tremor ran through her. "What's this?" The question emerged a bit on the high side, but faced by the undeniable threat hovering in front of her, Amrita didn't dare react further.

Caleb was frozen in place, his eyes wide, as a second fiery blade hovered above his carotid, poised with lethal intent.

"Now," Piper said pleasantly as she circled the immobile duo, "do we play this out, or shall we move on?" She stood behind Caleb and looked at Amrita. "I can guarantee that this close, I won't miss."

The foul magic tightened so fast and so viciously, I wavered on my feet. I didn't know what Piper felt, but my breath caught in my chest as I concentrated on staying upright. Thankfully, neither Amrita nor Caleb noticed my revealing movement as their attention was riveted on the Sentinel.

Piper, on the other hand, stood strong, the only sign of strain the white lines that fanned out from her eyes and mouth. Her reaction was to nudge the hovering blades a fraction closer to both the Sibyl and her follower in warning. A bead of crimson appeared on Caleb's skin.

"Fine!" Amrita snapped, and the coils of power locked around me receded with a startling quickness.

The release of pressure almost had me slumping in relief, but somehow, I managed to hold my position and did my best to unobtrusively suck in air.

Piper kept her focus on Amrita and Caleb. Her blades held their position for a long, telling moment before they winked out as if they'd never been. Then she came back around to stand next to me. Caleb's stiff shoulders sagged, and his chest heaved as he noisily dragged in air.

Piper waited until Amrita turned to face her before saying, "My patience is wearing thin. Are you in possession of the stone or not?"

The older woman brushed her hands over her hips, but the movement did nothing to disguise the fine tremor in her hands. "I am."

"Then shall we finish this?"

Amrita straightened her shoulders with a jerk and gave an abrupt nod.

"Good," Piper's earlier polite smile was back, her eyes hard.

Amrita managed to stop her sneer before it fully formed and waved back toward the door. "For obvious reasons, I keep it stored in a vault. If you'll follow me."

Piper considered her for a long moment before inclining her head. "After you."

Spinning on her heel at the unspoken order, Amrita all but stomped toward the door, Caleb scuttling behind her.

Caleb had just disappeared through the door when Piper asked me in a very quiet voice, "You okay?"

I managed a shaky nod and answered in an equally soft undertone, "I don't like this."

"Neither do I, but leaving is not an option."

With that, the two of us headed into what was definitely a trap.

NINE

THIS IS BEYOND STUPID!

No shit, Sherlock, but unless you have another bright idea on getting your hands on the Council's target, it's our only option.

Despite the silent argument occurring in my head, I gamely followed Piper down Amrita's hall of creepy things. I did one last scan of the enclosed passageway, and when nothing pinged on my magical radar, I closed my psychic eye. Hopefully, the brief respite would curtail the looming burnout that threatened, because every step was bringing us closer to a certain trap.

I didn't like how the magic here all but lived and breathed within these walls. The echoes were so thick, it threatened to leave me magically blind. My quirk might help, but without knowing exactly what we were walking into, I couldn't risk not being able to use it. Instead, I double- and tripled-checked the protections around Piper and me, as the Sibyl had already proven she couldn't be trusted, leaving me with zero doubts that something bad lay ahead.

We'd covered about half the hallway when the walls rippled, and an opening appeared to our left. Of course, Amrita waltzed right through it, leaving us to trot along behind her. There was another one of those mirage-like ripples, and I looked back to see the opening was gone, replaced by a painting of a stern-faced woman who appeared to watch us. It took a lot of willpower to turn away from that unnerving artwork.

In front of me, Piper continued at a steady pace. Nothing indicated that she noticed the strange goings-on, but since she was inside my shield, I wasn't fooled. A faint hint of wary tension drifted around the Sentinel, likely a trait of her job, as they weren't known to be the trusting types. It was strangely reassuring, probably because Zev tended to carry the same aura, and if I couldn't have him at my side, I would take Piper. Especially since something whispered that escaping Amrita's sticky web would be a challenge.

Guess I owe Mateo a thank-you.

In front of us, the illusion mage came to an abrupt stop next to an innocuous door. "Before we enter, I feel compelled to warn you that this room is heavily warded." She turned and waited for us to join her. "The only way in or out is to be accompanied by me."

"Wise to have safeguards in place," Piper said.

Amrita gave a delicate sniff, pushed open the door, and disappeared inside. Caleb stepped inside then held the door in a silent bid for us to enter, his gaze inscrutable.

When Piper went to enter first, I heeded my instincts and brushed past her, taking the lead. If something lay inside this room, it was better that I walk into it instead of her since she could turn things to ash and all I could do was hold it at bay.

Like many parts of the Sybil's weird house, the room was unexpected. Marble floors with pale-green veins stretched out farther than the space should have been able to hold. There were a few seating areas here and there, but the room's true focus was the pedestal positioned at the far end. The distance made it hard to determine what it held, but since Amrita was headed that way, I was pretty sure it was the object of the hour.

I took in the cream-covered walls lined with niches that held human-size statues, but there were no other doors or windows to break up the space. My Prism hitched then shuddered. The unexpected reaction caught me off guard. It took me a moment to realize that something in the room was determined to get past my Prism. I dared to open my psychic eye for a quick sweep and immediately wished I hadn't.

Corrupted magic swirled through the space like some demented storm, leaving me all but psychically blind. Amrita had warned us the room was warded, but she'd failed to mention what powered the ward's magic. This was no simple Arcane construct. Not with this much fouled energy flowing through the interlocked sigils. It warped the Arcane symbols until they slashed at my brain like well-honed knives. I dug my nails into my wrist, the small bite of pain holding back my shudder of revulsion. My vision swam as the nauseating crush of magic battered at my shield. It was so disorienting that it took teeth-gritting concentration before I could shut it down. So occupied with blocking out the horror, I missed the door closing us all inside.

"Shall we?" Caleb's voice broke through my jumbled thoughts.

I caught the cold amusement in his upwardly tipped lips, but he said nothing, simply turned and began to cross the room, leaving us to follow. I blinked to clear the gray-and-white spots from my vision as I tried to calm my panicked pulse and rioting gut. Something brushed my arm, and I barely refrained from jumping out of my skin.

"Ready?" Piper asked as she stood at my side, her gaze holding an altogether different question.

Not even a little bit. Since that wasn't an answer I could voice, I forced my lips to curve upward, praying it didn't look like the grimace it felt. "Of course."

I forced my feet to move, even though every instinct I had screamed at me to grab Piper and get the hell out of there. The small glimpse I had was enough to warn me that I had neither the time nor the skills to navigate the twisted magic caught between these walls. Whatever deals Amrita had made—and I no longer had any doubt of their hellish nature—I did not want to mess with them. In fact, my only goal now was to make sure that Piper and I got out of this breathing.

In complete agreement, my Prism gained a harder presence as it tightened around me, and I nudged it to do the same with Piper. I didn't need the gift of foresight to know things would not end well.

We crossed the space, and I noted that the alcoves were filled with full-sized figures that ranged from the humble to divine. It was like walking into a museum hall of Roman-Greco statuaries. Rather than bare torsos draped in gauze, they sported more modern fashions that spanned the last few decades. It was beyond unsettling, and unease skittered down my spine in a constant wave.

When we got close to where Amrita and Caleb waited for us by the pedestal, Piper commented, "Interesting collection."

"A personal favorite," Amrita replied.

Piper made a soft, noncommittal hum.

We came to a stop on the opposite side of the pedestal, facing the demented duo. Piper studied the palm-sized chunk that sat under a recessed spotlight. It looked remarkably similar to the earlier rendition, with one marked difference—it lacked the unearthly glow from within.

Piper's voice was droll. "I commend you on your illusion."

Amrita folded her arms, raised a brow, and said with a heavy dose of snark, "Thank you."

"I find it fascinating that so many stories revolve around such a simple object, don't you?"

"Stories?" The illusion mage cocked her head, a glimmer

of true curiosity peeking through the arrogance. "Do you not believe the historical recountings of its power?"

"I would never discount such things," Piper replied as she angled around the stone until her back was to Amrita. She flicked me a glance. "Especially as I've learned that the most dangerous things tend to come in humble packages."

Rattled though I might have been, I didn't miss her unspoken direction. It didn't say much that my first thought was *Oh hell to the no!* But we were here for a reason, so I did my part. I bolstered my shield and focused on the lone artifact on its pillar. I could hear the murmur of Piper's voice as she kept up her role as an appraiser, asking questions of Amrita and keeping the Sibyl's attention on her. I braced and cautiously reopened the lens that saw between worlds.

The hellish storm still raged, but I stayed on target, narrowing my focus to just the stone. Here on this plane, that unearthly luminescent green glow was back with a vengeance. Not the virulent green that warned people away as I'd expected, but a mesmerizing deep green that was easy to get lost in. In fact, the contrast between its beauty and the surrounding ugliness was so stark, it was startling. The stone emanated such *power* as it sat alone in a sphere untouched by the chaotic magic.

I didn't realize I was inching closer until a sharp warning pulse tore through my temples. Heeding it, I stilled and forced my gaze off the stone and down to the floor, doing my best to unobtrusively breathe through the lingering ache. Released from the hypnotic pull of the stone, my Prism thickened, strengthening the barrier between me and the stone's influence.

Yeah, this was the real McCoy.

So absorbed in what I was doing, I took a second to realize Piper had asked me a question.

"Don't you think, Ms. Costas?"

I met Piper's gaze as my brain caught up to the

conversation. "I have to agree with your initial assessment. It's a little underwhelming, but there's something inherently gorgeous about it too."

A darkly satisfied glint hit Piper's eyes, but she simply nodded as if agreeing with my assessment.

Amrita watched us both, her smile just this side of sly as she folded her hands in front of her. With a masterful hint of piousness, she said, "It's the touch of the divinity."

Divinity, my ass.

"Looks can be deceiving." Piper's response sounded distracted as she resumed her study of the stone.

Amrita's lips thinned with insulted anger, and a muscle in her arm flexed as if she was fisting her hand.

Piper ignored her reaction and reached out as if to touch the stone, only to stop with her hand a hair's breadth away. She looked to Amrita. "May I?"

Anxious seconds ticked by, then Amrita gave a slow nod of assent.

Air stuck in my chest, and my muscles locked as chains of anxiety wrapped around me. My head pounded. From dread or from abusing my magical senses, I wasn't sure, but what I did know was that I really, really, really didn't want Piper to touch that damn stone. Even knowing that it was the only way to set the wheels in motion and take out this piece of dangerous magic, I couldn't help but dig a little deeper to bolster the shield around us.

Piper inched closer to the pillar, and it felt like everyone, including me, held their breath as her fingers closed around the stone.

I wasn't sure what I expected, maybe a flash of clashing magic or a vicious spell whipping out, anything but the disappointing nothing that actually happened. Piper carefully took the stone from its pedestal, cupped it in the palm of her hand, and angled it under the light. "Stunning," she murmured as if enthralled. She lifted her gaze to Amrita. "To authenticate the stone, I must cast a simple test that gauges its power. Do I have your permission to proceed?"

As hard as it was, I resisted taking a peek to make sure that the spell Piper carried in her bracelet was doing what it had been designed to do, but with so much magic already in play, it wasn't worth the risk of being unable to react when shit hit the fan, because shit *was* going to hit the fan. It was just a question of when. I inched closer to Piper. The movement was small, but Caleb's gaze flitted to me before boomeranging back to the conversation.

That's right, I'm just a mere driver. No threat here. Dumbass.

Amrita studied Piper like a snake eyeing its unknowing prey. "You may, but understand that the stone protects itself, so I caution you to be careful."

Piper inclined her head, a small cynical smile on her lips, as if she considered Amrita's warning trivial. She traced a sigil on the stone. The symbol lingered in a burnished copper as its edges lost their definition, and the color slowly shifted to a deeper orange then morphed to gold.

Caleb's attention remained riveted on the stone, while Amrita's was focused on Piper. Using their inattention, I snuck another inch or two closer to Piper and tightened the shield around us.

Piper's spell slowly spread over the stone, as if an invisible hand were carefully dipping the stone into gold paint. The minute the last bit of chalky green disappeared under the golden glow, all hell broke loose.

An invisible shock wave tore through the room, shoving so hard against my Prism that I was forced back a few feet by what felt like a sucker punch to the gut. I let out a pained hiss. Across from me, Caleb's body bowed back in a painful arc as he rose up on his toes, his head thrown back, his mouth open in a silent scream. Next to him, Amrita stood tall, only her scarf and clothing whipping in the invisible wind as a dull-crimson circle erupted under her feet. Piper stood with the stone still in hand, her eyes filled with the same gold that covered the stone, her hair blown back by the force of the competing magics, while a storm of blue and gold twisted around her.

Even as I tried to breathe through the pain threatening to disembowel me, I prayed I was the only one able to see that whatever had caught Piper didn't have a solid grip. In fact, my shield held it back. Just barely, but that was enough to keep her safe. For now.

Unrelenting pressure battered my Prism, each blow rattling me down past bone and blood. Just when I was sure it would shatter, the pressure blinked out. The invisible wind disappeared, and Caleb collapsed with a groan at Amrita's feet. Piper and Amrita stared at each other, one surrounded by gold, the other by an ugly crimson. For a long moment, the only sounds were the harsh breathing of the four of us.

Without looking away from Amrita, who was staring at her with a small, creepy smile, Piper asked, "Are you okay?"

Taking the question as mine, I managed a rough, "Yeah, I'm good." To prove it, I reclaimed the space I'd lost and stood next to her. "You?"

"Same." She then addressed Amrita. "What was that?"

Amrita's smile widened. "Did the Council truly think I wouldn't *see*?" the Sybil taunted. "That I wouldn't know exactly why they sent you? That as the chosen caretaker, I wouldn't ensure that the stone entrusted to me would remain protected from ill intent?"

Unruffled, Piper held her position. "I'm not sure what you think is happening." She sounded remarkably calm considering the situation. "But I was sent to verify that the stone is real. This cast was nothing more than a simple test of power."

"No simple cast creates this," Amrita all but snarled as she threw her hand toward Caleb, who was shakily getting to his feet.

"It does if the object I'm testing is an old power."

Damn, she's good. If I hadn't known Piper was bullshitting, even I would have believed her.

"Now—" Piper's voice hardened. "Are we through with the dramatics?"

The crimson circle Amrita stood within flared brightly, her face flushed with temper, her mouth twisted into a sneer, and her hands fisted at her sides. "Dramatics?" The one word came out in a deep, menacing tone that did not fit the woman who'd uttered it. Her fingers flexed, the crimson flames rising to meet them. "You inept—"

Caleb spun and stepped into her as if to hug her close, and whatever she was going to say cut off on a sharp gasp, her eyes flaring wide as she stared at him. Her lips moved, but nothing came out. It wasn't until Caleb stepped back that I understood.

For a long, endless moment, Amrita stood there, her hands clutching a hilt that protruded from her gut, a dark-red stain spreading across her stomach. On the magical plane, a dark fire ate at the edges of her unholy wings. Then, as she started to fold, that crimson fire flashed blindingly bright as it shot toward the ceiling. The unearthly column of flame hung in midair on both realms, hiding Amrita from view. I did my best to clear my vision of white starbursts as my heart raced and dread crawled over my skin. The column snapped out with a worrying abruptness, revealing Amrita's lifeless body, which was bad enough, but what scared the ever-loving crap out of me was the portal that began to take shape next to her.

"Oh shit."

TEN

FOR A MOMENT, I thought the words were mine, but when Piper grabbed my arm and all but hauled me back, putting as much space between us and the portal, I realized it had come from her.

"We need to get out of here." I'd stated the obvious as ominous crackling sounds began to fill the room. I didn't dare take my attention off the portal, which was nearly complete. I didn't want to be here when it finished.

She didn't answer but shot me a "duh" look before turning back toward the newest nightmare. Like cracks on a sheet of glass, black lines filled with a dull pulsing red snaked through the air. The harsh snaps and cracks grew to a deafening roar as Amrita's illusions shattered. The museum hall disappeared, replaced by warped wooden walls, crooked windows, and pitted floors, but what locked a scream in my throat was what had replaced the statues. Desiccated remains of what had once been humans began to crawl from the edges of the room.

I couldn't stop my horrified whimper or my instinctive jerk to get away.

Piper's fingers dug in so deep that I knew, if we made it out, I would have bruises. "Don't move," she hissed.

That was an easy order to follow, considering my muscles were all but petrified by fear.

Unfortunately, Caleb wasn't as affected. With a snarl that was half fury and half fear, he swiped out at a lumbering figure reaching for him with hands that were claws of bone and dead flesh. It did him no good, because another zombie slithered with inhuman speed across the floor and wrapped around his lower legs. The wannabe truth sayer screamed and struggled desperately as the undead duo held him fast.

I was unnerved by the fact they weren't taking Caleb apart piece by piece but appeared to simply be keeping him in place.

"What are they waiting for?" The question came out on a panicked breath, but I knew the answer. I just didn't want to face it.

The portal was nearly complete. Another minute at most and zombies would be the least of our worries.

"Rory!" Piper jerked on my arm, breaking my horrified trance. "Focus!"

I forced my attention away from Caleb and onto her. "I'm here."

"We're going to have to make a break for it." The true face of the Sentinel was showing, her jaw set, her hazel eyes grim with determination, and her voice was harder than steel. "How strong is your Prism? Can you hold it until we make it out?"

My brain ticked over like a stalled ignition, but it finally caught. I moved only my eyes as I gauged the distance to the only exit and the shambling horde that appeared to be making their way toward the portal and Caleb.

"Out of here, yes. Out of this entire nightmare?" I wasn't sure, not with whatever illusion Amrita had woven together falling apart, releasing gods knew what, and a demon on our heels. Since I had no intention of becoming someone's dinner or losing my soul, there was only one answer to give. "Yes."

A wave of stench hit me, and my gorge rose. I fought back the urge to gag as one of the undead shuffled a few feet from us. I clocked it as female only because of the tattered remains of a skirt that clung to decaying hips. I wasn't sure if it was because we were playing statue or because half her face was nothing but bone, but she paid us no mind, her focus on the still-screaming Caleb. I held my breath as she continued on her path, passing by so closely that if I dared to reach out, I could have touched her.

As soon as there were a few feet between us and her, Piper tugged on my arm in a silent order to move. This time, when she took the lead, I let her. I sank every bit of my stubborn will into my Prism as we started to carefully make our escape. We had barely cleared the pedestal when a deep boom resonated through the room. I dared to look back and sucked in a sharp breath, acute terror leaving me nearly numb.

The portal was complete. The warped sigils glowed a menacing crimson as they ran along the unnatural doorway. Inside was a deep, endless black. It took a moment for me to realize that the trembling under my feet wasn't me but the echo of something coming resolutely closer. The stench of sulphur deepened, and caught in his chains of undead, Caleb whimpered.

Piper gave another painful jerk on my arm, and I tore my horrified attention away from the incoming threat to stay at her back. Swift and silent, she didn't waste any time picking a path through the wreckage. The only way to function through my fear was to concentrate on following in her footsteps while a silent reminder to be quiet looped endlessly through my head.

She stopped short as one of the undead managed to yank the chain holding him free of the wall. He pulled it behind him like a dog on a leash, his head swinging back and forth as if scenting a trail. An amber glow formed over Piper's hands and rose up her arms, her mage fire held close and tight. The zombie froze and lifted its head. It was only then that I realized there were no eyes, lips, or nose, just a nightmarish mask of a man. He tipped his head back, revealing a ragged line across what had once been a throat. It was so deep, that for a hysterical moment, I thought his head would fall off. It didn't. He did the disturbing scent thing by sniffing at the air.

Next to me, Piper slowly, painstakingly began to form a pair of lethal blades out of her fire, clearly preparing to remove the threat if necessary. Desperation fueled my Prism, deepening it, as I prepared for the inevitable attack.

It didn't come. Instead, the nearly beheaded zombie spun around with a disconcerting quickness and leaped across the floor to land next to the others clustered by the portal.

Taking it for the ominous sign it was, Piper and I gave up on stealth and sprinted for the door. Our sudden movement caught the attention of a couple of lingering corpses. One went to grab us. Its clawed fingers slid off the Prism as Piper shoved a fire blade into its eye socket. Flames erupted from the zombie's skull as it dropped. I clumsily skirted around it as I stuck to Piper's heels.

Behind us, a deep roar was building. Or at least it sounded like a roar. It silenced Caleb and the moans of the undead, then it disappeared, leaving behind an unnerving silence.

We were feet from the door, and I knew I shouldn't do it, but I looked back. My brain scrambled to make sense of what I was seeing, but it was no use. The form was too monstrous to even paint a coherent nightmare. Everything in me panicked and lent me unknown speed. I wrenched my attention away, caught Piper's wrist, and all but dragged her through the doorway as an inhuman presence began to seep through the room. "Go, go, go, go!"

We burst out into an unfamiliar hall. Ominous creaks erupted around us as Amrita's house, no longer held together by her power, began to collapse. Outside, something huge slammed into the ground hard enough to cause the weathered walls to tremble. I shied to the side so hard, trying to evade whatever it was, that I bumped off the wall. The resulting cloud of dust and grit was thick enough to leave a thin layer over everything, including my eyelashes. I coughed and spat as I stumbled down the dilapidated hall, doing my best to clear my airways. Without losing hold of Piper, I used my arm to cover my mouth as I dodged what appeared to be a gnarled tree root that had ripped through the floorboards.

Determined to get the hell out of there, I took a few moments to register that Piper was trying to yank free of my hold and was yelling at me. "Rory, for fuck's sake, stop for a second!"

Lungs aching, heart pounding, half-blind, and with a stitch in my side, I tripped over the uneven ground and caught myself with a hand on the wall.

"What?" It came out a croak of sound.

Piper took advantage and twisted her wrist, forcing me to let her go. "You're going the wrong damn way."

My eyes watered, and knowing that if I rubbed my face, it would only make it worse, I shook my head like a dog throwing off water then used the underside of my collar to wipe the grit from my lashes. Blinking away the last bit of dirt, I took in Piper's appearance. She was covered in a thin layer of dull-gray dust. I had no doubt I looked just as bad, which meant the two of us could easily be mistaken for the undead.

She scrubbed her hands through her short hair, creating a small cascade of dirt and grit. "I thought you had the damn shield in place."

"It is," I snapped back. "But it's designed to hold back magic, not..." Unable to find words, I just waved my hand around the disintegrating house.

A loud crash sounded nearby. I jerked away from the wall

I was leaning against as Piper spun around. Just behind us, one of the many doorways Amrita had led us past just an hour before disappeared under a wave of stone, wood, and rotted drywall. Despite the newly formed mini-mountain of rubble, the permeating feel of evil slithered in its wake and spurred us back into action.

"Come on." Piper darted toward an archway that was falling apart piece by piece in a slow rain of brick. She put her arms over her head and hunched her shoulders as she dashed through.

Not about to get left behind, I mimicked her and followed, praying I wouldn't get brained by a piece of the house. I almost made it, but one lucky brick scraped the back of my shoulder. The painful burn was nothing more than a blip on my radar. We continued our run, dodging all sorts of things both physical and magical. Some made zero sense, but I wasn't about to take the time to ponder the mystery of their existence. I kept my eyes on Piper's back, refusing to repeat my earlier mistake of pulling a Lot's Wife move and looking back, not even when I could feel something malevolent breathing down my neck.

If you don't look, it's not real.

I wasn't sure I really believed that, but it kept me from panicking. Finally, fucking finally, shafts of sunlight started to pierce the haze and peek around Piper. The lure of light added a needed boost to my sore muscles, and I picked up the pace. The dust clogging the air slowly cleared, and the welcome sight of open skies beckoned just beyond the glassless frame that I was pretty sure had been the entryway. Piper had stopped and was shoving at a door that appeared to be torn off its hinges and now blocked the final exit.

Harder, deeper vibrations ran underfoot, and the floor in front of me disappeared. Still barreling forward, I did the only thing I could to avoid being swallowed by the demonic house —I jumped. "Piper!"

She turned, her eyes widening as I all but flew toward her, but she didn't hesitate. She pivoted and reached out, giving me something and someone to grab. Although my feet found solid ground, it didn't last long. The second my weight hit, the floor began to crumble. I windmilled my arms and grabbed onto Piper, holding on for dear life. With a hard yank, she jerked me away from the pit, and we both fell back against the fallen door. Another crack sounded, then we were both on our asses, staring in horrified shock as the floor crumbled away like a relentless tide. Like landed crabs, we both scrambled back on our hands and heels, ignoring the layer of skin we lost from our palms in the process. Neither one of us was in a hurry to test the depths of the growing pit.

Piper made it across the threshold and to the porch first. I was halfway there when our luck ran out. Or should I say, *my* luck ran out.

ELEVEN

A VAPOROUS ROPE coiled around my legs between one blink and the next. Shock held me for a timeless moment as my brain fought to make sense of how this was even happening. I didn't have time to ponder why my Prism wasn't working, because hundreds of invisible teeth sank into my skin and all but shredded my legs. But it wasn't done. The vicious cord yanked my legs out from underneath me, sending me crashing to the floor with no time to brace. I tried to avoid giving myself a concussion and instead bit the hell out of my tongue. Copper filled my mouth as the breath whooshed out of my abused lungs. Hot, bright pain lit up one wrist as I landed on it, and skin tore from my chin as it scraped over the floor. I scrabbled desperately for a grip on the uneven floorboards. Whatever held me kept pulling, and I kept twisting, ignoring the sharp bits and pieces that shredded my shirt and lacerated my skin. Panic was stealing what little air I had, but one last wild grab found purchase. I dug my fingers into the solid wooden post that had once supported a staircase. Now, it was the only thing between me and certain death.

The agonizing rope bit deeper then yanked hard, like a demented fisherman determined to drag his trophy aboard. Just like that doomed fish, I fought, digging my nails into the rough wood despite the sharp sting as they tore under the relentless pressure. That was nothing compared to the other, more immediate agony in my shoulders and back. I couldn't get my legs free, but I kept trying, even as my spine contorted, and my shoulders felt as if they would pop out of their sockets. My fingers started to slip, and fear, dark and petrifying, slithered through my panic. I wasn't going to be able to hold on.

Then Piper was there. Her hands locked around my wrists as she braced her feet against the remains of a nearby doorjamb and pulled. Agony flared along my injured wrist, but I didn't care, more determined than ever not to lose my grip on her. Her arms strained as she played tug-of-war with the equally determined demon. "Kick, dammit!" she all but snarled.

Desperate rage mixed with the deep, visceral fear of what would happen if she lost this demented tug-of-war. I locked my bloody palms around her wrists and sank every bit of my magic and desperation into fighting back. For a breathless moment, I swore those invisible teeth loosened. That infinitesimal action triggered a small, capricious jump in logic. *The demon wasn't locked on to me but my Prism.* Buoyed by that reprieve, I blocked out the acidic touch of the demon's magic that felt as if it were etching deep scars into my shield and poured the last remnants of my power into my Prism.

I will not go out like this!

Piper's foot slipped. "Fuck!"

I slid back another inch closer to the pit.

She got her foot set again, and with a harsh grunt, she dragged me back, regaining lost ground. "I need to use my magic," she gritted out.

I met her gaze, recognizing the flickers of copper brightening in her eyes, and understood her plan of attack. *Magic follows intent.* Zev had thrown those words at me during our hours of defensive practice.

"Ready?"

I sank everything I had into holding on and pictured my magic draining from the shield I had locked around her. I redirected it into my Prism until it was diamond hard, with razor-sharp edges that would cut anything it touched. The air around us shivered as I forced my magic into its namesake, a reflective Prism that covered both of us. As ready as I would ever be, I ground out, "Do it!"

She disappeared in a column of eye-searing icy-blue flames as an intense heat washed over me. My Prism may have held back the burn, but my skin was filmed with sweat in seconds. Not good when a sure grip was all that stood between me and losing my soul. Piper's flames spilled over my Prism and wound around and around the demon's chains. A high-pitched squeal came from somewhere in the depths of destruction behind us. For a hopeful moment, the pressure on my legs eased as a noxious odor filled the air. It was just long enough to fool me into thinking we had a chance.

Then a hair-raising, deep chuckle filled the world. That voice would haunt me for years. "Foolish little mage."

Staring up into Piper's strained face, I saw her skin pale and her eyes widen. In that split second, I tightened the magic around us both, ignoring the agony that arrowed through my head and down my spine. I gathered every last bit of power at my disposal and poured it into my Prism because I was not going to let either one of us die here.

Piper's incandescent flames roared back at us like an angry phantom, the blue disappearing under a disturbing crimson tipped in ebony. Piper's mouth opened in a silent scream, and I echoed her as that unearthly inferno swept around us.

It was instinct, not thought, that saved us, because just when I thought we would both be turned to ash, the curtain of demonic flames swept back, like a tide being sucked back for a tsunami. This time, there was no squeal, just an ear-shredding bellow of fury as the demon's magic was turned back on him. The ropes on my legs disappeared, and because Piper had never stopped trying to haul me over the threshold, the sudden release sent us both sprawling. Piper slammed into the wall, and I ended up between her and the remains of the staircase.

We both wasted no time scrambling to our feet. Supporting each other, we rushed out the door, tumbled off the edge of the porch, and limped-ran our way to the car, chased by a horrendous howl. Then came the sound of the world ending. Bone-breaking snaps, ground-shaking explosions, and the horrifying roar of an inferno followed. There was a sonic boom, and its echo smashed against us like an invisible wave, picking us up and all but tossing us forward. Somehow, we managed to land without killing ourselves and scrambled around the far side of the car. As lame as it was, some protection was better than none.

Once behind the dubious protection, my legs gave out, and I collapsed to my ass in the dirt, my back to the front tire. I tried to reengage my brain, which wasn't easy. My body was in shock, my head pounded, my ears rang, my lungs ached, and everything hurt. Something nicked my cheek, and I batted it away before I realized falling debris was ricocheting off the car. Not about to get brained by something, I covered my head with my arms as the stinging barrage continued.

For long, interminable minutes, the sounds of all hell breaking loose filled the fall afternoon. The noise was horrendous. I swore there were anguished screams intermixed with the house's death throes. The oppressive weight of dark magic was suffocating, making it not just hard to breathe but also hard to think beyond the primitive fear flooding my veins. The only reason I wasn't crawling out of there was I hurt too much to move.

Eventually, the noise and the press of power receded. As the last echoes faded, an unnatural silence settled in. Not the kind that meant we needed to run but the kind that came from stunned shock.

When nothing more pelted me, I let my arms drop and sent up a grateful prayer that the storm of bits and pieces was just that and that nothing huge managed to get past the car. It would suck to escape the house of death and the raging demon within only to be squished by the fallout. I leaned my head back against the wheel well and looked at Piper sitting next to me.

She had bent forward over her upraised knees and was now shaking out her short mix of brown and gold strands. Sweat, dust, blood, and other things left her hair a damp, dark, tangled mat. She leaned back against the driver's door as she shoved a hand through her hair to pull it back from her equally streaked face. Her eyes were closed, and her legs were sprawled straight out as she sucked in air.

"You okay?" My voice sounded muffled, my ears still not working right.

The fire mage opened her eyes and rolled her head toward me. She stared at me for a moment, her gaze a little dazed, as if my question didn't quite register, then she managed a "Yeah, you?"

"Alive, thanks to you."

She closed her eyes. "You're welcome."

I didn't know how long we sat there, my mind numb and my body one big ache, but eventually, I asked, "Is it over?"

"Since nothing's come to grab us, I'm guessing we're good," Piper said without opening her eyes.

Deciding it was best if I checked, I forced my body to

move. It wasn't pretty, and it took more effort than it should have, but I finally got to my feet and checked out the house. "Holy Mother—"

"What?" Piper regained her feet with impressive speed. "Oh, hell's bells."

All that was left of the Blessed Amrita's abode was a pile of rubble, and even that was slowing sinking into the ground as if being swallowed by quicksand. The two of us stood there, unable to turn away from the disturbing sight. It wasn't until the ground gave a soft sigh and resettled that I realized that there was nothing left to indicate Amrita or her undead following had recently called this place home. No traces of power. No echoes of demonic laughter. No nose-curling fumes. No shattered furniture or relics. Just scattered piles of hard-to-identify debris and some broken, aged timber that could easily be mistaken as remnants from some long-ago structure. In fact, a single bird dared to sing out and was soon joined by others.

I stared at the now-empty spot, wondering if Amrita's illusions were stronger than I'd thought. "What happened to the portal?"

"Gone."

"Are we sure?"

"You want to go poke around and find out?" the Sentinel drawled.

"Not really."

"Yeah." She sighed. "I don't blame you."

I cautiously made my way around the car, using one palm against the warm metal for balance until I was sure my legs weren't going to give out. The car's once-pristine exterior was now dull with dirt and dust, but it was the myriad of dents and scratches, including a rather deep one across the passenger-side rear panel, that made me groan.

"What?" Piper asked.

"How good is the Council's insurance?"

She made her way over and stood next to me, studying the damage. "That's actually not too bad. A little buffing, some paint, it'll be fine."

Uh-huh, sure. Deciding to leave that little stitch until later, I turned my attention to the real concern. I felt Piper do the same. We stared at the patch of dirt with an unholy appetite. My voice was quiet when I asked, "Seriously, Piper. What just happened?"

"If I had to hazard a guess?"

When she didn't say anything more, I nodded.

"The stone was an old, old power." There was a grimness to her words that I didn't quite grasp. "Accessing such magic takes immense skill, and Amrita didn't strike me as the patient type."

"You think she made a deal with a demon to access the stone's power."

Even though I didn't mean it as a question, she still said, "Yeah, I do. I'd also bet part of the deal used the stone's power to supercharge her innate ability as well."

I stared at where an impossible structure had once stood. "Hence the magical fun house?"

"And likely the road of misdirection we first encountered."

"That should make getting out of here easier."

"Maybe."

Not liking her careful tone, I repeated, "Maybe?"

She grimaced then admitted, "Some of the older magics don't react well to sudden changes."

"So does that mean we're trapped here?" *Please say no. Please say no.*

"No," she said, but before I could heave a sigh of relief, she continued, "But depending on what her illusions were built upon, we might find ourselves trying to drive out on an animal track or a dirt road."

The poor Beemer is in for a rough ride home. "I'm going to hold out hope for a dirt road."

She snorted and scratched her nose. The once-bright-silver bracelet at her wrist was now a tarnished matte, and her skin around it looked bruised.

Thinking about her comment on old magic and sudden changes, I rewound recent events and lined the pieces up in order. "Can I ask you something?"

"Sure."

"When you triggered the Council's counterspell, you not only broke her bargain, but you snapped whatever bound Caleb, didn't you?"

She nodded. "And I managed to shatter her illusions."

A flash of decaying bodies that shuffled with inhuman speed zipped across my mind's eye, and a shudder rippled through me. "The zombies? Who were they?"

Piper's shoulders slumped, and she wiped a hand over her face. Her sigh was soft. "Since no one is rushing in to see what happened to their beloved leader, I'm going to have to say, her followers."

A ripple of horror pierced my exhausted haze, followed by pity. "There had to be at least, what? Fifteen? How do fifteen people go missing and no one notices?"

Piper waved a hand at where the house had once stood. "Illusion mage, remember? Not to mention, cult followers? I'm thinking they aren't the type to ask questions to begin with."

"Still..." I just couldn't comprehend that kind of blind devotion.

She folded her arms as she leaned her butt against the car. "Did you notice the statues when we first entered? How each one was dressed? I'm guessing she picked them off one by one. Most likely using each of them as payment to her demon."

Just when I didn't think things could get any worse. "As in their souls are trapped in hell?" The thought was beyond horrifying.

Something dark washed through her face and hardened her voice. "Yes."

"Can they be saved?" Even as I asked, I knew the answer.

Piper said nothing, but a muscle ticced in her jaw.

We stood there, side by side, for a long, silent moment, both of us lost in our thoughts. I didn't know about hers, but mine were downright dark. My body was a symphony of aches and pains, and the headache that had set up shop in my skull threatened to turn my brain into soup.

Finally, she straightened. "Come on. We need to get out of here and get cleaned up."

Her words rattled around my skull, not quite connecting through the pulsing pain that was slowly taking over my world. "What?" The word came out thick through my numb lips.

She got close, grabbed my chin, and stared into my eyes.

I blinked rapidly, trying to keep her in focus, because she kept blurring around the edges.

Whatever she saw made her frown. She let me go and held out her hand, palm up. "Keys."

The demand echoed in my ears, and even though I knew what it meant, but I couldn't get my hands to move.

Something warm covered my cheeks and held me in place. Piper's face filled my vision. "Rory, where are the keys?"

There was a deliberateness to each word, and her question finally penetrated. "Left pocket," I mumbled.

I felt her hand at my hip, and I looked down to see it emerge with a key fob. Then she wrapped her arm around my waist and tugged me away from the car. Far, far away, something was trying to get my attention, but a dull fog was slowly creeping in. I stumbled and heard some mumbled cursing, then there was pressure at the top of my head. I went with it and found myself all but shoved into the car. My head lolled back without permission. There was a tug and a faint click, then the door slammed. Between one blink and the next came the sound of an engine then movement. At least I didn't have to walk anywhere. I let my eyes drift shut, then nothing.

TWELVE

"RORY, WAKE UP!" Someone was shaking me. "Come on, dammit, or I'll throw you over my shoulder and haul your ass inside."

The heavy darkness rolled back, and awareness sputtered to life.

Amrita's house of horrors.

Zombie statues.

Demonic portals.

Piper burning alive.

"Like you could." My tongue felt thick, but I was pretty sure I got the words out.

"I will if you don't wake up!"

"Fine." I forced heavy lids up and found a pair of irritated hazel eyes. "Happy now?"

"Nice to see you awake. Now get out of the car."

When she pulled back, I got a good look at where we were, not that it helped any. Since my abused body needed a minute before I asked it to get with the program, I asked, "Where are we?"

"Just outside Flag."

Okay, that explains the trees and the buildings that look like they belong on some old west movie set. I slowly leaned forward to look out the windshield. We were parked at the back of a two-story building. Burnt sienna in color, the bottom floor had a door marked Service Entrance and a set of metal stairs that led up to a second floor with a wide balcony that spread under four arched windows and a door. The building was bookended by two single-level structures. The one on the left was an older cinder-block house with a yard full of even-older RV campers corralled by a wooden fence. The scent of spice and sweetness made its way into the car. Wondering if my nose was playing tricks on me, I took a discreet sniff and identified the scent emanating from the place on the right. More in line with the forest motif with its thick log walls and pitched green roof, it didn't exactly scream BBQ, but that was what was cooking over there.

"Are we stopping for lunch?" I wasn't sure my stomach was ready for it, even if it did smell divine.

A very unladylike snort came from Piper where she stood by the open door. "No." Her unspoken *dumbass* came through loud and clear. "That"—she nodded toward the two-story building in front of us—"is a safe house. Now, come on, out."

Since she clearly wasn't going to let me just sleep in the car, I mustered the strength and got my legs out of the car. I braced one hand on the doorframe, the other on the seat, and went to get the rest of me out. Instead, the muscles along my back cramped with wicked swiftness. I let out a pained hiss and forced myself to keep going. With the speed of an arthritic snail, I managed to escape the car with only a few more groans and a couple more curses. By the time I was on my feet beside the car, sweat was a clammy film on my face and spine. Piper did the supporting-arm-around-my-waist thing again, and together, we headed toward the stairs.

Concentrating on not tripping on thin air, I focused on my feet and the cracked concrete under them. "Not sure I can make the stairs."

"Don't have a choice," Piper said, her voice low even though no one was around. "No elevator."

Great. I set my hand on the railing. Even though fall was in full force, the iron was warm to the touch. That warmth felt good against my sore fingers, but the minute I went to grip it to pull myself up, it was a different story. The railing, pitted with weather and age, was rough against my battered palms, but step by step, I dragged myself up each one. Piper stayed behind me, and every time I started to wobble, her hand would settle against my back so I wouldn't send the two of us tumbling back down.

When we finally hit the top, I moved to the side and hung onto the balcony railing as Piper squeezed around me. At the door, she set her palm against the wall, and I didn't even catch the flare of resulting magic as she triggered the ward. *Uh, I must have burnt myself out.* "Dammit."

She turned back to me with an enviable quickness, her gaze darting around to locate the incoming threat. "What?"

"Nothing," I muttered, uncomfortable at being all but magicless right now. "How long can we stay here?"

"A few hours." She opened the door, then she came back, collected me, and pretty much dragged me inside. "We both need to clean up and catch our breath."

Cool air greeted us, and I shivered at the change of temperature. The AC was kicking butt, which would have been lovely in the height of summer, but right now? Not so much. Piper stayed at my side as we shuffled across a dark wood floor and a rusty-red rug held in place by a dark-gray sofa and an eclectic half-moon cushioned chair with footstool. Our goal was that wide footstool.

I sank down onto it with a soft whimper. Piper cautiously let me go, hands out as she waited to see if I would topple over. When I didn't, she asked, "You good here? I need to grab a couple things from the car and then reset the ward."

"Yeah."

When she left to head down to the car, I studied our temporary digs. The space was surprisingly modern, considering the outer exterior. Exposed brick stretched along the far side, where a compact kitchen sat, and the remaining walls were a soft cream decorated by a pair of old window frames holding wall sconces. Refurbished barrels made up the end tables, and something green and leafy spilled from a planter, adding a touch of the outdoors inside. Beyond a doorway to my right, I could make out the iron footboard of a bed with a quilt. Another door within that room most likely led to the bathroom.

As if the beckoning shower and facilities were a mirage, I found myself struggling to my feet, determined to wash off the layer of grime and the even more uncomfortable sensation of being covered in something corrupt. I wasn't sure how, but I managed to get to my feet and make it partway through the living room before Piper caught me in midshuffle.

"Where are you going?"

I kept my eye on the prize. "Shower."

She closed the front door. "You going to be okay on your own?" Her skepticism spoke volumes.

"Yep." *Even if I have to crawl.* The bedroom doorframe was right there. I lurched forward, my abused palms slapping against the frame as I caught myself. *Owowowowow.* I waited for the stinging pain to ease before shoving off to resume my trek because I wanted that shower, dammit.

"If you don't come out in fifteen minutes, I'm coming in," Piper warned.

"Twenty," I shot back. My next goal was a four-drawer dresser on the wall between me and the bathroom.

"Twenty," she agreed. "There should be some clean clothes in the top drawer."

I used the breather at the dresser to pull out a pair of sweats and a faded T-shirt with a brewery logo on it. The tag on the shirt said XL, and I didn't bother checking the sweats, because if they didn't work, the shirt alone would be long enough to do for now. Shoving the clothes under one arm, I managed to clear the last few feet without resorting to crawling.

Yay me.

Once in the bathroom, I closed and locked the door before setting the clean clothes on the closed toilet lid since there was no real counter to be had. Standing in front of the pedestal sink, I finally got a good look at myself in the ornate mirror above it. It was a good thing Piper and I managed to get inside the safehouse before we ran into anyone, because one look at me, and they would've been speed-dialing 911.

My shirt was toast. The seam at one shoulder was ripped and the sleeve barely holding on. The rip revealed the raw, ugly scrapes underneath. There were other tears, where cloth and skin had met the unforgiving floor at Amrita's, and I was missing a couple of buttons. Miracle of miracles, the ones that would have me flashing all and sundry were still intact. My hair was a tangled mess and looked more gray than dark brown. There was a good-sized knot just above my left eyebrow, the colors an angry purplish red. The scratches along my cheek and chin were joined by streaks of dirt, dust, and sweat.

I turned on the faucet and was about to throw water on my face when I reconsidered. I shut off the water at the sink and turned to the tiled shower that took up the back side of the modest bathroom. I opened the glass door and turned the knob on the wall to hot. Water fell from the rain showerhead in the ceiling. I closed the door and moved the clean clothes to the shelf of towels next to a towel rack. Then, using the sink for support, I lowered my ass to the closed toilet lid. Muscles protested, and a moan escaped, but I persisted.

By the time I got my shoes off then stripped what was left of my clothes, steam was filling the space. I opened the glass door and let the billowing heat wrapped around me as I adjusted the temperature then stepped inside. Warm water fell over me, and everywhere it met a scrape or cut or bruise, it stung. I stood there, head down, letting the water wash off the worst of it as I breathed through my body's discomfort. Only when the water ran clear did I reach for the liquid soap tucked inside the little shelf and finish the job. When metal brushed my fingers, I realized I had forgotten to take off my necklace with Lena's pendant.

Too late now.

By the time the last of Amrita's house disappeared down the drain, my arms felt like lead, but my head felt a little clearer. The persistent headache had downgraded to a dull throb, and every inch of my body simply ached instead of screaming for mercy. I stood there for a moment, mind blank, eyes closed, drifting in the heat's embrace as water washed over me. It was only when that heat started to lessen that I forced myself to get out so Piper could have her turn. I had patted myself dry and pulled on the oversized T-shirt before I unfolded the sweats and realized they were for someone much taller. I'd just decided to stick with only my underwear when Piper knocked on the bathroom door.

"Two minutes," I called out.

I dug through a small basket on the linen shelf, and when I found a comb still in its package, I claimed it. I dumped my used towel in a wicker basket set on the floor and kicked my ruined shirt and pants into the corner under the sink. Comb held between my teeth, oversized sweats under one arm and shoes in one hand, I opened the door with the other. Cool air rushed in, shoving out the lovely humidity, and my skin pebbled.

Piper, sitting on the side of the bed facing the bathroom, looked up. "Did you leave me any hot water?"

I dropped my shoes next to the dresser and pulled the comb from my mouth. "Yep. It's all yours." I held out the sweats. "You can use these if you want, but fair warning, based on their length, they belong to a giant."

"Thanks, but I'm good." She picked up another big T-shirt that was lying next to her and got to her feet.

The stiffness with which she moved was a stark reminder I wasn't the only one who'd been to hell and back today. I got out of the way so she had a direct route to the bathroom. "Anything serious?"

"No." In stark contrast to her answer, she was probing gingerly along her ribcage, just under her bra line.

I pointedly looked at where she was touching herself.

She grimaced and dropped her hand. "Okay, maybe a cracked rib. How's your head?"

"Hurts like a bitch," I told her honestly. "I'm pretty sure I've got a mild concussion, but I'll survive."

"Good enough." She stepped inside the bathroom.

"Twenty minutes," I reminded her as she started to close the door.

"If the water lasts that long." She shut the door, and as I turned to leave, she yelled through it, "Try and stay awake, would you?"

Before I could reminder her that *try* would be the operative word there, I heard the shower go on. Leaving her to it, I went back to the living room. I lowered myself onto the couch and inched my way back into the corner. It took a few uncomfortable moments and a couple of pained hisses before I found a position that didn't hurt. Settled in, I started to work the comb through my hair. It took longer than normal because I had to stop every so often to unknot the worst of the tangles without aggravating my headache. When I was done, Piper was down to ten minutes. I set the comb on the barrel table and curled deeper into the couch. I rested my head against the pillowy arm as I waited for Piper to finish. It was a risk, but I closed my eyes and listened to the shower running.

Now that the adrenaline was a distant memory and my

body's complaints had died down to disgruntled murmurs, I was able to determine that knot on my forehead wasn't the only reason my head felt stuffed with cotton. Part of the exhaustion I felt was because I'd all but drained my magical battery to nothing. It was disconcerting to feel so vulnerable. Magic was such an integral part of me that its absence was uncomfortable. A paranoid part of me that had grown during the challenges of the last year had me testing to see just how drained I really was. Truthfully, I was probably safe for now, but it was better to know for sure.

Just in case, I don't know, one of Amrita's zombies managed to track us. An unexpected snort of amusement escaped at that improbable thought, and it struck me that I might be skirting the edge of delirium.

Corralling my thoughts, I tried testing my magical stockpile. Picturing a heavy door held in place by a thick bar of iron that lived deep in my psyche, I went to lift the bar and found that it took teeth-gritting persistence to get the door unlocked. The effort reignited the pulsating ache in my temples, but I finally got the bar up and off. I stood there until the pain receded, then I grabbed the door and dragged it open. I stood in the psychic doorway, stunned. Instead of the typical vibrant hum of power lying in wait, what little magic remained curled cautiously around me, its potency dulled by overuse.

Zev would kick my ass if he ever found out how far I'd taken myself. *Thinking of which, I should probably find my phone.*

The thought drifted through my head without finding an anchor, and on some level, I knew I was coming close to disobeying Piper's order to stay awake. A heaviness took over my limbs, pressing me into the couch. The shower shut off, and in the resulting quiet, I could hear the soft tick of the ceiling fan. The breeze it created ruffled the T-shirt I wore, and the hem fluttered against my thighs. Drops from my still-damp hair rolled underneath the loose material and down the back of my sore shoulder. Sleep was beckoning when a soft pulse of heat flared against the base of my throat then slowly faded.

On some level, I knew Lena was trying to ping my location, and I needed to get up, get my phone, and let her know I was relatively okay. Unfortunately, though the mind was willing, the body was ready to call it a day. I drifted along until another pulse had me fighting the fog of fatigue and grasping the stone. I didn't know how long I sat there like that, but the next pulse coincided with Piper's sharp, "Rory, wake up."

"I'm awake," I mumbled.

"No, you're not." The cushion next to me shifted as she joined me on the couch. "Open your eyes."

I forced my lids to lift and found her looking at me.

With her hair combed back, the small cuts and bruises decorating her face were vivid bits of color against her pale skin. Her gaze held obvious concern as she studied me.

Seeking to reassure her, I said, "See, I'm awake."

She didn't look convinced, but said, "Good, because we need to talk."

"About?"

"What happens next."

I didn't think that was a big mystery. "We go home."

"Actually, no. We're not done with our assignment."

Something in her voice all but shoved the foggy haze of weariness to the side. I frowned and struggled to sit up. "We got the Council's stone. What more is left?"

"First, we need to call in a cleanup crew for Amrita's, to make sure nothing makes a reappearance. Then we need to check with Matt to see if there's been any movement reported."

I might have been bruised, battered, and drained, but my brain still worked. "You seriously think the Heretic was watching everything go down at Amrita's?"

"You don't?"

Honestly, dealing with the demented Sibyl had sidetracked my worries about the Heretic. But someone that arrogant, that focused on obtaining what he wanted, yeah, I could see him having some way to monitor Amrita and the stone. Now that she was out of the picture, my role as bait would be too tempting to pass up. Not just for the Heretic, but for the councilman as well. Since I wasn't exactly the trusting type, I had a better idea. "Fine. You call in the sanitizers and talk to Mateo."

Clearly reading between my words, she narrowed her eyes. "And what are you planning?"

"I'm going to call Zev."

THIRTEEN

INSTEAD OF CALLING, I shot Zev a two-word text: *CALL ME.* Not exactly subtle, but I didn't have the luxury of fucking around right now.

Piper had dumped our phones, the keys, and a containment box that held the Court Stone on the counter. I had managed to escape the clutches of the couch and reclaimed my phone, while she moved to the bedroom to make her calls. Now I was on the edge of the half-moon chair and could see her sitting on the side of the bed, her phone to her ear.

"That's right," she said. "You'll need at least a level-four team on site, but if a red team is available, send them in."

If the Council's cleanup crews mimicked the Guild's sanitizers, level four would consist of the basics: a Key who specialized in demonic casts; a casting mage to purify the earth, either fire or water or both; and a combat mage to take care of any lingering threats. I was betting a red team would include a Necromancer. That meant Piper was making sure all the bases were covered. Good thing, because it would suck for some innocent hiker to end up a zombie snack or become the idiotic object lesson that stumbled into a deal with a pissed-off demon.

I checked my screen and saw the text had been delivered —just like the one I'd sent in the wee hours this morning when I was wide awake after my conversation with Lena.

Only this morning? Damn, it felt longer.

Piper moved deeper into the bedroom, and from the deference in her tone, I assumed she'd moved on to call Mateo. Although I had an idea what the directive from the councilman would be, I knew getting Zev's perspective on the whole situation would make me feel better about everything. It wasn't unusual to go twenty-four hours without talking to him, not with our respective jobs. Sometimes, we just couldn't risk breaking radio silence. I got that, but after my near brush with death—and a demon—I was feeling a little shaky and could really use some reassurance from my boyfriend. Leftover insecurities from growing up on my own raised their ugly voices with taunts of how weak it was to depend on anyone. I shut them down with a stern reminder that it had nothing to do with being weak but being human and couldn't quash a burst of pride when they immediately fell mute. A year spent relearning that love and family came in many different guises was definitely paying off.

The fleeting distraction didn't last long before pessimistic worry set in about his continued silence. He wasn't the type to go dark unless shit was getting real, and he was out there with no backup. Considering how things were going so far on my end, I couldn't help the dark thoughts that were gaining strength. Panic was starting to nip at the edges of my composure when my phone vibrated with a familiar number.

The pressure of unexpected tears hit hard, and I closed my eyes and rested the phone against my forehead, taking a moment to breathe away my precarious reaction. When I was sure I could answer without revealing my mini-breakdown, I opened my eyes, pulled the phone down to slide my thumb over the screen to answer, and put it to my ear.

"Hey, you." When nothing came back, I frowned, pulled the phone back, and checked the screen. The call showed connected, so I put it back up. "Zev, can you hear me?"

Dead air answered.

I tried again. "Hey, Zev, can you hear me?"

Nothing.

Then came the repeated monotone beep of a disconnected line. Sure enough, when I checked the screen again, it showed the call had ended. Reminding myself not to overreact, especially as reception could be spotty outside the valley, I checked my signal. Three out of five bars. I called him back, hoping to get through. Instead, I got his voicemail. "Hey, your call dropped. Call me back." Even I could hear the hint of worry in my voice, but it couldn't be helped.

I tried to hold off the unease with logic, but it wasn't working. I was gripping the phone and staring at the screen, waiting for Zev's number to pop back up, when Piper called my name. I tore my attention from my phone to look at her. "Yeah?"

She cocked her head and studied me with a small frown. "What did Zev say?"

"Nothing. The call dropped."

She checked her phone. "Uh, I've got a signal."

"I've got three bars on mine, but I tried calling back and got his voicemail."

"Maybe he's just in a bad spot. Give him a few minutes. I'm sure he'll call back."

I wanted to believe her, but the little cloud of doubt stuck around. "Yeah, I'm sure he will." I deliberately set my phone on the chair's arm. "How'd your calls go?"

She came into the living room, set her phone down on the nearby end table, dropped onto the couch, and grabbed a decorative pillow. "The first one, good." She tucked the pillow into her lap, folded her legs tailor style, and leaned back against the arm of the couch. "Got a crew coming in to clean things up at Amrita's."

"Okay." I drew out the word then asked, "And your call to Mateo?"

"Well…" She plucked at some unseen thread on the pillow and avoided my gaze.

Not good. "What?" The word came out sharper than I intended.

She grimaced and looked up. "He wants us to go back until the crew shows up."

It took a second for her answer to register, but when it did, the resulting irritation was fast and hot. "Wait, so we have to go back to the house from hell and—what? Wait around a partially opened portal to hell as the sun sets?"

"Unfortunately, yes." Whatever she saw on my face made her add, "Look, I'm no happier than you—"

That's debatable.

"—but the Council wants eyes on the site until the crew arrives."

It was on the tip of my tongue to say something snarky about the Council's edicts and where they could put them when she pinned me with a hard-eyed stare and reminded me, "We're both under Council's orders."

It chafed the hell out of my ass, but I couldn't argue her point. "Fine," I bit out. "How far out is this crew of yours?"

"They're being redirected from another job, so I'm guessing a couple hours at most."

My phone vibrated, and I picked it up as I asked, "I'm guessing we have to head back over there now?" A text bubble from Zev was on my lock screen.

"We can get something to eat and then head out."

"I'm assuming we'll grab and go?" I pulled up the text.

"Yeah, there's a little burger shack we can hit…"

I missed whatever else she said, because I was staring at

an image of Zev, bound, bloody, and unconscious, accompanied by a gemstone and an hourglass emoji. The message was unmistakable. My blood chilled even as my mind raced.

"Hey, Rory? You okay?"

Piper's questions finally penetrated, and I forced my voice to stay calm. "Yeah, just got dizzy for a second." I sent back a thumbs-up, my decision made in an instant. Then I set my phone face down on the chair's arm. "Zev says he's tied up for a bit." Hysteria threatened to erupt on a shrill giggle, but I ruthlessly locked my emotions down and managed a passable smile. "So you mentioned something about food?"

"Yeah, just on the edge of town." She studied me quizzically. "You sure you're not going to pass out on me?"

"No, I'm good. I'll be better once I eat." *As if; my stomach was a knotted mess.* I grabbed my phone and got to my feet. "Let me get dressed, then we can head out."

I was almost to the bedroom when she said, "Don't take this wrong, but I'm driving."

I grabbed the doorframe and dug my fingers in, using the sting of pressure to help corral my urge to yell at the unsuspecting Sentinel, not that this was her fault. But what I wanted was to grab the keys and the stone and hit the road, leaving Piper behind, but that wasn't an option. Not yet. "I'm good with that. A couple more hours and some food, and I should be golden." I realized I hadn't asked a very important question. "How long does Mateo expect us to hang around and play bait?"

"He wants us up here until tomorrow, at least."

That didn't give me long to come up with a plan, but desperation was a great motivator, and I would figure something out. I had to because the alternative was unacceptable.

A while later, I sat in the passenger seat, this time, fully aware, and stared out the window. After downing a couple over-the-counter painkillers to tame the aches and pains, I'd found a pair of baggy cargo pants in one of the drawers at the safe house and paired it with my oversized T-shirt. A knot at the hip took care of the billowing shirt. I had to roll up the hems on the cargos and use a tie as a belt to keep the waist in place, but at least I wasn't in danger of flashing my ass when we left.

Unfortunately, my recently ingested hamburger sat in a nauseating lump in my gut. I wanted to blame it on the lingering malevolence that hung on the air, but I knew better. Thankfully, Piper wasn't overly chatty, likely because she was nice enough to be mindful of my headache. Whatever the reason, I would take it because it gave me time to plot. With what I was considering, I had to make sure I covered every possible what-if, because this had disaster written all over it.

Yeah, I could have come clean with Piper, and if I knew her like I knew Lena, I would have, because I wasn't that stupid. Taking on the Heretic was a suicide mission, but despite our recent bonding experience with Amrita, I couldn't risk sharing and then having her lock my ass down, leaving Zev in the wind.

What I was considering left my conscience a mangled mess, but the image of Zev was burned into my brain, and the resulting cracks in my heart hurt. I tried to channel my great-aunt's ruthlessness with reminders that handing over such a powerful magical object to someone like the Heretic wasn't just lethally stupid but also cataclysmically dangerous. He'd already proven he had no qualms over leaving a swath of destruction and bodies in his wake. That was how he'd ended up being targeted by the Council Hunters in the first damn place.

But weighing that knowledge against the possibility of losing Zev was akin to balancing a feather against a stone, with the scales landing decisively with Zev. It was selfish. I recognized that and knew going through with this would destroy something important in me, but I couldn't leave him there. Either way, I was damned.

Better me than him.

Zev deserved better. He'd spent his life protecting those under his care, in particular Emilio, the powerful head of the Cordova Family, and Jeremy, Emilio's orphaned nephew. Zev's role as the Family Arbiter defined his life, and I understood his innate honor demanded he sacrifice all he was to keep them safe. But in this moment, that didn't work for me. I knew exactly what would happen if I didn't figure this shit out. The minute Piper knew the Heretic was in contact and why, she would lock my ass down until Mateo told her otherwise. Then, at the Council's behest, Zev would be playing bait for the good of the cause. It wouldn't matter what the Heretic did to Zev, including killing him—the Council would consider the cost justified.

I did not.

So I needed a solid plan. Even if it meant I would spend whatever time I had left being hunted by the Council and the man I loved. At least Zev would be alive to hate me.

Granted, there was a microscopically thin chance that if I asked, Mateo would let me play this out my way, but I sincerely doubted it. Not only was there the little fact that he didn't seem to like me, but there was no way in hell the councilman would let me get anywhere near the Heretic with the stone. The risk was too big, even for the Council. Still…

It's not like the stone's a threat, not after Piper used the spell to neutralize it.

For a moment, clarity pierced my frantic thoughts. Clearly, the Heretic had no clue that the Court Stone was no longer functional. Otherwise, he would never ask to exchange it for Zev. The fact that he thought the stone still worked was a point in my favor. I could hand over the defunct object and save Zev. No harm, no foul, right?

Except for the fact that you'll have to betray Piper.

Well, yeah, but she would get over it.

And the Council.

I winced at that one because I wasn't so sure they would ever forget, much less forgive, such a transgression.

And Sabella and Zev, who stood up for you. Will they understand?

I was fairly certain my aunt would, but Zev? That one hurt. I knew he would be beyond furious with me for doing this, but I wasn't as self-sacrificing as he was. I was selfish as fuck, because it was becoming quite clear I would cross whatever lines necessary to save someone I loved. Honor, reputation, saving the unknowns, they all paled in comparison to a world he was no longer in.

My decision made, my heart remained heavy, but my mind cleared, leaving behind a cold practicality that I knew Sabella would have been proud to witness despite the circumstances. I started to work through my options. First, I had to swap out the stone, then get Piper out of the picture. That had to happen sooner rather than later. There had been no more communications from the Heretic since the initial exchange, and I knew there wouldn't be until I confirmed I had the stone and was ready to trade. I was working through the first part of my problem when Piper broke the quiet.

"You're awfully quiet over there. You still awake?"

"Yeah, just thinking."

"About?"

There were a couple things I needed to verify, so I started with the most important one. "I know the counterspell you set broke the demonic pact, but are we sure it negated the stone's power?"

She shifted in the driver's seat so she was angled toward me. Night had set up shop, so the only illumination came from the dashboard, leaving us both half hidden by shadows. It made reading her expression difficult, but her tone was thoughtful. "Since the Council wanted you here to verify the stone's authenticity, I think you're more able to make that call than me, which means I have to wonder why you're asking. Is there something that makes you think the cast didn't work?"

I wasn't expecting her to turn the question back on me, but maybe I should have, and now that she had, I found I had to think about it. Finally, I said, "No."

"Then why ask?"

That was easier to answer. "You said it yourself—the stone is an old, old power. The counterspell may have broken whatever bonds tied it to the demon and destroyed Amrita's illusions, but would it be enough to wipe out its innate magic? I mean, its power is all about perception, right? And we know that some magics can act almost independently." I was thinking of my Prism and how it would sometimes react before I knew what was happening.

"Influence, actually," Piper corrected absently, clearly considering my question. "You think the magic might protect itself?"

"It is old," I reminded her. "How much is really known about its capabilities? Could it fool another mage into believing it was inert?"

This time, she took longer to answer. "I don't know, but I know one way we can find out."

It was hard to stay casual, but I managed. "How?"

"We take it out of the containment box and test it."

FOURTEEN

"NOW?" I asked even as my pulse kicked up.

Piper shrugged. "Why not? It's not like we're doing anything else right now. Besides, you're uniquely qualified to keep us safe, right?"

Suddenly, my voice didn't want to work, but I forced out, "Right."

I knew the containment box with the stone was warded in a hidden compartment in the trunk. I'd watched Piper set those wards in place when we left the safe house. I didn't have the skills to navigate that security, even if my magic hadn't been as depleted as it currently was, so I needed her to undo them, hence my question on whether or not the nullification spell the Council had given her had actually worked. I was banking on magic's capricious nature nudging Piper to double-check that the stone was no longer a threat. Part of me was a little surprised it had worked, but I wasn't about to look a gift horse in the mouth. "All right."

We both got out of the car and met at the trunk. She popped it, and the interior light came on. The normally muted light appeared overly bright in the darkness. I held up the cargo mat as Piper released the wards on the hidden space. At the first brush of her power, my Prism woke with a complaint and slid clumsily into place. I spared a moment to be grateful it had responded at all.

Piper took the containment box out of its cubby and waited for me to lower the cargo mat before she set it down on top of the mat. "You sure you're up for this?"

"Yep."

"Okay." Taking me at my word, she traced her finger over the top of the containment box. Sigils ignited, flaring briefly before blinking out. She lifted the lid to reveal the stone inside. It still looked unimpressive. The streaks of green that had been highlighted under Amrita's artfully placed lighting now appeared dull and closer to gray. It reminded me of a raw hunk of quartz. She took it out carefully, set it on the cargo mat, then looked at me. "Now what?"

For a second, I wasn't sure why she was asking me, then I got it. She had no idea how I knew if the stone was real or not. What she did understand was that as a Prism, testing the stone against me wouldn't work. That meant she would have to be the guinea pig.

Brave of her.

Before I could answer, we both heard the sound of a car and turned. There was no missing the sudden, predatory stillness that settled over Piper as we watched it approach or the icy glow that came from her hand still half hidden inside the trunk. She grabbed the stone, dumped it into the box, and closed the lid, though she didn't reset the wards.

Headlights appeared in the darkness and grew larger as the vehicle got closer. The height of the lights and deep rumble of the engine told me it was likely a heavy-duty SUV. I held up a hand to block the glare, but the vehicle's outline told me my guess was spot-on.

Piper's stiff stance eased, her magic snuffing out as if it had never existed. "Cleanup crew's here."

The SUV turned to park nearby, but Piper stayed in front

of me as the headlights flicked off, the engine shut down, then the doors opened. A stocky figure emerged from the passenger's side first, and a clear baritone rang through the night. "Someone called for a cleanup in aisle three?" The speaker threw his door closed and started our way.

Piper laughed. "Dano, always a pleasure." She started toward him then stopped. She shot a look at the trunk then at me.

Reading her unspoken request, I dipped my head in a nod, assuring her I would stick with the Court Stone.

She turned back to the man who'd spoken and was now joined by three others. I tuned out their meet-and-greets and took advantage of the unexpected opportunity presented. I repositioned, leaning a hip against the car so I could keep the stone and the crew in sight, then I threw open the door in my head. It was a Hail Mary, because I had no idea if I would have enough mojo to pull this off. The dull pulse in my head spiked with malicious glee, but I powered through and focused on the containment box. The box itself lit up, but not with the clarity I was used to. Instead, it was a soft glow that sputtered here and there, as if affected by an electrical short. Another sign my magical battery was low. Not good since I was hoping I would be able to identify a backdoor to one of the wards to use later.

No such luck.

I pushed a little harder and got a swipe of pain just behind my left eye that made me wince. I rubbed the ache away, and when I looked again, my breath stalled. So did my brain.

In the center of the containment net, a barely-there pulse of deep, deep green burned. Realization kicked in without mercy, pummeling my already-bruised-and-bloodied conscious into submission. Despite the counterspell, something still existed in the Court Stone.

Something I could use, whispered a dark voice in my head.

"Rory," Piper called. "Come here."

I let go of my psychic sight, blinked away the tiny spots in my vision, straightened, and headed over to join the huddle.

"Guys, this is Rory Costas. Rory, this is Dano, Marge, Lettie, and Trev."

Dano was the first to hold out his hand. "Nice to meet you."

"Same." I shook his hand then did a repeat with the other three. Marge's grip was all business, Lettie's was quick, and Trev did the careful squeeze thing some males did when they were worried about their strength. The waning moon gave some light, but the shadows kept their faces partially masked. Other than build and height, I wasn't sure if I would recognize any of them in the daylight.

Clearly in charge, Dano rubbed his hands together and turned toward what was left of the house and churned-up dirt. There wasn't much to see, just a collection of misshapen shadows from the broken bits sticking up like porcupine quills from a small hill, while bigger pieces were scattered bits of darker dark where the house had stood. "Right. So, Piper, tell us what we're looking at."

"A long night" was Piper's dry response.

"Ha, ha." That came from Marge, who shifted a backpack up on one shoulder. She wandered over to the pile of dirt and kicked at it, causing a few chunks of stone to ride a stream of loose dirt down the mini-hill. "I'm not sensing anything trying to claw its way up."

Piper watched her. "Probably because they're buried under the house near the portal."

"Portal?" Lettie perked right up. Clearly, she was the Key of the group and now anticipated a challenge.

"Partial portal," I corrected. When all eyes turned to me, I shrugged. "If it helps, it comes with a pissed-off demon."

Trev bumped Piper's shoulder. "You always give the best gifts."

Piper heaved a sigh. "Whatever."

"Show us around." Dano clearly wasn't asking.

Obviously used to his abruptness, Piper nodded then turned to me. "You want to hang back while I walk them through?"

My pulse sped up, but I nodded. "Sure."

"Once I get them set up, we can finish up and head back."

"Works for me."

Piper addressed the small group. "Come on. Let's walk through this mess."

I casually made my way back to the car and almost fell on my face when a good-size stone rolled underfoot. I picked it up to pitch it farther into the woods, only to stop and study it as it rested in my palm. A vague idea took form. I looked back at Piper and company, but they weren't paying me any attention. I could hear them talking, but their voices were indistinct. I made it to the trunk and, before I could reconsider, flipped open the lid of the containment box. Under the trunk's interior light, I compared the rock and the Court Stone. They were close in size, but there was no way the deeper gray and blacks of the rock I'd found could be mistaken for the grayish-green mix inside.

But that's not the only stone out here.

Another visual check of the others confirmed they were still occupied. In fact, it looked as if Marge was getting herself set up, likely to make sure whatever was buried in that dirt stayed buried. I waited until the others disappeared into the night and their voices grew even fainter before I went to the far side of the car and deeper into the tree line that stood a few feet away. Hopefully, Marge would be too involved in setting up her stuff to look my way for the next few minutes.

It will never work.

Ignoring that snide mental comment, I thumbed on the phone's flashlight function and held it close to my thigh to block the light as I scoured the nearby ground. I just needed one stone, one close enough in shape and weight that, in bad lighting, could pass for a piece of quartz. If it held some hints of green, all the better.

Discerning colors in the limited light wasn't easy. I'd discarded a couple of potential rocks and was about to give up when I hit pay dirt. I took my covert prize back to the trunk and did the visual comparison. The shape was close enough. *The weight…* I held the Court Stone in one hand, my replacement in the other. *It'll work.* The coloration was a long shot—no green, just whites and grays—but it might be enough to fool a casual glance.

"Hey, Rory?"

Startled, I nearly dropped my stone into the trunk. Instead, I slipped it into my pocket then leaned to the side to see around the trunk lid. "Yeah?" I called back to Marge.

"Can I borrow you for a second?"

"Sure, give me a second." Since I couldn't reset the wards, I did the next best thing to secure it. I hurriedly replaced the Court Stone in the box, put that back in its hidey-hole, and closed the trunk. Then I headed over to Marge, this time using my phone's flashlight to its full potential so I wouldn't trip. As I was skirting around the small hill, I realized that although my cargos were baggy, they weren't baggy enough to mask the shape of the rock in my pocket. So I undid the knot in the oversized T-shirt, releasing the hem to brush just above my knees. It was big enough to be a dress, and between it and the pants, the rock was just another wrinkle.

I met Marge over on the side closest to where the house had stood and fought back a shiver. "What do you need?"

"I need you to hold this for me." She handed me a thick stick.

I shut off the light on my phone, slid it into a back pocket, and accepted the stick. "Okay." Only when I pulled it back did I realize what I held wasn't wood but bone. "Tell me this doesn't belong to the zombies."

"It doesn't belong to the zombies," she repeated unconvincingly.

Clearly, being a smartass was a requisite to being a member of the cleanup crew.

"Don't worry. No one's coming back for it," she said as she bent to the backpack near her feet and pulled out an oversized spool of black thread.

"If they do, they can have it," I shot back, trying to ignore the fact I was holding a bone that had once belonged to a human.

"Probably best you don't drop that," she warned and started to unwind the thread with quick movements.

As she did so, it became apparent the thread wasn't normal thread, thin and easily broken. This was thicker, somewhere between a ribbon and a cord, and would take serious work to break. It made me wonder what she was expecting, and my mind helpfully supplied images from half-forgotten zombie movies and my recent real-life encounter. Not inclined to tempt fate, I pictured a giant eraser wiping my mind blank.

Hard to do when you're holding a femur.

When she had what she needed, she grabbed the top of the bone, tipped it toward her, and started to wrap the thick thread around the top, while I held it at the other end. "This is the anchor," she explained, her tone brisk. "So I need you to hold it steady while I set the other three points. Once I complete the circle, we can set it in the ground." She tied off the securely wrapped thread and started to walk clockwise from me, letting it trail behind her.

For the first couple of steps, nothing appeared to happen, but then things changed. The night seemed to gain a stygian depth that chilled my skin, and an oil-slick sheen started to bead along the thread. At first, I thought I was imagining it, that the sporadic moonlight was playing tricks with my eyes. But when my Prism rose like a bad-tempered toddler to bat an invisible pest, I realized Marge was raising a containment circle with necromantic magic.

She got to the first quarter point of her circle, bent down, picked up what I was betting was another bone, shoved it into the ground, then coiled her thread around it three times. Power rang down the binding and into the bone I held. An unsettling sensation of being stalked by something unseen whispered over me, stretching my nerves tight as ice coated my spine. I gritted my teeth, refusing to resort to the too-stupid-to-live trope and look back.

Instead, I focused on Marge as she started for the halfway point. With each step, the ice lying over my skin sank deeper. She did a repeat at the halfway point, and when she straightened to hit the last point, the encroaching cold carved itself deeper, leaving behind a numbness. Unable to feel my fingertips at this point, I had no choice but to add my other hand to hold the bone steady.

Marge got to the last point and glanced my way. Whatever she saw caused her to frown, but she didn't alter her movements. She was close enough now that I could see her lips moving even though no sound emerged. Clearly, she was setting her wards. I could only pray she would hurry the hell up before my hands ended up frostbitten. By the time she made it back to me, I had sweat rolling down my temples and spine, my muscles were shaking, and my bloodless hands were all but fused to the bone. She coiled the last of her black thread just below where it was initially anchored, and the second the last coil of oily-sheened cord hit the bone, it went from subzero to white-hot.

I sucked in a pained hiss. Now facing me with the bone between us, Marge shot me a sympathetic wince, but instead of taking the bone from my abused hands, she tied off the thread, wrapped her hands around mine, and squeezed.

Pain ricocheted through my nearly numb hands, and I

couldn't stop my whispered whine of protest before it escaped.

She held my gaze with hers even as she continued to chant under her breath, a silent command to suck it up. Then she slowly sank into a crouch, pulling the bone, and because I was attached, me, down with her. Together, we shoved it into the earth. As soon as the bone sank a couple inches into the churned-up soil, the magic that had locked me to the bone released.

I fell back, my hands flying out behind me to hit the ground, soon followed by my ass and tailbone. The last made contact with bruising force. "Owowowowow." I half reclined on the ground and shot Marge a dark look. "Warn a girl next time."

"I'm guessing you haven't worked with Necros before." She dragged over her backpack and dug through it.

"No, you're my first." And if I had my way, she was also my last. Gingerly, I started to push myself upright. Dirt and debris bit at my palms, and it felt like I'd landed on a boulder. Muscles protested as I shifted my hips, and I felt stones roll underneath me.

"Careful," Marge said without looking up from digging through her bag. "There's bits and pieces of the damn house everywhere."

"Gee, thanks," I muttered, moving with even more care. The numbness in my hands was starting to ebb, leaving behind a deep burning ache and painful tingles, but I still managed to brush the ground under my ass clear. My fingers encountered the rock that I was sure had cracked my tailbone. I brought it around so I could see it, because I swore it had to be bigger than it felt.

Marge pulled out a small white bag from her backpack and traced the simplistic red cross etched on its front with a murmured "Heal." Then she handed it over. "Use this. It'll help."

"Thanks." I dumped the rock next to my hip and took the portable healing pack, holding it gingerly between my still-stinging palms as I braced my arms on my thighs. A warm, soothing balm washed over my hands, slowly easing away the resulting tingles and aches. "Please tell me you're good now."

That earned me a grin. "Yeah, I've got the rest, but thanks for the help."

"I'd say, 'My pleasure,' but I'd be lying."

She laughed.

The ache in my hands was almost gone, but I was loathe to give up my new security blanket. I lifted my hands, the pack pressed between. "You good if I keep this?"

"Totally, I've got more." She cocked her head. "Ready to get up?"

I nodded, and she helped me to my feet with a hand under my elbow. When I was standing, I asked, "What now?"

"Now, I have to set the second and third layers so I can start sifting through this mess and make sure everything's where it's supposed to be."

I held my hands at chest level, the healing pack between my palms. "Right, well, I'll just leave you to it then."

She grinned then bent back to her seemingly infinite pack of holding, probably looking for items for her next trick.

Rolling my shoulders, I tried to ease the twinges in my back. When I was sure I could walk, I turned to head back to the car and almost ended back on the ground when my foot slid off something and my ankle twisted. I almost lost hold of the healing pack and hissed a curse as I glared at the culprit on the ground. Thinking it was another damn rock, I bent over with the grace of a ninety-year-old with arthritis and picked it up, intending to throw it. Except when I straightened and shifted my hold on it, pale-green flashed in the moonlight.

Frozen in shock, I stared at what I held. *Oh my go...*

"You good, Rory?"

Startled by Marge's question, I almost dropped the fake Court Stone. Instead, I clumsily shoved it into the side pocket of my pants then lifted my hand. "Yeah, I'm good. Just taking my time."

"Don't take too long, or I'll press you back into service."

"I'm going, promise."

I made my way to the car. By the time I reached it, my muscles had stopped protesting, and only a few faint tremors remained in my hands. I gingerly opened the passenger door and dropped into the seat, the exhaustion from earlier making a comeback. I set the healing pack on my lap, dug out the first rock I found, dumped it on the ground since I no longer needed it, then closed my door. I leaned my head back, cradled the healing pack between my hands, and marveled at my luck.

I'd all but forgotten the Sybil's faux Court Stone, what with trying to escape the zombies and demon and all. I had no idea how it had ended up where it had since the last I'd seen of it was in the house. Mind spinning, I watched Marge create another circle, this time with white thread, and totally missed Piper coming back until she opened the driver's-side door.

The overhead light came on as she leaned inside. She took me in with a frown. "What did you do?"

I rolled my head toward her and mumbled, "Helped Marge."

She gazed around the interior. "Where's the stone?"

"Trunk." I closed my eyes and rolled my head back to center. If she wanted to double-check, she could be my guest. I was going to just sit here another minute or five. "Want me to grab it?"

"Nah, I got it."

There was a shift in the air, so I forced my heavy lids up and saw her disappear. The trunk went up. A long moment passed, probably as she doubled-checked it, then the trunk was slammed down. She came back to stand in the open driver's door, box in hand. "Marge, I'm heading out. Let Dano know he can text if he has any questions."

I didn't hear Marge's response, but I roused myself enough to sit up. When Piper dropped into the driver's seat, I stuffed the healing pack into the pocket on the passenger door and offered with determined casualness, "I'll hold it."

I barely dared to breathe as she handed me the box, closed her door, did a three-point turn, and started back toward the safe house.

FIFTEEN

THIS IS IT. If I was going to switch out the stone, it had to be now. Of course, I could just keep the fake one and use it. The Council might be pissed that I ditched Piper, but at least I wouldn't find myself on a most-wanted bulletin for stealing a magical artifact. That had to count for something.

And if the Heretic realizes it's not real? whispered that dark voice in my head.

Images I didn't want but couldn't shake pierced my heart because there was no doubt Zev would pay the price. Then it would be my turn.

Logic piped in with the reminder that Amrita's fake was damn good. Good enough that it might even fool the Heretic.

Or the Council, that dark voice whispered, tearing through my fraying conscience. *There's something left inside that stone. You can't fake that.*

The flicker of emerald that still beat at the heart of the Court Stone filled my mind, twisting and turning as my mind spun with various scenarios.

My dilemma was more than whether to switch out the stone. There was also the fact that the woman sitting in the driver's seat next to me was the type to take her job seriously, and I could totally see that as soon as we got in tonight, Piper's first piece of business would be to reset the box's wards, screwing my access six ways to Sunday. If I was going to make a switch that even a skilled pickpocket would think twice before doing, it had to be now.

I held the containment box in my lap, my exhaustion lost under the onslaught of guilty nerves. A burst of resentment triggered by self-disgust made me wonder why she hadn't just locked it back up in the trunk. Was it some kind of test? Did Piper know what I was contemplating?

Paranoia was a harsh taskmistress, and right now, she was whipping my ass. Even knowing that asking that question would open a can of worms I really didn't want to deal with, I couldn't help but break the quiet. "Why not leave it in the trunk?"

Her head turned toward me for a moment before her eyes went back to the road. She shrugged. "I figure we should do our little test before something else pops up."

"In the car?"

"Why not?"

"Um, maybe because, well, you're driving, and I'd rather not end up roadkill." As if to emphasize my point, the car bounced over the dirt road, and both of us swayed in our seats. I could've told her that taking it slow made the jostling worse, but that was the least of my concerns at the moment.

"Neither do I," she said. "Which is why we're going to put some distance between us and the crew before we pull over and do this."

I checked the side mirror. Behind us was nothing but darkness. The trees and shadows hid any view of where Amrita had made her last stand, but I couldn't dismiss Piper's implication even if I wanted to. "Is there something you're not telling me?"

"Oh, there are tons of things I'm not telling you," she answered cheerfully. "But in this, I'd rather be safe than sorry." Her eyes didn't leave the road as we bounced along another set of ruts. "Poking at items that are demon touched generally doesn't end well. Today has been a total bitch, and Matt isn't paying me nearly enough to go another round with Amrita's friend."

That was not something I had considered in my duplicitous plotting. Granted, my understanding of demonic deals was extremely limited, as in nearly nonexistent, but I thought once the portal collapsed, the demon's reach was blocked. Hearing otherwise made me eye the box in my lap. "Are you telling me this is still tied to the demon?"

"Probably not."

"Probably?" My question came out a little on the high side.

"How about 'most likely'?" When I huffed, she grinned and shot me a glance. "Relax. I'm just being cautious."

"Cautious is good," I muttered. "Especially when dealing with residents from the underworld."

Her humor leaked away. "Was that your first?"

"First?" I repeated, not quite following.

"Demon encounter," she clarified.

Remembering another time and another face that haunted my dreams, my fingers tightened on the box in my lap. "Second, actually, but the first time around, it was somewhat contained in a binding circle before it was banished."

"From the sounds of it, this situation is totally different." Thankfully, she didn't pry. Instead, she did her best to explain. "I can't be a hundred percent sure, but based off what we saw, I'd say that Amrita probably tried to access the Court Stone's power to grow her following and failed. Since the Council was so keen on keeping the stones' power in check, I'm betting that information on how to go about using them was either sketchy, at best, or complete and utter bullshit, at worst. I'm guessing whatever reference she found indicated someone else tried the demon route first and managed to get the stone to work."

The amount of sheer arrogance needed to fuel that kind of attitude left me dumbfounded, but from my brief and unpleasant experience with Amrita, it wasn't exactly a stretch to believe. "So she—what? Just decided, hey, let's dial 1-800-Let's-Make-A-Deal?"

Piper snorted. "Pretty much, except I'm betting she was smart enough to add a clause that allowed her to keep the demon happy so it would remain on its side of the portal."

I thought of the zombie horde. "Like feeding it her followers?"

"Probably," Piper agreed, her tone both soft and grim.

I followed the logic to its next conclusion. "We were supposed to be the next meal, but then Caleb killed her."

"Which likely broke whatever lock she had on it, giving the demon room to make a break for it while the portal was collapsing."

Echoes of pain shot up my leg as phantom claws dug deep once more, and I shuddered. "If I haven't already, let me say it again—thank you for frying its ass."

She shot me a look then went back to driving. "Thank you for not letting me burn when it hit back."

We both fell quiet. Piper concentrated on the dirt track that was supposed to be a road, while I sat in my seat, waging an emotional war as guilt and practicality tore each other to shreds. As much as I wanted to come clean, I couldn't do it. Not when the price was Zev. It didn't matter if Piper was someone I could see being a friend. This entire situation sucked ass, and no matter what I decided, I was going to fuck her over. "So how are we going to do this test?"

"We'll find somewhere we can pull over, then I'll set up a

protective ward we can work in." The car hit another set of potholes and shimmied.

I braced my foot against the wheel well and one hand on the armrest so I wouldn't slam into the side panel again. "You sure that's a good idea?"

"Even though I'm confident the spell did its job, I think it's better we know for sure."

There were a couple of arguments I could've made, but none would end up helping me, so instead, I gave in. "You're the expert."

A particularly rough bounce nearly knocked the box out of my hand, and Piper slowed even more.

"You sure you don't want me to drive?" I asked.

"Nope." Without taking her eyes off the dark road, she added, "Hurts, doesn't it?"

Her unexpected question left me battling back a spike of confused anxiety that she was somehow reading my mind. I looked at her and frowned. "What?"

Her lips curved. "Not being the one behind the wheel." The ride smoothed out once again, and she picked up speed.

I let go of the armrest as an amused snort escaped, bolstered by a surge of relief that she remained oblivious. "Yeah," I admitted, because normally, it would drive me bonkers, but tonight… it gave me an unexpected opportunity.

"Well, just sit back and relax. It'll be over before you know it."

Appreciating her dry humor, I chuckled, hoping only I heard the nervousness in the sound.

I wrapped both hands around the containment box and considered how to go about swapping out the stones. It was doable, as was fooling Piper while she had me test it for active magic since Prisms weren't exactly thick on the ground. Ignoring the additional weight of self-disgust, I had to admit that the fact she had no real idea of how I would determine if the magic was active was a huge plus. I could put on a show, or not, and she would never know.

Then there was the fact that Piper had seen both stones. Had she noted the differences earlier? Would she pick up on them again? Maybe it was a good thing we were doing the testing in the middle of the night, with shitastic lighting. Less of a chance for her to catch on once I made the switch. If I made the switch.

And if I did go through with this, the trickiest part would be the containment box's ward. I had no idea of the parameters it worked within. Wards were crafted, and the one on this box could be from Piper or Mateo. Either way, I was fairly certain it went way beyond a standard ward. It could be keyed to keep specific people and magic out. Or, worse, keyed to the actual Court Stone's power or some unique signature I was completely unaware of. Basically, I was about to play Russian roulette with the damn box.

As I ran through scenarios, quiet settled back into the car. Drained though I was, my magic was an intrinsic part of me, which meant it was always active on some level. Hopefully, it would be enough to protect me from whatever power still lingered in the Court Stone. I knew I couldn't risk losing my chance to swap out the stone, so even as I plotted, I waited. Sure enough, it wasn't long before we hit another bone-rattling set of bumps. This time, I let the car's motion toss me around, so my shoulder slammed into the window, and the box slid from my lap and tumbled to the floor.

"Shit." I used the ride's movement to hide the fact I'd pulled out the faux stone from the side thigh pocket of my borrowed cargos. I just had to wait until the car smoothed out before the seat restraint loosened enough to give me room to move.

"What?"

"I dropped the box." I used my foot to nudge the box

toward my seat and realized the Court Stone was no longer in it.

The car slowed. "Do you need me to stop?"

Hell no. "Nah, I can get it." I felt my seat belt loosen and bent forward. The box was half hidden behind my leg and the seat, which made it easier to mask my movements. Just then, the car hit another bump, and the faux stone tumbled out of my hand to roll under my seat.

"Dammit." This time, my curse was real.

I patted around the shadowed footwell, first finding one stone, then the other. I left the box behind my leg and tucked one stone under my heel. "Found it." I held up the stone, angling it so I could see it in the light from the dashboard. *This is it. Decision time.* For a moment, I considered letting fate make the choice, but my pesky conscience wouldn't let up. My fingers tightened, and I dared a small dart of power into the stone.

A faint zing answered.

My heart bled because I knew what my choice had to be. My mind screamed in denial.

"Just got to grab the box." I shifted my legs toward the console and leaned in deeper as if reaching far under the seat. Instead, I nabbed the box. The tires found another rut and almost dislodged the faux stone under my foot. Being bent over the way I was allowed me to drop the Court Stone back into the box, retrieve the fake version, and slip it into my pocket without giving away the game. After a few seconds of fumbling, I flipped the lid closed, sat back, and straightened my legs, the containment box safe once again in my lap.

"You good?"

No. "Yep."

We continued our trip, neither of talking as we bumped along. Finally, we joined the paved road, and everything smoothed out.

"There was a truck stop a couple miles from here," Piper said. "We can pull in there."

Considering I'd been unconscious during previous trips along this route, then lost in my head as I plotted, I would defer to her on the location. "Works for me."

All too soon, Piper was pulling off the road and into one of those large truck stops that held fuel pumps, a small diner, and a convenience store. Since we weren't looking for an audience, she picked a spot way off to the side and near the back, where a couple of picnic tables sat apart from the comings and goings. She shut down the car, undid her seat belt, then opened her door. "Come on."

I grabbed the box, got out, then followed her as she strode toward the three picnic tables.

She bypassed the first two and stopped by the one set the farthest back, where the building's security lights barely reached. "This should work." She waited until I took a seat and set the box in front of me on the table's top. "Right, give me a few minutes to set up the ward, then we'll get this done."

Buffeted by my chaotic emotions, I waited as she pulled a piece of chalk from a pocket to etch warding sigils on the asphalt at the four main points around our table. When she was done, she pocketed the chalk, went to the initial sigil, crouched, touched a finger, and whispered a word I didn't catch. A sharp snap of power zipped around us. In my head, a soft hum ignited as my Prism primed itself.

Once the ward was set, she got up and took a seat across from me, folding her arms on the table. "Okay, how do you want to go about doing this?"

Not the question I expected. "I figured you had a plan."

"Aren't you the one that can tell if it's the real deal or not?"

"Well, yeah, but aren't you the one that knows how to make it work?"

She shook her head. "Nope, to me, it's just a stone. Even back at Amrita's, it was just a stone."

I was a tad bit stunned, but maybe I shouldn't have been, considering my assigned role in this mess. Silly me, I had assumed that the Council would send in someone who knew how to handle the damn thing. Obviously, I was severely mistaken.

Shit, maybe I should've stuck with switching it out for the fake one. "So, you don't know how to make it do what it's supposed to do?"

She eyed the box, clearly thinking it through. "No, I have a couple of ideas, but if I'm wrong…"

"Yeah, let's not go there, then." That was the last thing I needed.

"What did you do before? To make sure it was real?"

Already super unhappy about lying to her, I stuck as close to the truth as I could without admitting I could basically "see" magic. "Part of being a Prism is being able to detect active magic."

She studied me. "And it was active at Amrita's?"

Thinking of the unholy chaotic mess of magic in the hall of horrors, I shuddered. "Oh yeah."

Her gaze dropped to the box then came back to me. "Is it now?"

It was my turn to study the object under discussion, because I wasn't sure I could pull this off looking her in the eyes. I could tell her yes, but that would invite questions I wasn't willing to answer and possibly force an outcome that included us making tracks back to the valley tonight. There was no way I could leave Zev behind, so I had to play this out to its deceitful end. "I'd have to take it out and hold it to tell."

She didn't say anything for a long moment.

I looked up to find her staring at the box, her brow furrowed as she thought something through. Finally, she appeared to make a decision, because she sucked in a deep breath then blew it out. When her eyes met mine, they were determined. "Right, so can you cover my ass while you're doing it, or are you all tapped out?"

It was a legit question, but it also meant Piper was putting a shitload of trust in me, which only added to my guilty conscience. I would be lucky if it didn't crush me under its weight. "I'm good, at least for this."

She unfolded her arms, shook them out, and rolled her shoulders. "Okay, then let's get it done."

I wasn't sure what would happen next, but I didn't want to risk it. If I'd replaced the stone with the fake, this wouldn't be so nerve-wracking, but it was too late now. Hell, it would not surprise me in the least if the stone decided to pull some unexplainable shit while I was trying to con Piper.

Better safe than sorry.

I extended my Prism over both of us, limiting it so it didn't brush the ward lines. It was uncomfortable, like stretching an overused muscle, but more than expecting the unexpected, I didn't want to take the chance that she had some way of being able to tell if my shield was in place or not.

When I had things as contained as possible, I flipped the lid and dumped the stone into my palm, closing my fingers around it. I let my inner eye widen until I could see the shimmer of Piper's power as it flowed around her. Beyond her was the ward, a translucent, blue-tinged dome. I recognized another, fainter shimmer that hugged the area nearest the building as a standard grid of a security ward. A throb just behind my eyes warned me not to press my luck, so I turned my attention to the stone cupped in both hands. Not really wanting to poke at the thing, I put on a show for Piper, pretending to study it.

That pulse of emerald was still there, deep in the heart of the stone. Again, the temptation whispered to nudge it, see if maybe I could use the stone to convince Piper to work with me. Maybe not tell the Council.

"Rory? You okay?" Piper's concerned voice cut through the tempting whispers like a knife.

I forced my gaze from that beguiling ember and looked at her, my thoughts a little sluggish. "I think so."

She studied me for a moment. "You sure? You don't look so good."

I shook my head, my mind clearing. "Yeah, I'm good, just tired."

"So? Is it active?"

There was only one answer I could give her, so even though the words tasted like ash on my tongue, I said, "Not that I can tell."

"You're sure?"

"As much as I can be, yeah."

Some of her stiffness disappeared as she stopped bracing for the worst. "Then I'd say the spell worked."

"So it appears," I choked out around the rising tide of guilt. Before it could take me under, I dumped the stone back inside the box, flipped the lid closed, and set it back on the table. My stomach rolled, and under the table, my foot bounced a couple times before I caught it and stopped. I pushed the box toward her. "You better ward it just to be safe."

She reached out and traced a complex sigil over the lid.

I held my breath as in front of my psychic eye, power ignited along the path she etched and locked the containment box inside a magical cage. Seeing the thick strands of the magical web that now held the box made me grateful I'd made the decision I had. The magic that bound the box was so complex, it made me dizzy and left me with no doubt this ward would not play nice with a fake object.

Across from me, Piper picked up the box and got to her feet. "Well, that was easy."

Luckily, she had turned away, so she missed my flinch. I cleared my throat as I pivoted on the bench to get up. "Yeah."

She went to the first sigil and used her foot to smudge it, breaking the ward. "Ready to call it a night?"

I got to my feet as a backwash of power swept over us then blinked out. "So ready."

Once she'd scuffed out all the sigils, she turned to head back to the car, leaving me to follow.

With each step I took, my conscience's whispers followed.

SIXTEEN

WE WERE minutes away from the safe house, and I had fallen into that kind of dull haze that happened after sitting in the passenger seat for too long. The adrenaline dump didn't help either. So when my phone vibrated with an incoming text, it startled me. I sat up and dug my phone out of one of the many pockets of the borrowed cargos. Heart in my throat because I knew it couldn't be anything good, I checked the screen.

For a moment, the world stopped. Then anguish-driven rage set in, icing through my veins and leaving my mind strangely clear.

It was another picture of Zev, and clearly, the Heretic was losing patience. Zev's head was hanging down, his dark hair damp with sweat or blood—I couldn't tell which. I had no idea how he was even sitting up, but his wrists were cuffed to the chair. His shirt hung in shreds from its collar, unable to hide the plethora of slices and bruises that now decorated his skin. I couldn't look away from those cuts. Something about them bothered me.

Was that—? I enlarged the picture, trying to see past the violence and blood.

Motherfucking son of a bitch. Those are runes. I was going to kill this asshole if it was the last thing I ever did.

"That Zev?"

Piper's question broke through my rage, and I concentrated on keeping my tone casual instead of snarling back the way I so wanted to. "Um, yeah, he's going to try and call me back in a little bit." I couldn't look away from the horrific image. My mind tried to unravel the markings and their intent, but I wasn't having any luck.

"Is everything okay?"

Her careful question made me realize that I didn't have myself as locked down as I thought. "Yeah." It hurt, but I cleared my screen, turned the phone face down, and held it against my thigh.

We drove under a streetlight, and I caught her frown before she turned back to the road. "You sure? You seem a little pissed."

"Just frustrated," I said as I forced my shoulders to lower and my spine to ease so I could sit back. "We need to talk, and we're not getting a chance to connect."

Clearly, my lame-ass excuse sounded plausible, because she said, "I'm sure he's not any happier about it."

"No, I'm sure he's not."

She pulled into the safe house's parking space, shut off the engine, and got out of the car. I grabbed the containment box from the floorboard and followed her up the stairs.

She waited until I joined her at the top before she released the security sigil, unlocked the door, and pushed it open. "Home sweet home." She stepped inside and hit the light switch.

The soft illumination spilled over the threshold and joined the pool from the porch light to nip at the night's shadows. Caught between the light and dark, I hesitated for a moment as the urge to turn and rush off into the unknown clawed at me, but cold practicality won out. I came inside and shoved the door closed behind me.

Piper dumped the key fob on the counter then turned, only to wince. "Ouch."

"You okay?" I set the containment box next to the key fob then headed to the sink.

"Just a muscle spasm." She twisted her torso to the left then to the right. There was another flinch, but she did the torso twist again then blew out a long breath. "So, are we flipping for it?"

I pulled out a glass from a nearby cupboard and set it under the thin spout next to the faucet. "Flipping for what?" I asked as I filled the glass with filtered water.

"The bed."

Glass full, I took a drink and turned to her, eyebrows raised.

She motioned toward the bedroom. "I'd offer to wrestle you for it, but I'm thinking we're both battered enough, we can try another option."

I leaned back against the sink, one arm folded over my waist, the other holding the glass. Under the bright lights, I couldn't miss the dark, bruised half-moons coming up under her eyes that joined her earlier collection of injuries or the tiny lines of strain radiating from her mouth. She looked like shit, and I was pretty sure I was a close second. "Since you were nice enough to let me nap earlier, why don't you take the bed. I'll stick to the couch."

"You sure?"

Despite her question, I could tell she was trying to be polite. "Yep, I'm sure." Especially since I had other plans for tonight. I managed a small grin. "Besides, I might be up late, waiting for a callback."

As if that were all the reassurance she needed, she caved. "Gotcha. Then I'll set the security and take this"—she picked up the box—"and call it a night."

Striving for casual, I said, "I need to get my charging cord from the car, so why don't I set the security." I turned back to the sink as I took another drink.

"Works for me." Piper set the box back down on the counter. "You familiar with a level-four ward?"

There were two types that the Guild used, so I asked, "Security or protection?" One would hold an intruder in place until the ward was released. The other would kick an intruder's ass then instigate a secondary level of lockdown. I didn't want to mess with either.

"Protection."

Right, my ass had been kicked enough today. "If it follows standard pattern, yeah."

"Good, then come here. I'll get you keyed in."

I set the glass aside and followed her back to the front door.

She traced a familiar protection rune just above the light switch inside the entryway. It lit up. She looked over her shoulder to make sure I was paying attention. "Watch."

I nodded.

She traced another symbol next to it, and this time, I recognized it as part of Mateo's Family crest. She connected the two with a familiar knot pattern. "*Babestu.*" Then she turned to me. "Did you get that?"

Silently, I repeated the word, paying special attention to the intonation that sounded vaguely Spanish. When I thought I had it, I said it back. "*Babestu.*"

"Good enough." She stepped back and motioned me to take her place. "To release it, reverse the order and say, '*Ireki.*'"

I did as directed, and the ward released.

"Right, then if you're good, I'm ready to call it a night." She went back to reclaim the containment box. "Need the bathroom?"

"Yeah, thanks." I headed in and did my business. While I

was washing my face and avoiding my eyes in the mirror, a familiar brush of power ruffled my Prism. Worried, I quickly swiped a towel over my face and yanked open the door.

Piper was standing with her back to me in front of an armoire in the corner. She looked over her shoulder. "You done?"

"Yep."

She turned back to the armoire, closed the doors, and did something I couldn't see, but that flutter of power was back. When she turned around and caught me watching, she said, "I was locking up the stone."

"Right." I half turned, dropped the hand towel on the edge of the sink, then turned back. "It's all yours."

"Thanks." She waited until I skirted the bed then made her way to the bathroom.

I was at the door when she called, "Night, Rory. See you in the morning."

I tried not to flinch and managed a "Night, Piper" before I pulled the door closed behind me.

A pillow and blanket sat in a neat pile on the couch. I set the pillow against the arm, shook out the blanket, and laid it along the back. I went to the kitchen, grabbed the key fob, then came back to the living room. I stood there for a minute, phone and key in hand, listening to the floor creak as Piper moved around the bedroom. Then a drawer opened and closed. I tried to time it before she got to the bathroom. "Hey, Piper, I'm heading down for my cord. Be back in a minute."

"Got it. Watch yourself," she called back.

"Always." I waited for the faint click of the bathroom door closing then headed to the front door. Outside, keeping up the pretense, I walked down the stairs, disarmed the car alarm, and slipped into the passenger seat.

I unlocked my phone and pulled up the last text image. I stared at the screen and prepared to blow up my life. Even though it wasn't the actual Court Stone, I was disobeying the

Council's orders. Not only was it career suicide, but the personal cost might be more than I could afford. If I hadn't been up close and personal to some of the Council's recent decisions during the last year, I might have been naïve enough to rope Piper into my rescue mission. Hell, I might have even tagged Lena for help. However, the Arcane Council was the kind of ruthless power that would write off Zev as collateral damage and punish anyone who helped me, so long as they could rid themselves of the Heretic once and for all. Mercy was in short supply, and they were the final say in the Arcane world. Even the powerful Arcane Families stepped lightly around the Council.

There was an inherent callousness to the Council's judgment. There always had been. They excused their decisions as necessary to protect Arcane society. That same attitude had all but decimated the entire mage class of Prisms.

Yet, I had risked my body, my soul, and even my friends to keep some insidious threats from wreaking havoc on a level that threatened to fracture Arcane society. Each time, I'd somehow managed to skate around the Council's censure. Granted, there had been additional help in the form of Sabella and the Cordova Family, but I knew this time, even that level of support wouldn't help.

I stared at Zev's image, my eyes burning but dry, and typed in two question marks before hitting Send. Then all I could do was wait for a response.

I didn't mind serving the Arcane Council, but I wouldn't do it blindly. Questioning authority was a default setting for me, and so far, it hadn't interfered with my Council assignments. I should've known that streak of luck would run out. I'd just never imagined it would run out like this. Contrary to the Council's dogma, there were some situations where the loss of one was too much. I understood that there was no excuse I could give them that they would accept, even if I was lucky enough to put an end to the Heretic, but I had my own family to protect. And sacrificing Zev was not an option.

Sabella would be disappointed, but she would understand. So would the intimidating head of the Cordova Family, Emilio, Zev's cousin. Whatever fledgling support I'd garnered from the Arcane Council would be gone, but maybe those alliances that Zev had bullied me into making would allow me to salvage something from the aftermath. *I mean, it's all about Family loyalty, right?*

My phone buzzed, and not expecting a call, I hit the answer button on reflex then realized it was Lena's name that had flashed on the screen. "Hey."

"Hey, you still alive?"

"So far."

There was a pause. "What's wrong?"

My best friend was too perceptive by half, and right now, I was kind of wishing I hadn't answered. "Nothing," I said, doing my best to sound normal. "It's been a hell of a day."

She wasn't easily discouraged, mainly because she knew me. "Spill."

"How about I fill you in later?"

"How about you fill me in now?" she pushed.

Even knowing she meant well, my response came out on the sharp side. "I'm wiped, babe, and seriously, it's been a day."

This time, the pause was a bit longer. "Why do I get the feeling you're about to do something stupid?"

Probably because I already had, but I couldn't tell her that. "Lena, it's fine. I'm just tired."

Proving how well she knew me, she gave a derisive snort. "Oh, it's definitely not fine, but I'll give you this. For now." She switched tracks. "Did you get what you needed?"

"Yeah."

"And Zev?"

That knot in my gut tightened, and my voice got tight. "He's been busy."

Whatever she heard left her worried, because her voice got soft. "Rory, what's going on?"

Knowing I wouldn't get her off the phone if I didn't give her something, I said, "Let's just say that Amrita wasn't the Council's biggest fan. Piper and I had to do some heavy-duty convincing to get her to comply."

"And you're not going to share details, are you?"

"Not now, no." I tried to soften my tone. "Let's get back to why you called."

"Cass."

Her answer came out of left field. "What?"

"Cass," Lena repeated. "You remember her? The bartender from Wonderland. Nice enough chick but a little weird. Okay, a lot weird." She didn't wait for me to agree. "Evan and I were out tonight, and she asked me to give you a message."

Confused, I frowned. "A message? From who?"

"Her," Lena answered. "She was adamant, scarily so, which is why I'm calling at unforgivable hours and sharing."

I'd met Cass recently when I made a drop off at an engagement party in Sedona. Max's and Devon's party, actually. "Sharing what?"

"Her message."

"Which was?"

"When shit gets real, don't drift."

Totally confused, I said, "What?"

"That's it, her message. 'When shit gets real, don't drift.' I don't get it either, but she was nearly rabid I get ahold of you and pass it along."

Both of us sat there, quiet. I didn't know what was going through Lena's head, but mine was spinning. The shit was so real right now, there was only one way forward. It didn't leave room for drift, so Cass's message wasn't making much sense, but that wasn't really a surprise.

"I know she's a little out there," Lena said, "and I can't explain it, but I couldn't shrug it off if I wanted to."

She didn't need to explain. I got it. Cass was an eclectic mix of bohemian and rocker chick, but there was also something else about her, something I hadn't quite been able to pin down, that made me believe there was more to the off-the-wall bartender than met the eye. She was easy to talk to, a skill inherent to her job, but then bam! Out of nowhere, she would say something that would stick with you until that undefinable moment when her serendipitous wisdom became critical. So, no, there would be no shrugging off her message, but I also didn't have the headspace to mull it over.

"Okay, you passed along the message, and I appreciate it," I finally said. "I'm not sure what it means, but I'll keep it in mind."

"Right," Lena muttered before heaving a sigh. "I get you've got things happening, but I hope you know, if you need me, I'm there."

And that was why she was my ride or die. No questions, just unconditional support. "I know, Lena-bee."

"Since you don't ever listen, I hope you hear this." Her voice took on a hard edge. "You get your ass in a sling, you call me."

There was no way I was dragging her along with me on this, but if I didn't give her some kind of reassurance, she would be there in a heartbeat. Since I was about to become a Council target, I needed her to stay free and clear of this mess, so I gave her what I could. "I hear you and appreciate it, babe, but I'm good."

"Whatever." It was clear she didn't believe me, but she knew me well enough to drop it. "Hurry up and get home, Rory."

Then dead air filled my ear as she disconnected without

giving me a chance to respond. I lowered my phone as I thumped my head against the headrest and closed my eyes. I'd been out here long enough that if I wasn't careful, Piper would come out to check on me. I sighed, checked my screen, and noticed the text I'd sent had been read, but that was it. I didn't like being at the mercy of the psychopath on the other end, but I didn't have much choice.

There was still one more thing I had to do before I headed up. I leaned over into the driver's seat and hit the hood release. Then I unplugged the charging cord, threw open the door, and got out. I came around the hood and lifted it.

Despite the nearby streetlights that provided some illumination for the parking lot, I flicked on the flashlight app on my phone, put it between my lips, and made quick work of pulling the automatic shutdown relay, ensuring the car wouldn't start. I dropped the switch into one of my pockets, quietly closed the hood, turned off the light on my phone, and headed back up the stairs.

Disabling the BMW would give me a bit more lead time, but it wouldn't take an experienced mechanic long to find the issue. Replacing the switch, in a town this size? Yeah, that might gain me a couple of hours, especially since high-end auto parts would be hard to come by.

Once I knew where I was heading, finding a ride that couldn't be tracked by the Council and wouldn't stick out on the road would be a necessary pain in my ass, but it wasn't insurmountable. I'd pinned a couple of rides parked in the spread-out homes as we drove up. A twenty-minute walk, less than five to rewire an ignition, and I would be on the road.

Now all I needed was a direction.

I headed back up the stairs and had crossed the threshold when a text came through. I didn't get a chance to read it because I turned from closing the door to find Piper standing in the bedroom doorframe, dressed only in the safe house's wardrobe staple, an oversized T-shirt, as she used a towel on her wet hair. "Did you get it?"

I held up the cord. "Yep."

She let the damp towel hang around her neck and folded her arms over her chest, her gaze shrewd. "You were down there for a bit."

"Got a call from my roommate."

"Things okay?" That too-perceptive gaze didn't lessen.

"Yeah." I walked over and plugged my cord into the socket on the kitchen counter as I mentally scrambled for a believable reason for Lena to call so late that wouldn't raise more questions. "She's a Guild Key, had something come up, wanted to touch base with me since our schedules are fluid."

That answer apparently worked since some of her tension eased. "Right, well don't forget to—" A big yawn cut her off, and when she was done, she pushed off the door. "Sorry, I was going to say, don't forget to reset the ward."

"Done." I walked over to the door to do just that.

"Night, Rory, see you in the morning," she called.

"Night, Piper." I was glad my back was to her, but I wasn't sure I could keep the guilt off my face since there was no way I would be here when she woke up. I set the ward and didn't turn until I heard the bedroom door close. Alone again, I went straight to my phone, pulled up my text, and found a set of GPS coordinates and a time. Using an app that pinpointed the semi-illegal night races I occasionally attended while hiding my cell signal, I plugged in the coordinates. The map did its thing, and a small red dot appeared on a spot that was normally two and a half hours away.

I wasn't completely familiar with this particular stretch of road, but I knew enough about the geographical surroundings to calculate I could cut that drive time down to just under two hours with a solid engine and a lead foot. Unfortunately, that didn't give me much time to wait, but I didn't have a choice. I looked back at the door Piper had closed and saw light seeping from underneath.

It wasn't easy, but I went through the motions of shutting off lights and setting up the couch with the pillow and blanket. Then I kicked off my shoes. I left my pants on but moved the stone to the other pocket before I drew the blanket over me. Then I turned to my side, so I was facing out to the room, and waited.

The minutes ticked interminably by, and it was a constant battle not to move as I waited for Piper's light to go out. It couldn't have been more than five minutes, even though it felt longer, before the light disappeared. It was another fifteen or so before that deep quiet, when everything and everyone slept, slipped in. Though it was hard, I gave it another five then slowly sat up. I slipped my shoes back on, tiptoed across the floor, and grabbed my phone. At the door, I released the ward with a near-silent whisper, opened the door cautiously, and slipped out, taking one regretful look back. I tucked away my guilt and spent a precious few moments to reset the ward, unwilling to leave Piper undefended, then rushed with silent stealth down the stairs and started to jog into the night.

SEVENTEEN

I ENDED up bypassing the two homes I'd initially tagged to "borrow" their rides. The first one had lights on everywhere while laughter and music spilled from open windows and doors. Not wanting to be spotted, I moved deeper into the shadows, hoping the partygoers were too inebriated to notice me. The second had a dog. I kept jogging, refusing to give up. I had one other option—the bar at the bottom of the road where we had turned into the neighborhood.

By the time I hit it, I was breathing hard, and sweat clung to my skin. *I really need to add more cardio to my workouts.*

Bikes were parked out front, including a couple that made me reconsider my initial plan for four wheels. That was, until I spotted the thick-chested, leather-clad, bearded sentry standing against the unlit side of the bar with an arm full of short-skirt, halter-top curves and a clear line of sight to the bikes, despite his companion doing her best to keep him distracted.

Nope, not pissing off the local bikers.

Music, loud and abrasive, spilled from the small-town bar. The accompanying din of voices, laughter, and shouts added weight to its popularity. Not to mention the large selection of jacked-up trucks that required a ladder to get into and the flashy custom bikes that belonged to the patrons inside. Who knew that such a sleepy town included a hopping night life?

I turned away from the two-wheeled temptations of serious speed and slipped into the dirt lot, keeping clear of the lone light pole. I slunk my way through the parked cars, aiming for the back, where the shadows were the deepest. I bypassed anything that was customized or too new, unwilling to add another layer of trouble to my evening. The Council was more than enough, thank you. I brushed my fingertips over metal hoods and fenders and used that sixth sense Transporters relied on to find what I needed. On the fifth one, I got lucky. It was an older four-door, its paint faded, but the engine was in meticulous shape. I tried the driver's door and found it unlocked.

A twinge of remorse hit, but even as I sent a mental apology out into the universe, I slid into the car and pulled the door shut before anyone noticed the dome light. After a quick scan for any magical tripwires that came up empty, I took the old-fashioned route and leaned down to do my business. Using the utility knife I'd had the presence of mind to pocket when I was plotting at the safe house, I had the wires exposed in minutes. A couple twists later, the gauges and systems flickered to life, then it was simply a matter of touching the starter wire to the battery wire.

The engine turned over with a smooth purr that almost brought tears of relief to my eyes. I blew out a shaky breath, sat up, casually pulled out of the lot, and headed down the road. As soon as the bar's lights disappeared, I checked the fuel gauge. Someone was looking out for me, because it was nearly full.

One handed, I pulled out my phone and switched to airplane mode. There was no way to fully hide my cell signal, not if someone, say like the Council, was determined to track me, but at least this way, it would take them considerable time to get access. I then opened the night-race app, pulled up the map, and hit the gas.

⁕⁕⁕⁕⁕⁕⁕⁕⁕⁕⁕⁕⁕⁕⁕⁕⁕⁕⁕⁕⁕⁕⁕⁕⁕⁕⁕⁕

The needle on the fuel gauge slid below the last line as the coordinates brought me to an even smaller town that sat a stone's throw away from the First Nations border. I lowered my speed and passed the unlit gas pumps under a metal awning, following the last bit of direction from the GPS. *Talk about the middle of nowhere. Maybe I should've pulled into that gas station I blew past fifty miles back.*

I hadn't seen another pair of headlights in the last twenty minutes. If not for the clear indication of the shared border on the app's map, pinpointing that demarcation line would be a crapshoot.

Visitors weren't prohibited on First Nations land, but they weren't exactly met with a welcome party, either. As one-third of the ruling powers in the United States, the First Nations tribes held equal power to the Arcane Council and the Traditionalists' government, but the three powers that be didn't always get along. They were what could be considered cautious allies. History was dotted with various bloody battles, and a decisive civil war in the 1800s had ended with the signing of the Mystic Accords by the First Nations and the descendants of the initial immigrants from the European-based Arcane Families.

Land was divided among the two powers, and life continued forward until those who had no access to magic demanded a voice, creating the Traditionalists. Politics was a necessary evil that I tried to stay clear of. Like most of the population, though, I knew that despite the depiction that all three powers were equal, the true power brokers were split between the First Nations and the Arcane Council, leaving the Traditionalists clinging to the illusion of power.

That made me wonder why the Heretic had chosen to hide so close to the First Nations land. It wasn't like they were known for providing Arcane fugitives with asylum. More times than not, they were merciless in keeping the unwanted off their lands. In fact, while working for the Arcane Guild, I'd witnessed evidence of that more than once when tribal authorities would contact the Guild Director to inform her to pick up the trash before they took it out on a permanent basis. They were a tight-knit society, loyal to each other, and outsiders were viewed with a very jaundiced eye.

Kind of like the Arcane Families.

And the Traditionalists.

Right, so why would a dark-web assassin and information broker hide here?

I had no answer, and honestly, it was the least of my worries right now.

The GPS directed me to a dirt lot off the highway that fronted what I first thought was an old single-level motel, but it turned out to be shops. There was a bakery, a feed store, and a drugstore. None were open. In fact, when I pulled into the lot and my headlights swept over them, I noticed that the bakery had plywood on the door. I parked near a graffiti-covered pay phone with a flickering light and shut off the headlights but not the engine. I peered around. Not that there was much to see. There were no streetlights except for the one back near the highway, leaving everything else cloaked in shadows. The sporadic moonlight didn't do much to help other than glint off the battered metal of the hanging store signs.

I debated walking around but decided that was just stupid. The horror-flick vibe was too strong, so I picked up my phone and typed, "I'm here."

Long seconds ticked by, and when nothing happened, I dared to lower my window, my ears peeled for any signs of life. I nearly jumped out of my skin when a harsh ring cut through the quiet. It wasn't until the second ring that I realized in a near miracle, it appeared the pay phone actually worked.

Two guesses on who's calling, and the first one doesn't count.

"Son of a bitch," I muttered under my breath as I undid my seat belt.

I opened my door and headed to the antique pay phone, my gaze darting around in case someone decided to jump me. I made it to the phone without incident and picked up the faded plastic receiver. I held it away from my ear, not comfortable with what may or may not live on the plastic. "Hello?"

"Shut down the phone, dump it, then head across the road to the cattle guard, and wait," a mechanical voice directed.

"Wait, wha—"

A dial tone cut me off.

This was so fucking stupid.

Frustrated, scared, and pissed way the hell off, I white-knuckled the phone and barely resisted slamming it back into the cradle. I stomped back to the car, wondering if I was being watched even though I couldn't spot any cameras.

I clutched my phone during the short walk back, and once at the car, I ducked inside, powered up the window, and leaned down to undo my makeshift key. Hidden by the dash and my position, I pulled up Lena's name in my text and typed out a message. What I didn't do was hit Send. Chances were high my phone was also being monitored, and since the Heretic's computer skills were legendary, I couldn't risk sending it. However, there was nothing to stop me from leaving Lena what crumbs I could since she had another way to track me. I powered the phone down and sat back up, the pendant under my T-shirt resettling against my skin. I dropped my phone into the cubby on the console and got out.

I jogged across the highway, which was easy enough with no traffic, and found the dirt road with the metal grate that kept the cattle from the asphalt near an accompanying yellow metal diamond with a cow in the center. The sign was unmistakable. There was nothing and no one around, but I couldn't shake my unease as I approached the cattle guard.

Something or someone was out there. *They have to be, right?*

I slowed as I got closer to the grate, my power tightening around me in reaction to my edginess. I was so busy peering at shadows that I stumbled over something—a rock, a weed, or a hole. Whatever it was, it sent me lurching forward, and I barely caught myself on the signpost, the metal cool against my palms. I regained my balance, straightened, and took a step back, and my heel met the metal of the grate.

Magic snapped around me with a breathtaking quickness, leaving me no time to react. All I could do was feel it lock on, heavy and thick as it coiled around and around my Prism. I forced my fingers to release the signpost as the night sky and the surrounding blur of the desert disappeared. It was soon replaced by a wall of blackness that stretched high overhead, blocking out the starry sky. It was like standing in the center of a silent tornado. Buffered by my Prism, it didn't touch me, but an invisible wind whipped my hair around my face, the strands leaving painful stings behind. I tried to move—an arm, a foot, anything—and discovered I was stuck like a fly in amber. Panic skittered through me at the unfamiliar helplessness as I tried to figure out why I couldn't escape. Only when I stilled did it hit me that the magic wasn't attacking, simply restraining, which meant the best my Prism could do was hold it at bay.

What if...

I edged my Prism outward, forcing the shield to expand in an attempt to get more space between me and whatever held me. I gained maybe an inch before the eerie silence was pushed aside by a deafening roar, and things changed. The magical pressure clamped down with cruel relentlessness, and I could do nothing but grit my teeth as I fought it back. Then an inky chain whipped around my waist and yanked me backward so suddenly that my arms and legs flew forward, and I screamed. My defiance was lost in the roar of noise as the magical tornado picked me up and swept me away.

EIGHTEEN

"RORY, WAKE UP."

There was something familiar about that voice, but I was so damn tired, and everything hurt, making it hard to string two coherent thoughts together, much less words.

"Rory, come on. Wake up."

Go away.

"Rory, dammit!" The rough voice got snappy. "Get. Up."

Zev. That was Zev.

The last bits of disorienting fog faded away, leaving me painfully aware that I was lying on a hard surface. A very hard and gritty surface. In fact, it felt like someone had bashed my shoulder and hip hard enough to bruise. I was so stiff, moving would take some serious effort. My head throbbed, my throat felt raw, and there was a coppery tang in my mouth.

Okay, let's start small.

Without raising my head, I forced my lids to lift. They weighed a freakin' ton, so it took a couple of tries before I got my eyes open. Not that it helped. Everything spun in a nauseating blur.

"That's it, babe, wake up." There was relief in his voice.

Since I was about to hurl, I reconsidered keeping my eyes open and squeezed them shut. The blur disappeared but not the spinning. That got worse.

"No, Rory, come on, open your eyes."

"No." As a protest, it was weak and came awfully close to a groan, but he heard it.

"Come on, baby," he cajoled. "I need to know you're with me."

No fair pulling out the pet names. "I'm here," I mumbled, thinking it should be obvious.

"I know, but I need you to look at me." When I didn't move, he added, "Come on, sweetheart, wake up."

Since he would keep pestering me instead of letting me sleep, I gave in. I kept my eyes closed and started to push myself up. Rocks and dirt bit into my palms, but that was secondary when every inch of my body started to protest. Vehemently. "Ow, shit!"

I groaned and cursed my way upright until I managed to prop myself up on my aching hip and one hand but had to stop and use my other hand to hold my skull together. My head pounded so hard, I was afraid it would shatter. Thinking was difficult, but it didn't stop the memories from leaking in. The cattle guard in the middle of nowhere, stepping on the grate, grabbing that stupid sign, and triggering a trap. The magical wind tunnel, the crushing pressure, the soul-freezing power that ripped me through the air. And now this, waking up with Zev nearby. I put two and two together and got a very unusual four.

Fuckin' lovely.

I'd survived my first teleport ride, which my Prism wouldn't counter since it wouldn't view teleportation as an attack. As far as I knew, teleport spells were few and far between. Originally designed to shift objects from one point to another, this one must have been a hell of a complex cast if it transported me. It also did not bode good things.

"Rory, hey, look at me."

"Trying," I croaked out. I let go of my skull and used my second hand to keep me upright. Those small movements set the world spinning again, and I really didn't want to open my eyes. Not yet. Then I sucked in deep breaths and waited for the spinning to slow. My sloshing brain finally settled, and when I was fairly sure I wouldn't vomit, I slitted my eyes open then winced when light set things off again. I screwed my eyes shut. "Hurts."

"Not surprised," he said from somewhere off to my side. "Your head hit hard when you landed. It worried me."

I was right there with him. Without opening my eyes, I stayed still, head down, propped up on my hands, weight on my sore hip, and swallowed a couple of times until my mouth was no longer dry. "How long?"

Clearly able to follow my question, he finished, "Were you out?"

I started to nod, but when the world slid sideways, I stopped. "Yeah."

"Too long," he answered. "I'm guessing about fifteen minutes, but it's a little hard to tell time in here."

His response spiked my pulse and curdled my stomach, but before I could say anything, he kept talking.

"Should I ask how you ended up here?"

Nope. Not ready to deal with that thorny problem, I forced my eyes open and stared at the hard-packed dirt between my hands. When things stopped sliding sideways, I carefully lifted my head and looked around.

It didn't take long to know we were royally screwed. There were stains on the floor. Some dark, some faded. I couldn't tell what they were, but it couldn't be from anything good. There were four walls, one holding a heavy slab of metal I figured was a door. Of course, no windows, just a flickering light bulb on a bare wire hung from the ceiling. It was hard to tell if the walls and ceiling were stone or cement, not that it made a difference really since it was basically a cell. Finally, my gaze landed on Zev. Back braced against the wall on the far side, legs sprawled out, looking like shit, he was sporting a heavy set of shackles and cuffs linked by a chain set into the ground.

I licked my dry lips. "Where are we?"

His chuckle was dry and pained. "I was hoping you could tell me."

"The only place I know we're not is Kansas." I got to my hands and knees because I wasn't sure how steady I would be on my feet.

"Thanks for that, Dorothy."

Gravel bit into my torn palms and ripped-up knees, but it was better than taking another header. "I'm assuming from your comedy routine we're alone."

"For now."

"Got any idea how long our good fortune will last?"

"Unfortunately, no."

His answer got me moving, and I started to crawl across the floor.

I hadn't gotten far when he said, "Babe, stop."

I stilled and lifted my head, doing my best not to wince as I took in his battered face and even worse-looking torso. "What?"

"You need to stay back."

"Why?"

"Because in about two feet, you're going to hit the asshole's circle."

I carefully inched closer, and sure enough, there was the first curve of a complex circle. If he hadn't warned me, I would've crashed right into it. "Is that for me or you?"

"You."

"That's what I was afraid of." Unable to go any farther, I got off my hands and knees until I was sitting facing him. Then I carefully twisted at my waist so I could visually follow the lines carved into the ground. Needing to know what I was dealing with, I pushed past the throbbing ache and reached for the magic that lived in me so I could use that other sight. Except nothing happened. My pulse sped up. I took a breath and tried again.

Nothing.

Panic skittered, and I switched tactics. This time, I reached for my Prism, only to feel it cling to my magical fingers like a cobweb, there, but barely. My breath stalled as dread crawled through me, and I couldn't help but look to Zev.

He caught my gaze, and there was worry in the dark depths, but his voice was flat when he asked, "Let me guess—you can't access your magic?"

Instead of answering, I asked a question of my own and couldn't stop my voice from shaking. "What is it?"

"If it's the same cast used on me, I'm not entirely sure, but..." He went to move, winced, and resettled. "Based off the fact that my magic has been drained until it's all but flatlined, I'm thinking it's some version of the Drainer's Circle."

So not the answer I wanted to hear. I could feel my face pale as anxiety and fear wrapped me in their cold arms. A Drainer's Circle was a corrupted spell that was as barbaric as it sounded. Initially created by the dark practitioners of the Cabal, it was designed to slowly drain a mage of their magic and then feed on their unprotected soul, leaving behind a wraith. The last time we ran into one of those, it'd nearly cost Lena her life, and it'd taken everything Zev and I had to break her free. There was no way, with the shape the two of us were in, that we could pull off a repeat performance. "A version? You're sure?"

"Since I'm not dead and soulless, yeah," he said, voice dry. Whatever he saw on my face had him adding with a bit more gentleness, "Breathe, babe. Whatever spell he's created, it's meant to keep you weak, magically and physically."

Well, it was fucking working. I sucked in air and tried to match Zev's calm. I snagged an edge of it and clung hard. "Okay, okay. So we've got some type of containment cast happening." And if the Heretic managed to take an oldie-but-goody mage spell and twist it into something new, that meant… "The Heretic is part of the Cabal?"

Fueled by greed for both money and power, the Cabal had come into existence around the late 1800s and early 1900s, when scientific advancement was on the rise. It was founded by a bunch of monied whiners who were jealous of the innate power wielded by the Arcane Families. The Cabal mixed science and magic through twisted ritualistic spells, and up until recently, I, like most of the world, had thought they were just another urban myth. Instead, I'd discovered the hard way that they'd gone way underground and were now coming to the surface like a bunch of hard-to-kill weeds.

"Well, since I'd just gotten the shit beaten out of me when I was dragged in here, I wasn't exactly able to ask him."

Clearly, Zev was in pain because his level of smart-assedness was hitting critical levels. "Never mind, that's something for later—"

"If there's a later," he cut in.

I ignored Mr. Glass Half Empty. "How do we break this circle?"

"Can you access any of your power?"

I shook my head.

"Can you reach Sabella?"

My hand went to my pendent. Typically, the charm acted like a direct line to my great-aunt, even with Lena adding in her tracking hex, so I tried to tap into the small power reserve. Instead of the normal hum of power, it lay inert against my skin. I pushed a little harder, but it was like standing outside a candy shop window with my nose pressed up against it. I could almost touch it… Pain shot through my head, and I let it go with a frustrated "No."

Resignation tightened his face. "Then I'm afraid we're fucked."

Not the response I expected. Zev always had a plan, and since his experience with magic far outstripped mine, I'd gotten used to relying on that fact. That he was all but resigned to his fate now worried and pissed me off in equal parts. I fisted my hands as the urge to snap back rode me hard.

One thing at a time.

I reached deep for patience, which was in short supply, especially as the sense of time running out crept closer. "Yeah, well, I'm not in the mood to be fucked, so stop pouting and work with me."

His temper broke under my sarcastic tone and darkened his bruised face. "I'm telling you, there's no way to break the circle. I've tried."

"There has to be some way out of this."

"Good luck finding it."

"Dammit, Zev, knock it off. You know spell work better than I do. Help me figure out a way out of this mess."

"I'm not being a shit to be a shit, Rory," he bit back. "The last time almost killed me, so excuse me if I'm not all that excited to give it another go and leave you alone facing a demented, narcissistic egomaniac."

The depth of his rage and self-recrimination flayed me, making my heart bleed, even as I wondered about his uncharacteristic fatalism. It was so unlike the man I knew and loved. Zev wasn't the type to give up, and we'd been in plenty of situations where the odds were towering against us. Normally, thinking the worst was going to happen was my role, not his. Maybe whatever warped spell this was had also done a number on his emotional stability. If that was the case, I needed to get him out ASAP before that black hole swallowed him whole.

But first, I needed to find a way out of this circle the

Heretic had dumped me in. "That's not what I'm asking you to do, Zev. I just need help figuring out how to get around this crap before that dick returns."

He dropped his head and fisted his hands. The movement caused the chain of his cuffs to wink underneath the overhead light.

The unusual glimmer caught my attention. "Zev, are those cuffs spelled?"

He lifted one hand, pulling the links tight, and twisted his wrist. The chain rotated, and sure enough, that glimmer came back, along with markings etched along the metal. "Yeah."

My heart cracked under the weight of resignation in that one word as understanding struck. Even if I could break the containment circles, getting around whatever magic infused those cuffs would be a whole other challenge, which he didn't think we could beat.

Well, fuck that.

Zev's abnormal attitude had to be the result of the magic binding him, which was even more reason to get us out of there. Since I wasn't ready to sit in my little circle of hell and wait for the Heretic to kill me or him, I got to my hands and knees and slowly crawled within the confines of the cast. Anger, frustration, and a healthy dose of dread kept me moving even as my already-abused skin tore on my knees and palms. I could see the carved runes that made up the cast and even recognized a couple, but the majority made no sense. I'd almost completed my circuit when Zev called my name. I turned back to him to see him watching me. "What?"

"How did you get here?"

I got off my hands and knees and sat facing him. Then, with studied casualness, I deliberately misinterpreted his question. "Teleport cast."

He pinned me with a hard stare. "Figured that out when you popped in here, babe. How'd he get you in a trap in the first place?"

Okay, this was not where I really wanted our conversation to go. "I was on a run for the Council."

"I thought you were with Sabella at Max's memorial?"

"I was, then I got cornered at the funeral by Mateo and Olivia. They needed a driver for an antiques appraiser."

Zev wasn't a fool, and I knew he was putting even those few pieces together and filling in the blanks like a damn Jeopardy champ.

"An antiques appraiser?" he repeated in a careful tone.

I'll take "doing stupid shit" for two hundred, Alex. I tried not to wince. "Um, yeah. Her name was Piper McMillan." I hurried on as recognition flared in his dark eyes. Clearly, he knew Piper's real occupation. "Mateo and Olivia wanted her to authenticate a stone held by the Blessed Amrita, so they asked me to take her to the appointment."

"Did they now." There was a dangerous purr to Zev's voice that warned me he was far from happy about this request. He looked down at his hands as he flexed them. "And you just agreed?"

Tension filled the space between us and pricked my professional pride. "As Mari often reminds me, I did sign a contract with the Council."

At that reminder, he looked up and met my gaze. A world of temper stormed in the depths, making it hard to hold, but I managed. "And Sabella?" He all but growled. "She was okay with you taking this job?"

"She wasn't exactly thrilled."

That earned a twist of lips, but there was no amusement in it. "I'm sure."

"I did try to call you," I reminded him in a quiet voice. "Many times."

A muscle in his jaw worked, but he bit out, "What happened?"

"Ms. McMillan managed to authenticate the stone, but

Amrita wasn't keen about turning it over to the Council. So things got a little tricky." *Understatement of the year.*

Something must have shown on my face, because his attention sharpened. "How tricky?"

"Well, let's just say that Amrita will no longer stand in the Council's way."

"And this stone?"

"It's safe," I hedged, feeling the weight of it in my pocket.

He studied me, clearly wanting to get into details. However, this was not the place or the time. "And where is Ms. McMillan now?"

"On her way back to Phoenix." Getting reinforcements, I hoped.

Despite the myriad of bruises around his face, he still managed to narrow his eyes. "Is that your way of telling me no one knows you're here?"

I looked away, using the pretense of studying the circles as my excuse not to meet his gaze. "I'm sure someone's either on their way or soon will be, but it's not like we can just sit and wait."

"What do you mean 'or soon will be'?" An underlying threat in his voice made me squirm. When I didn't say anything and continued to avoid his gaze, he demanded, "Rory, what did you do?"

Defensive, I snapped, "I did what was necessary."

His voice went arctic as he bit out, "What. Did. You. Do?"

"Leave it, Zev." I knew he wouldn't, but I didn't dare tell him the truth, not without knowing, beyond a shadow of a doubt, that we were alone. I couldn't risk it.

The man was beyond stubborn. "Rory, what the fuck did you do?"

Knowing he wouldn't let it go, I blurted out, "I made a trade."

There was a significant pause, and I swore the temperature in the room dropped a few degrees.

"For the love of all that's holy, tell me you didn't," he demanded, his voice a harsh whip of censure. "Tell me you did not bring him the stone."

I stayed silent, my heart beating hard as I braced.

"Are you fucking kidding me?" Like an avalanche gaining steam, his voice started low and cold and rose to a roar. "Why the fuck would you do that?"

"Because I'm not willing to lose you!" I yelled back, holding his furious gaze with mine. "I won't sacrifice you for some stupid relic."

NINETEEN

"DAMMIT, RORY!" A vein popped alongside Zev's temple as he stared at me, fury in every abused line of his face.

"Don't, Zev," I warned, seeing he was biting back words—words I knew would cause lasting damage if he let them loose. "Don't you dare."

Whatever he heard in my voice had him looking away as he visibly fought to rein in his temper. His torn-up chest rose and fell with his rough breaths. When he finally looked at me, his dark eyes burned with banked emotions, and his voice was a low whip of reprimand. "That wasn't your choice to make."

"Wasn't it?" I shot back.

He growled, the sound a rumble of anger and frustration. "The Council will not forgive this."

Wasn't the Council I was worried about. "I know."

Zev and I stared at each other, both of us pissed but each for entirely different reasons. Me because the dumbass should know me well enough to trust my judgment. Him because he was a thick-headed idiot who thought he knew everything and had no problem jumping to the totally wrong conclusions.

"You can't give it to him."

Since, in this case, he was wrong, I stayed silent and held his gaze. It wasn't easy, especially when disappointment joined his fury. It hurt, having that directed at me, and it hurt even more when he muttered a curse and looked away. He shoved his emotions behind a mask, leaving me feeling more alone than ever. "Zev—"

"Don't," he bit out as he turned back. "Look, I get it. There's no good move here, but you can't give him the stone, Rory. That kind of power in his hands…" He shook his head. "It's not worth it."

"You are not expendable, Zev. Not to me."

Something flashed through his face, but it was gone before I could decipher it. "Neither are you." His gaze locked with mine. "You go through with this, you know what that will do? What that means?"

I knew he wasn't talking about the Heretic or the Council but us.

He didn't wait for my answer, not that I had one, and kept laying me out. "You hand it over and we get out of this, the Council will sic a Hunter on your ass. Want to take a guess at which Hunter they'll use to hunt you?"

Oh, I knew the Council would come after me, but not for the reasons Zev believed. The fact I was handing over a false relic might salvage a couple of brownie points, but the simple fact that I would defy the Council, in principle if not deed, would require they make me an example. I had hope that because of my ties to Sabella that the example would be marginally less painful, but honestly, once I'd seen the images of Zev, my decision was made. That didn't mean there wasn't a resentful little demon fuming in my heart that wouldn't allow me to stay quiet, because I was a glutton for punishment.

So even though I didn't want to ask, I did. "And you would hunt me?"

He grimaced as emotions tore through his expression, but I was watching him so closely, I saw his answer, and my heart broke. Was there a small part of me that wished Zev would choose me above all others without hesitation? Of course, because I was in love with him, and I knew he was in love with me. I was also realistic, though. This wasn't some fairy tale love story. It was very real and very messy, and there were no easy answers to be had, not when he was held fast by multiple bonds of love and loyalty, some of which did not belong to me. I opened my mouth to cut him off before he could say it out loud and make it irrevocably real, but I didn't get a chance as another voice joined our conversation.

"Oh, this is too perfect." A man stepped out of the shadows by the far wall, doing a slow, condescending clap. His gaze swept over both of us.

Despite my battered body and aching head, I scrambled backward like a drunken crab. My Prism pulsed, and I winced as I put a good foot between me and the circle's edge before I stopped. That shocked burst of instinctual magic hurt, and my heart was doing its best to beat its way out of my chest. Across from me, Zev, who after an initial jerk that rattled the chains holding him, stilled and stared at the man with the intensity of a wolf preparing to attack.

The stranger's attention stayed on Zev, and a silky menace replaced his mocking disdain. "It almost makes me want to risk letting you live, Aslanov, just to see how twisted up the Council can get you. But, alas, I have other plans for you." Done taunting Zev, he turned my way and gave me a smile that sent a shiver down my spine. "Rory Costas, Arcane Transporter, Secure Delivery for your Arcane Needs, right?"

Even though there were no images of the Heretic, I knew who we faced. A couple inches under six feet, he was older than I expected. I'd thought he would be in his late twenties, maybe early thirties, probably because the one time he had been caught on a security camera, he'd been wearing a hoodie and hanging at a computer café frequented by the college-age crowd. But going by the lines in his face and the strands of gray just starting to touch his brown hair, he was likely closer to forty. If I didn't know what a monster he was, he might have been considered attractive in a haughty, mature sort of way. He was well put together, wearing dress slacks, a collared shirt, spiffy shoes, and an aura of self-possession that could easily fool people into believing he was a good guy. That was until they looked into his eyes. That was where the real Heretic lived—cold, calculating, and merciless.

Those soulless orbs continued to study me despite my silence. Then he smiled, and it sent a shiver down my spine. "So lovely to have you join us."

"How could I refuse?" It sucked that when fear took the lead, because my mouth gained an attitude, but there it was. I settled on my ass, gingerly brushed off my scraped palms, and folded my legs. Best to get comfortable since I wasn't going anywhere anytime soon.

A flicker of something—interest maybe—lit his eyes, and his smile downgraded to amusement. "I believe you have something for me?"

I shifted my weight to my sore hip, reached into my pocket, and pulled out the stone. "You mean this?" I resisted the urge to look to Zev and did my best to ignore the weight of his recrimination.

The Heretic froze for a moment. His attention riveted to the stone as I held it with both hands in my lap. When he raised his gaze, it carried a keen light. "You surprise me."

I tilted my head in silent question, wondering what it would take to get him to step into the circle so I could physically take him down. It was a long shot, but a long shot was better than no shot.

Correctly reading my nonverbal cue, he said, "I'll admit, at first, I wasn't sure you'd come through. Even with my… incentive." He waved a hand in Zev's direction.

Keeping his attention on me was uncomfortable, but if it drew him in, I would suffer through it. So I focused on something he said and repeated, "At first?"

"Mm-hmm." He strode closer and stopped just shy of the circle's edge.

Clever bastard.

He dropped into a crouch, which put us at eye level. "When I realized who you were, I did a little research. Which is kind of my thing, you know."

His inherent arrogance galled the hell out of me, but I didn't break eye contact. Instead, I held his gaze and tried to ignore the deep chill that set up shop in my bones. "I'm not sure there's all that much out there about me, since I'm not that interesting."

"Oh, don't be so humble, Rory." He braced his arms on his knees and cocked his head. "You don't mind if I call you Rory, do you?" He didn't wait for my response but kept talking because he obviously liked the sound of his voice. "I was quite impressed with your online reviews, especially since you've only been in business for—what? A year, maybe? But still, you've managed to create quite the reputation for exceptional customer service. Considering who your clientele are, I wasn't sure I'd be able to get you to agree to my request, but then there were your voicemails to Aslanov."

The ache in my head, exasperated by nerves and dread, made it a challenge, but I tried to recall the messages I'd left Zev. I'd done my best to keep them short and sweet because he was working. Realization struck, and I winced because it wasn't the messages themselves but the simple fact that I'd left them that had clued this asshole in to Zev's importance to me.

The Heretic's chuckle wasn't about amusement but a sadistic kind of enjoyment. "I see you figured it out. Though I'm not quite sure how someone like him was able to gain such devotion, at least it gave me the leverage I required to get what I wanted." Without rising, he pivoted on the balls of his feet so he could face Zev, who was glaring at him as if he could set the Heretic on fire by will alone. "Normally, you'd be the last person I'd agree with, Aslanov, but I have to admit —the Council will not be happy with her, or you." His grin widened until it was a baring of teeth as he looked between us. "Which, of course, makes me absolutely ecstatic."

When Zev continued to watch him without uttering a word, the Heretic turned back to me. "You know, considering things are about to go very, very sideways for you, you might want to reconsider your career options."

Is this guy for real? "Are you offering me a job?"

"Would you take it if I did?" He seemed genuinely curious.

I really didn't have to think about my response. "I don't think I'd like your benefits package."

"That's too bad." He stood up and brushed out his pants. "Since it seems the Council's severance package can be quite brutal." He studied me for a long moment.

It took everything I had not to look away, but my fingers tightened on the stone. It was like looking into an endless pit —cold, empty, and pitiless. I didn't dare move. Hell, I was barely breathing. I had no idea what he was looking for, but whatever it was, I prayed to anyone listening that he wouldn't find it. Finally, unable to take it, I snapped, "What?"

"I don't see it."

Even though my common sense screamed to shut the hell up, I asked, "See what?"

He waved a hand in the direction of my face. "The family resemblance."

Not following, I frowned. "What resemblance?"

"Don't be insulting, Rory." He looked down his nose at me. "According to my sources, you're related to Sabella Rossi, but she's"—he gave another wave of his hand, this one accompanied by a sneer—"and you're you."

My lip wanted to curl, but I didn't need Zev's slight head shake of warning to check it. I could only get away with so much, and I had a feeling I was closing in on that limit.

Not done with his disparaging assessment, he continued. "And a Transporter, no less. Not that I'm denigrating your profession, but I'm curious. How have you managed to wiggle your way into the upper echelons?"

"Luck?"

He chuffed. "Please, you know there's no such thing as luck." He motioned over his shoulder with his thumb at Zev. "Just ask your boy toy over there. He thought luck was with him when he stumbled onto my inquiries with the Blessed Amrita. It didn't take long for him to realize luck had nothing to do with it."

"No, that wasn't luck." Zev's tone was acerbic and mocking. "That was you being sloppy."

Clearly, Zev was done with the silent treatment.

The Heretic turned to Zev and folded his arms over his chest. "Sloppy? I'm not the one who informed dear old Matt and Ollie that I was interested in the Court Stone. That was you, taking the bait and making sure the Council retrieved it for me."

"As I said," Zev drawled. "Sloppy."

Since I tended to agree with Zev's assessment, I decided to keep the narcissistic mage talking. "Why not just take the stone yourself?" Maybe if we kept him distracted long enough, the stars would align, and Lena would manage to track my ass so Piper could make an appearance. Or, even better, Zev could pull a unicorn out of his ass and get us out of these damn circles. Hell, I would even take Amrita's pet demon showing up and providing a distraction.

Zev snorted. "He tried that. She told him to fuck off and made it stick."

Happy Zev was joining the game instead of sitting there like a dark thunder cloud of judgment, I caught the conversational ball he tossed me as color rose under the Heretic's skin. "Did she trap him in one of her illusions? Because that, I could understand."

"She was that good?" Zev asked, as if the Heretic weren't standing there glowering at both of us now.

"Yeah, she was."

"Huh, she should've stuck with that," he said. "Instead, she set him up."

Wow, Amrita really thought highly of herself, because I couldn't see the Heretic walking away without retaliating in a big way. "Really?"

"Really." Zev rested his head against the wall, bent his legs, and rested his cuffs on his knees. "He tried to turn one of her followers against her, but they double-crossed him."

I absently rolled the stone between my hands. "I bet it was Caleb." I looked at the Heretic, who was not amused by our little comedy routine if his dark scowl was any indication. "Was it Caleb? Or did Amrita try to feed you to her pet demon?"

Strangely, he didn't call us out on our back-and-forth. Instead, he actually answered my question as if we were having a conversation at a dinner party. "She tried, but I wouldn't be where I am today without mastering the fine art of negotiation."

"What did you offer her?"

"After I made it painfully clear to her that I wasn't on the menu, I pointed out the precarious position she'd find herself in if I made the demon a better offer."

"That's all it took?" That kind of threat didn't seem like something the delusional Illusionist would brush off.

His smile made my skin crawl. "She and her demon share an interesting trait. They're all about their own interests and self-benefits." He cast a sly glance at Zev. "Unlike Aslanov here." Then that creepy gaze came back to me, pinning me in place. "And you, it seems. I'm curious: how did you and the other one escape her pet?"

That snark in the face of death took control of my mouth. "We ran really, really fast."

A laugh burst free before he shook his head in a resigned sort of way. "You know, in any other circumstances, I might like you."

In any other circumstances, I would want to sink a knife into his black heart. *Oh wait, I still want to do that.*

His amusement faded as he began walking around the edge of my circle. "The woman with you. Who was she?"

Since I didn't trust him, I kept an eye on his movements. "According to Councilman Medina, she's an antiques appraiser."

He stopped, faced me, and raised an eyebrow. "An appraiser? Really?" He shook his head, took something out of his pocket, and sank once more into a crouch. "I would've thought you'd be more selective in the jobs you took, Ms. Costas." He tipped a small glass bottle and began to pour what appeared to be water into the etched line of the circle.

Power brushed over my skin, setting my teeth on edge. *Not good.*

Oblivious to my reaction, he continued. "That woman isn't an appraiser." He stopped what he was doing and gave me a look. "Correction, she's not just an appraiser." He went back to what he was doing as he directed the next to Zev. "But I bet you know that, don't you, Aslanov?"

Zev didn't answer. His attention remained locked on the Heretic and his movements, but a muscle in his jaw flexed.

Undaunted, the Heretic continued around my circle, moving farther away from Zev. With each drop that filled the lines, the power tightened. "Not that it matters, I guess." He finished emptying the bottle and rose to his feet. "There, that should do it."

I sat there, mesmerized as the clear liquid tumbled along

the circle's lines, more than could logically fit in that tiny container, but then, magic wasn't about logic. The liquid picked up speed and turned milky as it raced through the circle and spilled into the sigils that crafted whatever spell was in place.

As soon as the last marking filled, invisible chains snapped closed on my wrists, yanking me up to my feet with an agonizing suddenness that left me gasping for breath and sent the stone tumbling to the ground.

TWENTY

CAUGHT IN THE MAGICAL TRAP, I twisted and turned, snarling in fury as more bindings wrapped around me, trussing me up like a damn turkey. The bindings tightened, cutting into my skin deep enough to leave welts. The Heretic flicked his fingers. The bindings clamped on my limbs and hauled me into midair like a real-life Michelangelo's Vitruvian Man, sending agony arrowing through my shoulders and hips. The rattle of chains barely penetrated as tears burned my eyes, but I refused to let them fall.

"The more you struggle, the worse it gets," the Heretic said as he watched me fight the spell.

"Asshole," I hissed, trying to subdue my instincts to escape.

"Yes, I am," he agreed cheerfully. "But I'm also not an idiot."

He made another motion, one I couldn't follow, and the magic shifted. The pressure wrapped around my arms and legs increased slowly until dislocation became a real fear. My spine bowed, and I locked my scream behind clenched teeth. I couldn't see what he did next, but I sure as hell didn't miss the fact that he was walking into the circle straight toward me and, worse, the stone.

There was an enraged growl coming from somewhere, then I heard Zev. "Stop! You're going to tear her apart."

I lost my battle with tears. They broke free and spilled down my face as a groan squeezed through my clenched jaws.

"Please," the Heretic scoffed as he bent to retrieve the stone. "I just want to make sure she won't try anything stupid." But the pressure on my limbs eased fractionally. He straightened, the stone held between his fingers as he raised it. A bright light flicked into life, throwing stark shadows through the room.

Panting, vision blurred, I blinked away the betraying wetness until I could make out what he was doing.

He rotated the stone slowly under that vivid light, his eyes narrowed as he clearly searched for something. Whatever he was looking for, he must have found, because the lines in his face smoothed away. Then his lips curved with satisfaction. "There it is."

The light winked out, leaving me blinking away tiny white dots. "There what is?" My question came out hoarse, but understandable.

"The mark I left on the Court Stone." The Heretic moved to stand directly in front of me. "To ensure you brought me the right one."

His words ricocheted through my brain and sent fissures snaking through my confidence. For a moment, I questioned if I'd swapped out the correct stone.

Stop, Rory. No way would Amrita have left him alone long enough to mark the real deal.

Despite my harsh self-reminder, trepidation vied with the pain. "What do you mean, the right one? There was only one stone."

"Was there?" he mocked. "Amrita was very attached to

her illusions. Unnaturally so." He closed the stone in his fist and shook it in my face. "I had to make sure she and, by happy coincidence, now you, couldn't fuck me over."

His smarmy insolence just pissed me off, and without realizing it, I jerked against the bindings, hissing as they yanked me back.

"Temper, temper," he chided before walking away.

Once he was back outside the circle, he released the bindings, and I crashed to the ground. My feet hit first. The impact was jarring, sending me to my knees. I barely caught myself on my hands, but even so, I still bit my tongue deep enough for it to bleed. The drop revived the ache in my head with a vengeance. All I wanted to do was curl into a ball. Instead, I managed to spit out the coppery taste of blood, then I carefully sat back on my heels, sucking in deep, harsh breaths. My vision was a mess—blurry one moment, pitching the next—but I could make out Zev's shape as he strained against his chains.

"Now then…" The Heretic's voice came from behind me, causing me to twitch.

I didn't dare turn to look. If I did, I might end up hurling or passing out. Neither result was particularly ideal.

"We have a couple more items to take care of."

I could hear dirt and gravel moving underfoot as the Heretic came around and stood between the two etched circles, the stone nowhere to be seen. "As entertaining as you two have been, I do have a schedule to keep. So this going to be a little rushed."

That was the only warning before he tossed something in the air and muttered a word I couldn't make out. Magic erupted like a Slinky let out of a can. It coiled up for a moment then spilled over, rushing through the etched runes and igniting the lines on the floor.

With my magic at an all-time low, all I could do was brace under the onslaught. Whatever curse he set in motion crawled under my skin and wrapped thorny vines into my veins. My vision whitened, leaving me blind, and time disappeared as I struggled to escape. His corrupted power dug through my magic like a horde of locusts, determined to devour every last drop, but desperation is a wonderful thing.

Somehow, I found a cache of power huddled deep inside, and being the stubborn bitch I was, I sank my will into it and threw the weight of both into my Prism. The additional power added a reinforcing layer and slowed the drain on my magic. It wouldn't hold forever, but it gave me the tiniest bit of breathing room.

I didn't know how long it was before I could make out the confines of wherever the hell the Heretic had stashed me and Zev, but I knew it had been a while. For one thing, I was sprawled on my back, and my aches had graduated to a whole new level.

Fuckin' great.

As much as I didn't want to, I forced my body to roll over. By the time I was on my stomach, I'd broken into a cold sweat. I pressed my damp forehead to the ground between my sore palms, barely registering the bite of grit against my sensitive skin. With a deep groan, I pushed up to my hands and knees, then I stayed there, weaving slowly from side to side. When the dirt underneath stopped rolling, I dared to lift my head.

"Shit!" It came out in a pained whisper as I spotted Zev, who appeared pinned against the wall, eyes closed, his face a twisted mask of agony. "Zev!"

No reaction.

Panic joined the rest of the emotional mess churning in my gut and added a sharpness to my demand. "Zev, look at me!" Despite the horrific role reversal and déjà vu, I kept hounding him until his eyes opened. Then I kind of wish they hadn't. I flinched under the storm of rage and torment staring back. The muscles along his arms, legs, and neck strained under the unseen restraints. Some of the cuts on his chest had reopened and were seeping blood. Sweat left streaks in the grime on his face, disappearing into his scruff. His lips were thin, his teeth bared, and it was obviously taking everything he had to endure.

I had no illusions about what the Heretic had set in motion with his twisted mess of spell work. If Zev and I were to have any chance of surviving this, I needed to act, and I needed to act now.

I dropped ungracefully to my ass, bending my knees to brace my elbows so I could hold my head in my hands. I closed my eyes and sank into that quickly dwindling reserve of will and magic. I shoved everything I had against that psychic door that allowed me to visualize active magic. When it barely budged, my desperation turned to fury. I shoved harder until something gave, and it cracked open enough to slip inside. Somewhere in the back of my brain, I knew I'd done damage of some kind, but that would be an issue for later.

In front of me glowed a knotted mesh of magic, but it wasn't the steady radiance I was used to. Instead, it was like looking at a decrepit power grid. Lights flickered here and there, lines appeared broken or fractured, and some areas did a slow strobe from painfully bright to barely-there spark. It was a nightmare.

How in the hell do I get through this?

A memory tapped my shoulder—an explanation Lena had shared when explaining how Keys navigated hexes. *"Think of your magical signature like a coat. Mages wear their magic in similar fashion, their specialties coming across in the fit and style. Damage to the magical coat generally indicates exposures to hexes."*

Using her example of magic coats made sense to me because my Prism acted like head-to-toe body armor. But for the majority of mages, their "coats" came in a variety of styles, each one customized to their family lineage. Although magic within the Arcane Families originated with their bloodlines, they were also will based. The stronger the will, the stronger the magic. This innate magic had three classifications: Elemental, Mystical, and Divine. Most fell under Elemental or Mystical, while Divine was rare. Then, based upon the type of magic wielded, mages were further arranged into types—like Air Mage, Combat Mage, Casting Mage, and so on. Within those were the specialties, such as Keys, Transporters, Nightmares, and Hunters.

Occasionally, there were outliers who were considered dual mages, those who could wield two dominant abilities, like me and Zev.

I had no clue what kind of mage the Heretic was, outside of pure dick, but I did know where Zev's abilities lay. As a Hunter and an animal mage, his predatory magic blended with his investigative skills, creating a highly lethal combat mage with a special affinity for all things creature and creature related.

Using Lena's advice, I ignored the matted mess of the Heretic's twisted spell and searched for the familiar pattern of Zev's magical coat. Panic was shredding the last bits of my composure when I finally caught a glimpse of it. The normally rich sapphire-blue glow was now a muted steel blue, but it at least remained mostly intact. Buried deep under a thick, dark heavy mass that resembled rusted vines, it was pitted with rips and frayed patches. Clearly, he was taking a magical beating.

With no particular skill or finesse, I imagined tearing my way through the jumbled weave, forcing it apart so I could get to Zev. Clearing the last briar-like layer cost me, and by the time I reached him, I felt as battered as his magic looked. With no time to rethink my decision, I grabbed his mangled power and pulled it close, forcing my Prism to stretch and reform to cover the additional magic. The minute the two powers touched, the vine-like spell redoubled its efforts, lashing at my Prism. It shuddered under the impacts but, thankfully, held. Knowing all I could do from here was hold on and endure, I huddled under my Prism's impenetrable mantle and safeguarded Zev's power.

I didn't know how long I remained inside that protective ball, but my awareness of the mortal world penetrated my dazed psyche in a slow drip. I was lying on my side, curled into the fetal position, with a direct line of sight to Zev, who was sprawled in his circle. A handful of inches separated us, but thanks to the magic still running through the etched lines, it could've been miles.

At least he wasn't pinned to the damn wall.

"Zev." I tried to call to him, but my voice didn't work, and my mouth simply shaped his name. A couple of hard swallows later, I had enough moisture to give it another shot. This time, I managed to croak, "Zev." For a never-ending moment, he didn't respond, but when I heard a soft groan, I tried again. "Zev, can you hear me?"

A part of me, nearly mindless with fear, pain, and fatigue, babbled that I sounded like that annoying cell phone commercial. I ignored that sliver of impending insanity and called his name again.

Finally, his long lashes lifted, revealing a foggy kind of awareness as he stared at me.

I held his gaze, relief a solid lump in my throat. "Hey, you."

Lines creased his brow, and he started to lift his head, only to wince and stop with a pained hiss.

"Yeah, I wouldn't recommend moving," I advised.

He resettled but kept his gaze locked with mine, and I was grateful to see that weird fog was clearing. He licked his cracked lips and asked, "What did you do?"

Since neither one of us was in any shape for a long explanation, I went with "Bought us some time."

"How?"

I managed a half-assed "Magic."

He huffed what I hoped was humor and closed his eyes.

Anxiety had me saying, "Hey, don't fall asleep on me, babe."

"I'm awake," he mumbled, and his lashes rose once more. "Heretic?"

"Gone." Then I thought about it. "I think."

We both lay there, staring at each other. I wasn't sure what he was going through, but holding my Prism in place for both of us was taking concentrated effort. The hex was relentless in its attempt to break through, and I was scared shitless I would lose my hold and kill us both. Needing a way out of my spiraling panic, I asked, "Any ideas on how to get out of this?"

"No." His gaze drifted over my face, and it was clear he was battling something.

Unable to watch, I let my eyes drift over the floors and walls. The dizzying mix of runes and sigils covering the ground were filled with that hazy white power. I visually traced the path of intertwined symbols that connected our two circles and realized it stretched toward the wall behind us. *Strange.*

As much as I didn't want to move, I really wanted to know where it led to. I put a hand to the ground, clenched my teeth, and pushed up so I could lift my head. That was when I spotted the stone sitting on top of what looked like an old wooden crate in the center of another, smaller symbol-infested circle that glowed with an ugly mix of iron-colored umber. "What the hell is that?"

"He's draining our magic to jump-start the stone."

My arm started to shake, so before I face-planted, I lay back down, unable to stop my bleak huff at Zev's answer. "Good luck with that."

"What?"

I avoided his gaze, hesitant to share the truth in case the

Heretic was lingering around somewhere, gleefully waiting for us to die. "Nothing," I mumbled.

Unfortunately, Zev wouldn't let it go. "Rory." My name came out on an honest-to-goodness growl.

Desperate to divert his attention, I asked, "How long do you think we have?"

"Enough for you to tell me what you're determined not to share." When I remained silent, he pressed. "Spill."

As much as I adored him, he could be a real dick sometimes. I glared at him and snapped, "Considering who our host is, I'd rather not."

"So there is something you're not telling me."

"There are many things I'm not telling you," I shot back.

Finally, he let it go, but I knew it was a temporary reprieve. The two of us fell quiet. I didn't know about Zev, but I was having trouble holding on to my thoughts. I was worried about my Prism shattering while I was trying to avoid panicking about how long we had left before the hex did its job and what would happen when the Heretic realized he was powering a dud.

"Is that the pendant Sabella gave you?" Zev's unexpected question broke through my chaotic mishmash of traumas.

I dipped my chin so I could see my necklace. Sure enough, the gold links that held the polished stone had slipped out of my T-shirt. "Yeah, it is." There was a faint pulse at the pendant's heart, and an idea flickered to life, sparking a firefly speck of hope.

Something must have shown in my face, because Zev asked, "What is it?"

I licked my dry lips and whispered, "Any chance one of your little partners in crime is lurking about?"

"I haven't had a chance to check."

"Can you? Now?"

"I can't access my magic," he reminded me, clearly not recognizing that he was now behind my Prism.

"Do me a favor and try." When he continued to look skeptical, I added, "Please."

He studied me for a long moment, then his eyes took on a weak glow and widened in surprise. His gaze, filled with questions, snapped to me.

I managed to shake my head in warning, and thankfully, he turned his attention back to connecting with any animal nearby. I wasn't expecting much. *Hell, I'd settle for a desert mouse at this point.* I just wanted something big enough to carry out the scrying stone, the same stone that held Lena's tracking spell. Maybe, once it was free of the circle, she would be able to pick up its signal.

Strain lined Zev's face and added a hint of gray to his battered features. I could feel him pulling on his magic, and it answered, like when a kid tried to suck a thick milkshake through a too-small straw. The attacking hex must have picked up some sort of signal, because suddenly, all those damn vines locked around my Prism and squeezed. On the magical plane, where he couldn't see, hairline cracks started to appear. Not willing to distract Zev, I brought my arms up to cover my face, as if to ward off a blow, but in actuality, it was so he couldn't see the tears of pain leaking from my eyes or the fact that I'd locked my agonized groans behind a clenched jaw.

I tried to seal the fractures, but the pressure from the hex was relentless. Just as little black spots danced around the edges of my vision, something with noticeable weight slid over my hips. I jerked and sucked in a sharp gasp.

"Easy," Zev warned.

I carefully moved my arms and found myself face-to-face with a snake. I froze, barely daring to breathe. The inhuman eyes were set in a black stripe above the rounded nose, and a distinctive dark-brown-and-tan pattern covered most of its body until it shifted into black stripes at its tail. The only thing that helped me not lose my shit was the lack of a signature rattle.

"Zev?" His name came out in a squeak.

"It's a bull snake," he said. "Give it the necklace."

Right, okay. Tearing myself away from the staring contest, I finally managed to undo the clasp even though my hands shook. "Okay, okay, we're good, aren't we, buddy?" I murmured as I gingerly wrapped the necklace around Zev's friend. It took a couple of loops and a bit of creative tucking, because it would do us no good if the necklace slid off during its ride. When I was done, I lifted my trembling hands and said, "It's on."

The snake's tongue flicked out once, then the snake pivoted and slithered across the floor. I watched, praying its movements wouldn't dislodge the pendant. Thankfully, my wrapping job seemed to hold, because it made it to a deeply shadowed edge of the wall and disappeared. Zev continued to pull on his magic for the next few minutes, and when he finally stopped, relief shuddered through me.

I worked on patching up the cracks in my Prism, an arduous task even though no new fissures appeared. The muted steel blue of Zev's magic had faded even more, but at least the hex's frantic pressure had eased off as well. It was still doing its best to bash through my shield, but it wasn't as rabid. That gave me time to work. By the time I finished, I was beyond exhausted, and my Prism had gained a fragile edge. I sank everything I was into reinforcing it, pitting my will against the Heretic's hex in a never-ending battle that I couldn't afford to lose. I prayed Lena would get the message and send help before it was too late.

TWENTY-ONE

I HUDDLED over Zev's magic, trying to make myself smaller as my Prism shrank even more. I dug through my bones and blood, deep into my soul, collecting whatever scraps of magic I could find to use it to fuel the protection that was slowly failing. I was so deep in my own mind that the aches and pains from my battered body were a distant memory. I wasn't sure I even had a body left at that point. My world was all about enduring the hellish bombardment of those vampiric vines.

At some point, I could hear Zev calling to me but couldn't afford to split my attention, and he eventually stopped trying. At least that was what the tiny bit of me that could still think hoped. Dark lines had snaked across the surface of my Prism and were irrevocably eroding through my shield. It didn't take a genius to understand that when they finally won, Zev and I would both lose. I stared dully at the deepest gouge and swore I could see venom actually eat away at the Prism, like watching, up close and personal, as acid eroded glass in slow motion. I reached for my power, wanting to reinforce that spot, but nothing answered. A spurt of alarm followed by a harsh whip of pain flared, but it was so far away, it barely made an impression. Automatically, I tried again, and this time, something whispered back. I gathered those final bits and cobbled them together. It took a bit to add it to the other patches, but I finally got it to hold.

Then I waited for the next crack to appear.

I drifted for a bit, losing track of what I was watching for, but a flicker of movement caught my eye. I blinked away the numbing haze and tried to focus. What I saw didn't compute. Bright blue-white seared through the muted tangle of vines that had become sickeningly familiar. It blazed through the mass, burning a path through as the coiling tendrils snapped out of its way.

What was that?

It rushed toward me, and survival instinct kicked in like a bitch. The resulting adrenaline rush shoved me back into the mortal realm with agonizing abruptness. The world reshaped around me in a dizzying rush complete with the deafening clamor of sound. Unable to do anything but squeeze my eyes shut, I rode out the chaotic current until it finally receded into something recognizable. A voice, specifically a voice yelling at me.

I dared to open my eyes. My vision swam then steadied. I was still lying on the ground, but I could no longer see Zev thanks to the eye-watering glare of a blue-white curtain of flames separating us. Horrific images tumbled through my mind, triggering a raging grief.

Zev!

His name came out on an intelligible grunt as I tried to push up but didn't get far. Still, I managed to inch toward the curtain. There was no logic to my movements, just pure desperation.

"Rory, dammit! Stop moving!"

I heard the words, but they didn't compute, not until they were repeated, this time with an unnerving bark of command. Recognition took a second to make its way to my brain. When it did, I looked around, seeing nothing but that unnatural flame, and croaked, "Piper?"

"Stop fucking moving, Rory, or I swear to god, I'll fry your ass." Her voice was a snarl of fury.

Shock and, even more scary, hope held me still. "Piper, is that really you?"

"Yeah, it's really me." The surrounding flames rose nearly to the ceiling then slowly began to draw back, revealing one very pissed-off Sentinel. Behind her, where there used to be a slab of metal, was a ragged hole, the edges torn and blackened as if someone had taken a blowtorch to it. Her attention wasn't on me but on the symbols covering the ground. Strangely, she had her phone out. "Right, what's next?"

Not quite sure what she was asking me, I frowned. "What?"

Her eyes came to me, a cold anger burning in their depths as she held up a hand in the age-old signal to shut up.

"Take me closer to your right," Lena said.

I blinked, and it took a moment to realize Lena's voice was coming through Piper's phone. Piper moved toward the stone and its surrounding circle.

"Can you find something that looks like two hourglasses hooked together?" There was an unmistakable urgency to Lena's tone.

"Hang on." Piper scanned the ground, inching around the symbols linking the stone to Zev and me. Then she stopped and angled the phone downward. "Like this?"

"Yeah, that's it. Now, see if you can find something that looks like a wide sloped mountain. It might have a broken line through it."

Piper studied the area around the stone and stretched out her arm over one of the sigils. "This one?"

"Perfect," Lena said. "You're going to have to force the magic in those two to separate, so you need to shift those two runes, so it breaks the connection between them. Turn the screen around so I can show you what I mean."

Piper turned the screen back and frowned down at whatever Lena showed her. "Got it. Which one do I start with?"

"The first one, here. See if you can erase the bottom marking, like this, then redirect it to the second one, like this, okay?"

"Got it. Okay, hang tight because this is going to be rough."

"Be careful you don't touch any of the other markings. I have no idea what might be buried in that thing."

"Yep, not in a hurry to blow myself up," Piper said. "I'm going to set my phone down so you can watch while I do this." Putting action to words, she grabbed what looked like a stone from the rubble around the metal slab, positioned it, then propped her phone against it. "Can you see it?"

"Yep."

Piper went back to the hex and crouched just outside of the circle that now carried her unique blue-white signature instead of the Heretic's darkly corroded milky one. A short rod of brilliant-blue fire appeared in her hand as power washed over me, raising the hair on my arms and nipping at my skin like burning embers. The magic deepened until it bled out her eyes like ghostly solar flares. She adjusted her grip, cracked her neck once on each side, then took a deep breath. "Right, chin up, tits out." With that incongruent comment, she set the tip of that rod to the ground.

I braced as magic slammed into me and wrenched open the psychic door, allowing a surge of blue-white flame to rush through and over the twisted vines that stretched across the mental landscape. The leading edge of the unearthly firestorm hit my Prism, and it shuddered under the impact. The magical wave crested, and I fought tooth and nail to keep the shield in place as worry skidded along my nerves. Sure enough, the magic hit a tipping point and tumbled down, the terrifying wave washing over my shield and over what lay beyond. Everything outside my protective barrier began to burn under the magical flood. Some of the thicker vines resisted, twisting and turning in a vain attempt to escape, but the fiery flood was relentless, eating away at them inch by inch.

A resounding crack echoed through my mental walls and jerked my attention upward. Just inches above my head, where my Prism curved around me, four thick vines, the same color as the spell siphoning our magic to the stone and the size of tree branches, undulated. They reared back, and I held my breath, unable to do anything but watch as they slammed into the top of the shield again. A fracture appeared, spidering out from the impact. More lines spread slowly, inexorably outward.

Inside my fragile dome, I fashioned a magical version of duct tape and slapped it up against the walls of my abused Prism, hoping it would hold. Magic was fueled by a mage's will, and right now, mine was scraping bottom. The vines continued to batter at my hasty bandages as if sensing just how close I was to buckling. I dug even deeper and balled Zev's magical coat deep into my stomach as I curled tighter, praying that whatever Piper was doing would kick the fuck in.

The vines reared back for another strike. Blue-white lightning erupted around them, striking the vines. Lines of white and blue ran deep within the vines, slowly burning from the inside out as the external hits kept coming, faster and faster, brighter and brighter. The dark tendrils flailed under the attack even as they began to splinter from the inside out as Piper's magic snapped them into pieces.

When the last vine toppled and disappeared under the current of wild magic, I remembered to breathe. Piper's preternatural flood receded slowly, lapping at the edges of my Prism. When it pulled back completely, all that remained was the carnage of broken magic, like the charred aftermath of a forest fire. The vines were blackened, burnt, and broken. No sign of the Heretic's power lingered. Even as I watched, some remnants crumbled to a dust-like layer, but under the detritus was movement. Things shifted and reformed. This time, though, there was no more ugly mix of umber and iron. Instead, it was shades of orange and red, with hints of luminescent blue.

Piper's colors.

Bit by bit, the spell around me reshaped as the lines regrew, sluggish at first, but reclaiming ground. Instead of thorny vines, they resemble cords that stretched toward Zev and me, but they couldn't find purchase on my shield.

"Rory, whatever the hell you're doing, knock it off." Piper's strained voice echoed around me.

Still in shock over what I'd witnessed, it took a long second to shift my awareness back to the real world, where Piper, now on her knees, face pale, sweat dampening her hair, scowled at me. The unearthly glow in her eyes was back to a simple flame, no tears in sight.

My brain stumbled, but I finally managed, "What?"

"If you don't let me in, you and Zev are going to die. So stop fucking around."

Holding that angry gaze, I bit back the urge to snap at her and instead called out, "Lena?"

As my best friend, she knew exactly what my question was and said, "Do it now, or it will be too late."

Heeding the urgency in her voice, I let go of my hold on my Prism, but nothing happened. I frowned.

"Hurry up, Rory," Piper bit out with a hint of desperation. "I can't hold this forever."

"I'm trying," I shot back, trying to ignore my rising alarm. I tried again, forcing my magical hold to uncurl from its death grip. It hurt. Like holding too tightly for too long. My Prism wavered then slowly shattered in a silent rain.

Piper's ribbons didn't wait. They struck, wrapping wherever they could touch, lighting up every nerve ending. I felt as if I were being burnt alive. Agony seared across my brain and soul, and somewhere, someone let out a pained shriek.

My spine arched as I clawed at the dirt, my mouth opened in a silent scream. A harsh, guttural yell from somewhere nearby echoed around me. My awareness wavered as darkness crowded in, but I couldn't afford to black out. I fought it back, and when my mind clicked back on, I was dry heaving. My head felt like it was going to explode as I lay on the ground, tears trickling into my hair. As irritating as that was, I didn't have the energy to brush them away. All I could do was lie there and stare up at the dangling light bulb that swung above me as I concentrated on breathing. It was the only movement I dared as voices and movement swirled around me.

"...burned away most of the hex," I heard Piper say, her voice rough.

"Good. That was the trickiest part. The next should go smoother," Lena said, all business. "But if the dick weasel set it up the way I think he did, the minute you break their containment circles, he'll know."

Piper made a noise somewhere between a derisive snort and a groan. "Of course he will, which means it's a fifty-fifty shot of him making an appearance or cutting his losses."

"He'll come back." That was Zev, his voice hoarse. "He wants that stone."

"No doubt, since he's got a major hard-on for you," Piper pointed out.

"And an even bigger one for that stone," Zev said.

Hearing him provided me the incentive to rejoin the living. I turned my head and hissed as pain slashed through my temples and down my neck then radiated through my spine.

Motherfucking ow! I clenched my teeth and slowly rolled to my side as the conversation continued.

"It's good to want things." That was Piper, who was now sitting on the ground.

Across from me, Zev was using the wall that anchored his chains to brace himself as he stood. Clearly, he was doing better than me.

How unfucking fair is that?

"We need to take him out." Zev turned until he could lean his back against the wall. His dark hair was a matted mess, his face pale and bruised. His eyes burned with a fierce light as he spoke to the Sentinel behind me. "If we don't, he'll switch targets."

Not keen about being the only one lying horizontal, I gritted my teeth and slowly, painfully pushed until I was sitting up. Piper was over to my left, no hint of her earlier friendliness in sight, and Zev glared at me from my right. Being caught between the two made me wish I were anywhere but there.

Yeah, yeah, I'm on everyone's shit list. Got it.

All my aches and pains were back, but this time, my bones felt brittle, especially my skull. A stiff wind would finish the job and shatter them into dust. Being so weak wasn't just scary; it was demoralizing. I didn't dare lift my hands from the ground because my balance was still for shit. And I could feel my torso slowly weaving from side to side as my head spun. I licked my dry lips and tasted wet copper.

I braced myself on one arm and swiped shaky fingers under my nose. They came away with a red smear. Staring at the blood on my fingertips, I knew it was a bad sign. I wiped the blood on my grimy pants then reached for my ear, just to check. Sure enough, I came back with blood.

Dread was a faint pulse, but I hurt too much to pay it

much attention. Logically, I knew what that blood meant, because I'd overextended my magic once before to save Sabella. Obviously, biting off more than I could chew was becoming a lethal habit. I discreetly wiped my fingers on my pants again.

Well shit.

With my magic beyond exhausted, I was nothing but a liability—which sucked big time.

Despite the obvious drain of using her magic to break the draining hex, Piper studied Zev, clearly thinking things through. "What are the chances he'll come back here instead of waiting for another opportunity?"

Zev eyed the remains of the metal door. "Considering your entry would be hard to ignore, I'm thinking they're on the high side."

"We need a plan," Piper said.

"He's a slippery bastard." That pearl of wisdom came from Lena and brought me back to the conversation happening around me. Both Zev and Piper ignored her.

"Can you help if he makes a reappearance?" Piper asked Zev.

He took a moment to consider it then said, "As a distraction."

"What about you?"

It took me a moment to realize she was talking to me. I didn't want to admit how bad things were with me, but not doing so in this situation would put Piper and Zev in danger. I swallowed and croaked, "I'm not even sure I can walk out of here, honestly."

"Fucking great." She pushed stiffly to her feet. "Since I'm not about to carry you, we should probably finish this." She started to move toward the containment circles, but Zev stopped her.

"First, you need to get the stone somewhere safe, where he can't get to it," he advised.

Piper gave him a puzzled look. "Trust me, it's out of the Heretic's reach."

Zev frowned as his attention went to the stone then returned to the frowning Sentinel. "What do you mean? It's right there, behind you."

Piper turned, picked up the stone, and held it in her palm, her voice careful. "You think this is the Court Stone?"

Inside his dark goatee, Zev's lips thinned as he looked between me and Piper. "It isn't?"

It was Piper's turn to look at me then back to Zev, her eyebrows rising. "Um, no, this is Amrita's fake. Otherwise, we wouldn't be talking right now because there would be no way for me to reverse that hex he set up." She slid an unreadable glance my way. "Not that the Council will care."

Ignoring the weight of Zev's gaze, I managed a shrug. "I'm sure they won't."

Piper studied me for a moment. Something close to pity flashed in her eyes before it disappeared as she shook her head. "You're a daft bitch. You know that, Rory?"

"Yeah, she's all about doing the unexpected." Lena broke in, reminding everyone she was still on the line. "Look, I'm sure there's a shit-ton of stuff to discuss, but unless you want to be caught with your pants down, I'd suggest we get things moving."

"Yeah, let's get this done." Piper put the fake stone in her pocket then flexed her fingers. "Right, so how do I get them out of this?"

TWENTY-TWO

AS LENA WALKED Piper through the steps to reverse the containment circles, I avoided Zev's gaze. I wasn't ready for this discussion or contemplating what lay in my future. I was fairly certain death was no longer an option. In the Council's eyes, that would be a mercy. Nope, whatever punishment they devised wouldn't be easily escaped, which left them with a smorgasbord of options. Hopefully, I would get time later to drive myself crazy trying to outthink the Arcane Council.

"Are you sure?" Piper's sharp question caught my attention.

"Considering what you hit in the last go-around, yes," Lena answered.

"Well, fuck a duck." Piper dragged a hand through her hair.

"What did I miss?" I asked.

"These circles he cast, they're hella difficult to break," Piper said as she studied the containment circles.

"And riddled with nasty surprises," Lena added.

Piper looked to the phone, her forehead furrowed with lines. "I didn't think he was a casting mage."

"He's not," Zev said before Lena could answer. "He's an information broker, which is worse, because anything can be bought for the right price."

"Like that damn teleport spell," I pointed out.

Lena said something particularly foul, while Piper's head snapped up, and she nailed me with a hard-eyed, narrow gaze. "Teleport spell? What teleport spell?"

Shit, right, kind of forgot to mention that part, didn't I?

I grimaced. "The one that dropped me here?"

Clearly, Piper questioned my mental stability, because she shot Zev a look. "Is she serious?"

"Unfortunately, yes," he confirmed grimly.

"You know, it would've been nice to know that earlier," she groused. "In case he decided to—I don't know—pop back in unexpectedly."

"We were a little busy not dying," I pointed out with an edge of sarcasm. "Besides, since he basically walked into the shadows and poofed as he gloated maniacally about his evil plan, I'm thinking your entrance screwed his return options."

"Which means it's likely he's already on his way back here," Zev added.

"Where is here, by the way?" I asked.

"You're about twenty miles from where you parked your car, in an abandoned homestead," Lena said. "Evan's monitoring the main road where you parked, but lucky for us, there's not much traffic on it."

"Any chance Evan can get eyes closer to us?" Zev asked.

"Um, no, because you're actually on First Nations land," she said then rushed to add, "The good news is that it appears there's just the one dirt road in and out to that place. I mean, Piper didn't spot anyone around when she came in."

"That's good news?" I wondered aloud.

"Considering we didn't have time to inform the head of the local force that we were coming in, yeah," Piper said.

"If they realize we're here, it's going to cause waves." Zev aimed his dour comment at Piper as he moved to the edge of the circle closest to mine.

She shrugged. "Yes, thank you, I'm aware. But considering Rory's friend all but threatened all sorts of nastiness, like messing with my credit score and putting deep fakes up on my socials, if I didn't help her *tout suite*, I made an executive decision."

I tiptoed around the ache in my head and decided to herd the room of cats back on track. "We can discuss the political ramifications later. For now, can we break these circles so we can get the hell out of here?"

"With the kind of magic this guy is throwing around, taking these circles down won't be like flipping a switch," Lena chided. "Piper has to basically unwind the binding cast of both circles at the same time."

That did not sound good. "You mean like trying to write with both hands?"

"Exactly like," Lena confirmed. "Plus, she won't be able to stop until it's completely undone, or all of you will be in a world of hurt."

"And Piper's not exactly firing on all cylinders right now," Piper added drolly. "Add that to the fact that Rory's got jack and shit to call on and Zev's running at less capacity than me, if the Heretic pops in, he's going to be a huge pain in our collective asses."

Zev rubbed the back of his neck. "Lena, what's your best guess on how long breaking the circles will take?"

"Fifteen, twenty minutes," she said. "Which goes back to my initial point—Piper's likely to trip at least one, if not more, nasty surprises. I mean, no offense, Piper, but the two you hit this last time did a number on you."

"No offense, and I'm aware," the Sentinel shot back. "But as we're out of options, let's get a move on."

Lena, once again, had Piper use the phone and walk around both circles, stopping now and then to go over some point. Meanwhile, I was struggling with a load of guilt because, as a Prism, my job was to be everyone's shield. When my skills were needed the most, though, I had no way to keep anyone safe.

"Got it." Piper picked up a fist-sized rock and dragged over the crate from the now-burnt-out circle, smearing the charred lines. When she took a position between the two circles, she put the crate in front of her, set the rock on top, then propped her phone against it. She asked Lena, "You good?"

"Yep."

Piper looked at Zev then me. "Ready?"

Both of us moved back to the centers of our respective circles and nodded.

Piper lit up once more like a human blowtorch and sank her magic into both circles. It was like igniting gunpowder. Her magic zipped along the outside rings of the circles, each one stopping at a different point before spilling into the runes and igniting the hex.

Once everything was lit, Lena directed, "Now, line up the foundational sigils."

Strain lined Piper's face, but her magic didn't falter. Instead, two long, fiery ribbons unraveled from both circles and leapt to her hands. Her muscles tightened as she gripped the ends and pulled.

That was when I realized the two ribbons were now sticks, and their ends, buried in the containment circles, were curved in a scarily scythe-like shape.

Magic shoved me backward as the circles began to rotate slowly, inch by inch. Minutes ticked by as, with Lena's verbal guidance, Piper continued to manipulate the two circles into alignment, her arms shaking with strain. With nothing to do but watch, I silently urged her to keep going.

"That's it, a little more. Okay, there! Stop!" Lena called out.

The circles stilled.

"Now comes the hard part."

Piper hissed, and I winced in sympathy. The Sentinel and the Key worked with focused urgency for what felt like forever but was probably closer to five minutes. Sweat had left wet stains under Piper's arms and down her front, but she kept going, and my respect for her grew.

Unfortunately, caught inside our respective traps, Zev and I were left to endure the push and pull of magic as Lena and Piper worked. It wasn't as painful as the first go-around, but the sensation of being constantly poked with sharp objects did take its toll.

"There, right there," Lena said with suppressed excitement. "Make that last mark, and the circles should snap."

Snap?

That was the last thought I managed before the world imploded and magic picked me up and tossed me through the air. My ears popped, my back slammed into something hard, then I was falling in a rain of dust and grit. My feet, then my knees hit the ground. When my palms hit, the impact sent jagged spears of pain from my wrist to my shoulders, but at least I didn't add another lump to my head. Instead, I tumbled over to my side with a grunt and a groan.

I took a second, or five, before I tried to move. At least this time, I hadn't lost consciousness, which was a small blessing. I pushed up and tried to find enough moisture to clear out my mouth. I coughed and spat until I was no longer chewing on grit. Dirt hung on my lashes and hair. I carefully shook my head, setting off a rain of dust and renewing the pounding in my head. New stings and twinges joined the old guard, and my arms shook under the onslaught.

"Rory? You—" Zev's voice was cut short by a hacking cough. "You okay?"

"I'm in one piece," I croaked, putting a hand to the nearby wall, and got to my feet. "You?"

"Same."

"Piper?" I called out, unable to see much through the dusty haze. When she didn't answer, I stumbled toward where I last saw her and tried again. "Piper?"

Through the thick curtain of dust-choked air came Zev's voice. "Over here."

Diffuse light danced with dust, turning my surroundings into a nebulous mystery. Orienting toward the light source, I stumbled forward, tripping over rocks and other unidentifiable debris. "Over where?"

"Here." His voice was closer and a little to my left.

I switched direction, took a couple of hesitant steps, and almost tripped over Piper. "Shit!"

She was on the ground on her side, facing Zev, who was kneeling next to her. I dropped behind her, put a hand on her shoulder, and looked at Zev, unsure what to do. "She okay?"

"She's breathing." He wore a mask of dust and dirt that probably matched mine. "Just knocked out, I think."

Seeing him from inches away, no chains in sight, it hit me. "It worked! The circles and your chains. They're gone."

"Yeah, they are." He reached for Piper. "We need to roll her over. Ready?"

I nodded then shifted my hands so I could help. "Was that supposed to happen?"

"I'm thinking no." He carefully nudged her to her back. "She likely tripped something."

I slowly let her weight settle against the ground, and she let out a soft groan without waking. "So, Lena was right, then."

I took in the smear of dark red under her nose and even more red matted in with her hair high on her forehead, and my worry sprang up. Her shirt was ripped up near the shoulder she'd landed on, and there was a tear along her pants below the knee. Concerned about injuries we couldn't see, I gently ran my hands over her and was relieved went nothing appeared to be broken, not even the fake stone, which was still in her pocket. "She took a hell of a hit."

"But she's alive," Zev said with grim practicality as he wiped his forearm over his forehead, smearing sweat with grime.

A faint breeze broke through the curtain of dust, and I sneezed. "Ow! Damn," I moaned, keeping my eyes closed until the resulting tilt-a-whirl stopped.

"Bless you."

I opened my eyes at Zev's absent statement.

He was looking back toward where the outside air was now fraying the curtain of dust and allowing sunlight to take its place. "We need to get out of here."

If I had to judge time by the angle of that shaft of light, I would put it at midafternoon. I turned my attention to what was around us.

"What are you looking for?"

"A way to carry her out," I said. "I don't think she's waking up anytime soon."

"I've got her."

I turned back and watched him shift into a squat without his usual grace. "Are you sure?"

"Yeah." He got an arm under her shoulders, then I helped position her knees over his other arm.

When he had her in a hold, I moved around to his side to offer whatever help I could as he struggled to his feet. After a few precarious moments, he was up with Piper's head against his shoulder, and he only swayed a little bit. For a second, I worried he would topple over. Luckily, he remained upright.

Face pale but determined, he said, "Ready?"

"After you."

He turned, and I went to follow, but something crunched under foot. I looked down and found Piper's cell. "Dammit."

Zev stopped and turned his head to look back at me. "What?"

I crouched, because bending over was not a good idea, and picked up the pieces of her phone. The shattered screen was dark, and the case was cracked and split, exposing the electronics. I straightened and showed him what was left of our lifeline. "We lost Lena."

"Not a surprise. That much blowback would fry any nearby electronics." He hitched Piper a little higher. "Come on. Let's move."

Not needing any further encouragement, I shoved the phone's pieces into a pocket and stuck close. His balance was off, from Piper's weight, his injuries, or both, and it made getting over the debris pile partially blocking the opening a challenge. There was a definite incline as we clambered up and, finally, out.

The afternoon light was piercing after the dimness of our cell, which didn't help my headache. I threw an arm up to hold it back as I narrowed my watering eyes and looked around. High-desert terrain stared back. Dried yellow grass spread across the yard and under the broken gray boards of what had once been a paddock fence. The yellow continued toward the rounded mountains lingering on the horizon. A scattering of ponderosa pine and some shorter, stockier trees I couldn't place broke up the space in between.

I turned back to where the Heretic had held us to find that Lena's word choice of *homestead* was wishful thinking. It was more like a shack with a hole dug into the ground. I had no idea if that addition was courtesy of the Heretic or just something he'd improvised upon. Either way, it was a cellar, like the ones found in the middle of the county. It also made for a daunting cage.

"There."

I turned toward where Zev had jerked his chin to see another structure. It looked like only two of the walls were still standing despite the gaps that had once held boards. The pitched roof was just a couple of charred beams, one strong wind away from collapse. The third wall was a weed-choked pile of old gray wood, and the fourth didn't even exist. Then I realized what had caught Zev's attention wasn't the falling-apart barn but what Piper had arrived in. Peeking out from behind the ruins was the hood of a car.

"Yes!" I started toward it, grateful we wouldn't be walking twenty miles back to town. Hell, I wasn't sure I would make it to the car. "Wait here," I told Zev. Then, without giving him a chance to respond, I did my best to hotfoot it to the vehicle. By the time I got there, my breathing was rough, as if I'd gone for a two-mile run, and my limbs picked up a tremor. None of that mattered because we had wheels.

It wasn't the BMW but a weird cross of station wagon and small SUV. I got to the driver's side and opened the door, which protested with a loud metallic shriek. I dropped into the driver's seat as I scanned the dash. There was a small screwdriver jammed in the ignition. It might not have been as inconspicuous as my wiring job, but it would work. A couple of jimmies later, the engine kicked over. I slammed the door closed, peered through the smeared windshield, and headed toward Zev. The ride was jarring since the vehicle wasn't exactly designed for four-wheeling and the shocks were definitely shot to hell. *At least it moved.*

Accompanied by a bunch of protests, some mechanical and some mine, I pulled to a stop near Zev and made sure the doors were unlocked.

I got out, went around, and opened the back passenger door. "Put Piper back here."

I moved back to the other side so I could help him get her

laid out along the back seat. Together, we got her in, and Zev used the middle seat restraint around her waist. Piper safely stowed, I got back behind the wheel as Zev folded himself into the passenger side. As soon as his door was shut, I hit the gas.

TWENTY-THREE

I GOT the mutant station wagon out of the yard and onto the dirt tracks that served as a road. As soon as the tires found hard-packed dirt, I sped up. Gravel spat from under the tires as we picked up speed, and the rutted dirt made the car rock in a way that sloshed my brain around, which didn't help the ache that had settled in for the duration.

In the passenger seat, Zev was going through the glove compartment. Napkins, straws, and what looked like an old, spiral-bound road atlas fell to the floor.

"What are you doing?"

"Looking to see if there's anything we can use."

"I don't think you'll find much." The car was too old for Bluetooth or any kind of wireless connection, as evidenced by the fact the stereo sported a CD player.

Who the hell owns CDs?

Undaunted, he continued his search, and more concerned about hauling ass, I left him to it. Between watching the sky ahead for any the tell-tale dust clouds of an approaching car, I checked on Piper via the rearview mirror.

Zev made a noise and pulled something out of the compartment.

"What?"

"Bingo."

I shot him a glance and caught the glint of metal and a black handle before I went back to driving. "Is that a hunting knife?"

"Tanto, actually," he corrected in an absent tone.

There was a blur of movement as he tested its weight with a couple of movements. One caused a pained hiss and a wince, then he shifted his grip and tried again. Whatever change he made appeared to work, because he slammed the compartment door closed and sat back with a satisfied air.

A spurt of amusement sparked. "Feel better?"

"Yep."

Boys and their toys.

The front passenger wheel hit a particularly deep rut, and the car bounced hard enough to slam my shoulder into the door. I bit back a curse and tightened my hold on the wheel. Not that it helped. We continued our teeth-rattling ride, and Zev grabbed the chicken handle as his body bounced off his window. From the back seat came a soft groan. He looked back to check on Piper.

Fighting the wheel, I didn't dare divert my attention. "She okay?"

"She's good." He twisted back around.

The front tires found solid surface once more, and the car's motion downgraded to jarring. "Do me a favor?" I flexed my fingers on the wheel, trying to release some tension. "Get your belt on."

His chuckle was soft, but he let go of the chicken handle and reached for his seat belt.

As he clicked it into place, I muttered, "Thanks."

"Welcome."

We rode in silence for a long moment. It wasn't uncomfortable, but it also wasn't easy. I didn't know what was on Zev's mind, but mine was darting around like a chipmunk on crack. There were things I wanted to say, maybe explain, but this wasn't the time or place. Maybe, when we got out of this, I would get a chance.

Not if the Council's waiting to haul you away.

I grimaced. Yeah, there was that little issue. Who knew what the powers that be would say or do. All I could hope was that Mari was a lawyer worth her hefty retainer fee. It would help if somehow, someway, the Heretic would be caught before I had to answer their questions, but that, too, was skating miracle territory. I had no doubt he knew Zev and I were out of his clutches, but I wasn't sure what reaction that would provoke. Either he would scuttle under a rock and wait for the next opportunity to strike, or he would storm back here, determined to erase his mistake. I wasn't sure which side I preferred he landed on, but I couldn't shake the anxiety that crawled along my spine. Nor could I stop myself from constantly checking our trail.

The fourth time I did it, Zev twisted in his seat to look behind us. "What's wrong?"

"We're leaving a trail," I pointed out unnecessarily. It wasn't like he couldn't see that for himself. We were in the middle of practically nowhere. The trees here were sparse and scattered, and the landscape this high up was fairly level. Then there was the hovering dust cloud caused by our aggressive passage, which was a neon arrow pointing directly to us.

"If Lena's assumption that this is the only road in or out is right, we're good."

"Until we're not." Despite Zev's apparent unconcern, I was a bit more pessimistic.

"What the hell?" The groggy question came from Piper.

My eyes went to the rearview again. In the back seat, the Sentinel had her hands to her head, her eyes screwed closed, and her knees drawn up, the closest she could come to the fetal position without the seat belt cutting her in half. One hand lifted, and she blinked slowly, her eyes dazed.

Some of my apprehension eased now that she was awake. "Hey, Piper." The tires found new ruts, and the car rocked, bringing my attention back to the road. "Welcome back."

Her response was a hissed, "Ow, dammit."

I winced, feeling for her. "Sorry about the ride."

"How are you feeling?" Zev asked, twisting so he could see her.

"Oh, just fucking dandy," she groused. "What happened?"

"What do you remember?"

There was a pause, then she said, "I got the last piece in place, and the world blew up."

"That about covers it," Zev said.

I heard the sound of the belt coming undone behind me. "I'd keep that on if I were you."

She ignored me, and more rustling sounds followed. When I dared to check the mirror again, she was sitting up. She met my gaze in the mirror, and when I deliberately looked to the shoulder belt then back to her, she huffed but gave in. "Fine."

I turned my attention forward, and a click sounded. "Happy now?"

"Very." At least this way, if we rolled, we might limp away. I did another scan of the passing scenery. I thought I caught something but wasn't sure. I eased up on the gas just a titch and leaned forward over the wheel.

"What is it?"

I didn't look at Zev but narrowed my eyes. "I don't know." The car bounced, the steering wheel knocking into my chest, and I pulled back. "Thought I saw something."

It was his turn to lean forward and scope out to our left. "I'm not seeing anything."

No amount of rolling my shoulders eased the knotted

muscles, but I still tried. "Maybe I'm just jumpy." I pressed back down on the gas, and the car gamely picked up speed again. Ahead of us, the dirt road started to arc in a broad curve.

"Where's my phone?"

I dared to take my hand off the wheel and shifted my weight so I could dig the pieces out of my pocket. I handed them back to her. "Here. Hope it's under warranty."

She made a disgruntled noise and took them from me. "Are you kidding me? I just got this."

"File a loss-replacement claim," Zev said as the car entered the curve.

"It'll be my fourth this year." Her tone was disgusted.

I lost track of their conversation when the road straightened once more, this time cutting between a patch of trees. Some bore scorched scars, probably from the summer wildfires that tended to terrorize this area. They were a bit more dense here, but I still caught a faint brown cloud a ways out but heading toward us. It weaved between the branches off to our left, where no road existed.

Wound up as I was, it wasn't skill but an instinct that had me hitting the brakes hard—something I knew better than to do. "Shit!"

The front wheels locked, throwing the car into a fishtail. Even as Zev's and Piper's curses filled the air, I kept my focus and put my foot back on the gas to accelerate—not much, just enough to shift the car's weight to the rear. I turned in to the skid until I regained control. Then I eased up but kept going, not willing to stop.

"What the hell, Rory?" That was Piper.

"Look." I pointed out the windshield.

Zev braced a hand on the dash and leaned in, trying to see. In a summation that was both grim and spot-on, he snarled, "Fuck!"

"Yeah, exactly." I picked up speed and listened to the

engine protest. Poor baby, it was probably used to puttering about, not redlining its way through the mountains.

"That's not a car." Piper was all business.

No, it wasn't, because a car would generate a bigger dust trail. "My guess, it's an ATV or dirt bike."

"You think it's him?"

"You don't?"

She grabbed my headrest, catching a few stray strands of my hair, as she leaned forward. "So why are you trying to get away? Car versus bike, car wins every time."

Not always, but instead of arguing, I pointed out, "Better question. If it is him, why would you go after a car on a bike or ATV?" That dust trail was definitely heading our way.

Clearly, Zev was following the same logic, because he bit off a curse. "Can you go faster?"

I wish. "Not without risking blowing the engine and one or more tires." And that would make things exponentially worse.

"Yeah, let's not do that." Piper pulled back without releasing her grip on the headrest.

Zev's hand fisted against the dash, his attention riveted on the incoming threat. "He's going to need a clear line of sight."

"How do you figure?" Piper asked, her tone just as grim as Zev's.

It was my turn to answer. "Because one, we can't outrun magic, and two, the minute he hits the road, he'll catch up."

"If we can't outrun him, then we need to do the unexpected."

I didn't have a clue what Zev was implying. "Like what?" I felt the moment Zev and Piper exchanged a look, clearly considering something above my pay grade. Not thrilled at being left out of the silent conversation, I snapped, "Like what, Zev?"

"We can't risk losing him," Piper pointed out, clearly talking to Zev.

He looked to her. "I know."

"Right, so…" She let go of the headrest. "Chicken then?"

I caught Zev's nod, and my stomach knotted as understanding struck. "Please, for all that's holy, tell me you're not considering what I think you are."

"You have another suggestion?" he asked. "She's right. We lose him now, gods only know when we'll be able to corner his ass. The Council wants him out of commission, no matter the cost."

Fuck the Council. Resentment simmered, but I managed to keep that sentiment locked behind gritted teeth. Barely.

"Rory."

The way he said my name, with a soft implacable edge, caused a lump in my throat, but I knew he wasn't going to back down.

"I've got barely enough magic to do damage, you're completely wiped out, and Piper's magic—"

"Isn't an option," she finished. "Zev's right—our only option is to do something unexpected." She paused. "What's more unexpected than playing chicken?"

I wanted to argue, to rail against the two stubborn asses in the car and remind them that we'd barely escaped our last encounter with the Heretic. It was a shit plan, but deep down, I knew they were right. We had to neutralize the threat any way we could.

I slammed my hands against the steering wheel and yelled, "Gods dammit! Fine! Fucking fine! Let's play."

TWENTY-FOUR

DECISION MADE, a tense silence filled the interior as the speedometer inched up in painful increments. I needed to put more distance between me and the Heretic. He was coming in at an angle. I couldn't risk taking the car off the road, so I needed to lure him onto it. To do that, I had to eke out more speed so it appeared as if we were getting away. I white-knuckled the wheel and chanted under my breath, "Come on, come on, just a little more."

The engine whined in protest, but bit by bit, I gained ground. It was easier for me since I was on a relatively straight shot, and he was having to zigzag across the rough terrain. Gravel pinged off the sides of the car as we barreled down the road.

In the passenger seat, Zev monitored the Heretic's progress by leaning over and practically ending up in my lap as he braced one hand on his seat back and the other on the dash, stretching his belt to its limit. My shoulder brushed his chest with every bounce of the car, and occasionally, his dark head obscured my view.

"Babe, pull back," I bit out. "I can't see."

He eased back. "Keep going," he urged. "He's falling behind."

"It's a bike," Piper confirmed. "He just passed through those trees over there."

I didn't dare take my eyes off the road. "Zev, find me somewhere I can get us turned around." The road was not only too narrow to handle anything less than a five-point turn but also sat a good half foot up from the forest floor. I needed a relatively flat area or a spot where the side grading wasn't so steep. "Piper, I need to know when you've got a clear visual." Because if she could see him, he could see us, and I might not get a chance to flip the car around.

"Got it."

We all fell quiet, each of us concentrating on our separate tasks. Time lost meaning. It could've been minutes or merely seconds before Zev leaned forward and pointed ahead. "How about there?"

I followed his finger and saw a relatively clear, flat space that appeared to be even with the road. *That'll work!*

I had opened my mouth to respond when Piper warned, "He's going to clear the tree line in about fifteen seconds."

I put the accelerator all the way to the floor and focused on my goal. The high-pitched whine of a dirt bike joined the protest of our ride's engine. Although my pulse picked up speed, my mind found that strangely clear state that was part innate magic, part instincts, and all of it unique to being a Transporter. The second I felt the tires hit the change in dirt, I angled into a controlled slide that lasted all of three beautiful, perfect seconds before magic slammed into the driver's-side rear panel, turning it into a nightmare.

An invisible force picked up the back end and flipped the car, tossing us like a two-ton quarter across the dirt road. The world spun in a dizzying rush as we went airborne for a long moment. The safety belt cut into my chest and shoulder, sending pain zinging along my collarbone as my arms went over my head in a lame attempt to protect my head. Then we hit the ground with bone-jarring force. An airbag slammed into my upraised arms, knocking me to the side. My head bounced off the headrest as my hip and shoulder bashed into the door and the world outside went sideways. There was a scream of metal shearing over gravel and the deafening crack of safety glass giving way as we slid over the road. We hit something then rolled one more time.

When the car finally rocked to a stop, the air was choked with dust, and harsh coughs filled the car. One was mine. Pinned by the safety belt, I punched weakly at the slowly deflating airbag with my left arm because lifting my right hurt like hell. My hips and knees felt battered, probably from hitting the dash and door, but after a couple of cautious tests, I was reassured that walking was still an option. My ears rang, and the powder from the airbag left me half blinded. My chest felt bruised, and my ribs ached, but at least they weren't broken.

A muffled curse came from nearby, and I croaked, "Zev?" I wasn't sure he'd heard me since I'd barely heard myself. I tried again. "Zev, Piper, you okay?" I carefully twisted in my seat, hissing at the resulting jolt, and realized that the car had landed upright. I looked at Zev and could make out his head hanging forward, his dark hair covering his face. I tried to reach out, but the belt held me back. "Zev?"

With a groan, Zev jerked in his seat then lifted his head. He reached up to his face.

"Hey, Zev, you good?" I tried to unlatch the belt, but it was stuck.

"I'm alive," he ground out as he turned to me.

I winced at the blood covering the lower half of his face. "Your nose."

He dabbed at it. "Not broken."

I thought he was being optimistic, but at least he was alive. "What about the rest of you?"

He wiggled, wincing here and there, but finally said, "Still attached."

"Piper?" I called back. "Piper, you okay?" I waited for her response, but it didn't come. Panicked, I tried to yank my belt off so I could see into the back. "Piper?" There was a frantic edge to my voice.

There was the sound of nylon snapping, and I caught the flash of a blade as Zev cut himself loose. Then he was using his legs to shove himself over the console as he twisted to check on Piper. "She's out but breathing."

Okay, okay, no one's dead. At least not yet.

The ringing in my ears was fading, and I could hear the radiator hissing and, even more worrisome, the rev of an incoming dirt bike. I peered through the myriad of cracks running through the windshield. The car was off to the side of the road at an angle, its hood pointed back in the direction of the shack with a view to what was headed our way. "Shit, shit, shit!"

Zev echoed my sentiments, but there was no time to fuck around. We reached for our doors. My fingers found the latch, and I leaned in to shove it open as a dark oath came from Zev. I turned. "What?"

"My door's stuck."

"So's my belt."

"Move your hand." He bent in and went to work on the belt. As soon as it snapped free, he slashed through the curtain airbag and tossed it aside.

I wasted no time shoving my door open and clambering out. I leaned against the car since my right arm was all but useless as I got out of Zev's way. He shoved his way across the console and crawled out of the driver's side. As soon as I could trust my legs, I went to open Piper's door. The handle gave but the door didn't. Setting my teeth, I gripped the handle in my left hand, angled toward the hood, and tried again. Nothing.

"Let me." Zev said, taking my place. After two sharp tugs, the door finally relented with a protesting shriek. He ripped through the airbag and ducked inside.

I took that moment to check where the Heretic was, because that engine sounded like it was almost on top of us. Sure enough, the bike was barreling toward us. I did a sort of stumble walk to the middle of the road with some vague idea of using myself as bait to keep his attention off Piper and the car. With no weapons, no magic, I did the only thing I could. "Zev!"

The next bit happened in slow, dreadful motion.

One moment, I was facing down the bike. The next, Zev was beside me. A stream of magic tore out of him and whipped toward the man on the bike. It hit the bike first, which came to an abrupt stop, the back wheel rising fast. The Heretic rode that bike like a bucking bronco to the apex, then he jumped. I had a momentary thought that it might all end in a few seconds before that foolish fantasy died a quick death. Somehow, the bastard managed to call on a wave of air and ride it like a surfboard out of the path of the tumbling bike.

What the actual fuck?

Stunned, all I could do was stare when his feet touched down, and he took a couple more steps then stopped.

"Fancy meeting you here, Aslanov," he called out as he stayed well out of reach. That soulless gaze came to me then went back to Zev. "You're both looking a little rough."

He waved his hand, and Zev grunted as magic sent him stumbling back.

I turned to go to Zev, but an invisible force shoved me back. I landed on my back, winded from the impact and the combined pain of every ache, cut, bruise, and broken bone. All of it coalesced into one breath-stealing moment. When I finally sucked in air, I heard the sound of gravel under foot then steps getting closer. After a heartbeat, then two, another pained grunt came from Zev. I rolled to my uninjured side, determined to get up and do—what, I didn't know, but lying around was definitely not it.

Zev landed on his knees nearby, and I stumbled toward him just as he flicked his wrist toward the Heretic, releasing the black-handled blade. It tumbled end over end, but the Heretic, slippery asshole that he was, managed to dive out of the way. But if the pained hiss was anything to go by, Zev had managed to score a hit. I didn't bother to look. My focus was on Zev, who was beyond pale, his face a contorted grimace, and blood leaked from his ears, nose, and eyes. I didn't know what spell the Heretic had used, but it was brutal.

I was almost within touching distance when I heard a distinct click. I spun around, and my heart stopped.

The Heretic had a gun pointed at Zev. "You've been a pain in my ass too damn long, Aslanov."

Undaunted, Zev stared back. "Right back at you, asshole."

"Fuck you, Aslanov!" The Heretic snarled as he recentered the gun.

I didn't think. I just acted. I dove forward as if I could stop the inevitable. At the same time, fire whipped around the Heretic's neck and tightened with brutal efficiency. Unfortunately, the bullet was already loose. I got to Zev just as the bullet got to me. It was like being punched. I stumbled under the impact and tripped over something. I thought it was Zev or my own feet. I felt myself fall and tried to catch myself, but my arms wouldn't cooperate. I swore someone called my name, but then pain bloomed bright and vicious, then nothing.

TWENTY-FIVE

"I THOUGHT you were going to choose yourself, dearest?" Couched in chiding endearment, Sabella's tone didn't fool me.

"In a roundabout way, I did," I assured my great-aunt. "I mean, I'm not on the Council's most-wanted list." *Just their shit list.* I didn't need to add that last part, because it was the reason for our current conversation.

"Was it worth it? Because from where I'm sitting, it appears as if you're paying a pretty steep price for doing the Council's bidding."

She wasn't wrong.

I'd been sent home from the hospital four very long days ago, and my magic was taking its sweet-ass time coming back online. The only reason I wasn't in a tailspin was because it *was* still there. Once I woke up from my involuntary two-day nap, Dr. Garcia, a Healer and friend of the Cordova Family, had read me the riot act for once again pushing my limits. "I don't know about worth it, but I'm pretty sure it's way better than the alternative."

Her sigh came through loud and clear over the phone, but thankfully, she let it go. For now. "How's your shoulder?"

Luckily for me, the Heretic was a shit shot when he was being choked by a rope of fire. His bullet had torn through muscle in my upper arm, missing anything vital. It was the broken collarbone from the rollover that was kicking my ass, along with the concussion. "Sore. The doctor says I've got at least another six weeks with the sling, then maybe double that for rehab."

That meant at least two long months before I could get back behind the wheel. Between medical and everyday bills, my savings account was going to take a hit. I shoved that away to worry over later, laid my head back against the couch, and closed my eyes. "When's your flight to Italy?"

"I haven't decided yet."

"Sabella—"

"Don't." She cut me off. "I'm not leaving until we hear back."

"You can't interfere."

"Can't I?"

"Okay, let me rephrase. Please don't."

"This is a farce."

Here we go.

Her voice took on an unforgiving edge. "You're the reason they no longer have to worry about the Heretic."

Not the only reason. If it hadn't been for Piper and Zev, Sabella would mostly likely be attending another funeral. "Stop. You and I both know they are justified in reviewing my actions."

"Why are you being so stubborn about this?"

I stifled my sigh. "It has nothing to do with being stubborn."

"Doesn't it?"

We'd gone over this before, and we always ended in a stalemate. It was time to put it to rest. "No, it has to do with taking responsibility. Good or bad, it was my choice to make, which makes it my consequence to carry."

She made a humpf sound. "It doesn't mean I have to like it."

Neither did I, but it was what it was. I just had to hope I could handle the fallout.

"Have you heard from Mari?"

"Not yet. She promised to call as soon as she heard."

"You'll let me know?"

"Of course."

We spent a few more minutes chatting about less stressful things then finally said our goodbyes.

I sat there, legs propped on the coffee table, eyes closed, head pillowed by the couch, listening to the quiet. I was finally alone since Lena was out spending time with her cuddle bunny, Evan. Thanks to the painkiller I'd taken earlier, I drifted for a bit. It was a nice respite from the near-constant worry that had dogged my heels since I opened my eyes in the hospital, which I couldn't remember getting to since I was down for the count, but Zev and Lena had filled in the blanks.

About the time I was making my dramatic move to save Zev, Piper had crawled out of the car and, despite seeing double, managed to lasso her magic around the Heretic. Her attempt couldn't stop the bullet, but it did throw off his aim. It also meant the Council didn't have to waste resources on a trial.

Meanwhile, Lena had called on reinforcements, in the form of her estranged family, to ride to our rescue. Since her father was a shaman in the First Nations, she had distant cousins she maintained contact with. In this case, it was enough contact to ask them to get to us without raising the alarm. From what she implied, it sounded like these cousins were all about bucking the rules, so they hadn't hesitated to get into their truck and haul ass to the coordinates she gave them, where they hit the scene shortly after everything went down.

At the hospital, Zev and Piper were treated for various injuries while they waited for me to wake up. Apparently, a person could only lose consciousness so many times before their brain decides to shut down. In my case, I'd lost forty-eight hours. According to Lena, Zev had sat next to me the entire time. He was also the reason I got to endure Dr. Garcia reading me the riot act. What I did remember was opening my eyes to see his dark head on the edge of my bed, his fingers tangled with mine, and relief sweeping through me that he was okay.

Then the real fun had started. Mari and Sabella showed up, both demanding details from me then from Zev. Somehow, Lena managed to slide out before they could turn their interrogation her way, which was a small blessing. Because she was a Guild employee, her involvement could get tricky as shit, which was why Zev and I tried to minimize her involvement as much as we could.

Hearing a knock, I blinked blearily at my ceiling. It came again, and my sluggish brain kicked in. Anxiety crawled through me, undoing the lovely buzz of the muscle relaxer. I carefully struggled out of the couch and made my way to the door as I called out, "I'm coming. Hang on."

I got to the door and opened it to find Zev on the other side. "Hey, you." I stepped back and held open the door.

"Hey," he said as he moved in, then closed the door behind him. He carefully pulled me into his arms, mindful of the sling, as his lips brushed over my forehead. "How are you doing?"

I let my head rest against his chest, avoiding the edge of a bandage under his shirt. "Hanging in there."

"Did you take a pain pill?" He herded us back to the couch.

"Yep."

"Good."

We settled in, Zev in the corner, legs sprawled, arm over

the back of the couch, and me next to him, using him as my pillow on my uninjured side.

"Heard anything?" His question rumbled under my ear.

Without lifting my head, I shook it, rubbing my cheek against his T-shirt and inhaling his comforting scent. "How did it go yesterday?"

It had been his turn to answer the Council's questions. The day before, it was mine, and Mari was the only one who'd been allowed to come in with me. There had been a bit of a scuffle about that decision, since she wasn't just a lawyer but also a Seeker. There was some discussion on the Council about a mage who could determine if a person was lying also acting as a witness's advocate. Whatever their concerns, Sabella had managed to address them, because in the end, Mari got to stay as my legal representative. I was very grateful for that, because even though I knew it was going to be rough—and it was—I had no doubt it could have gone much, much worse. Instead, I'd walked out emotionally and physically drained with no idea where the Council stood. And I'd passed Piper heading in as Mari and I headed out.

He dropped his hand to run his fingers gently through my hair. "About as expected. Did you see Piper?"

"Yep."

"And?" he asked when I didn't say anything more.

I sighed. "It was awkward at first, but I got a chance to apologize and thank her." The first had appeared to mollify her lingering anger; the second had amused her. "She was pretty cool about everything, considering."

He chuckled. "You sound surprised."

"Probably because I am."

"Why?"

That made me tilt my head up, which meant he stopped playing with my hair and instead cupped the back of my head. I rested my hand on his chest and took in the fading bruises and healing cuts, all visual reminders of something we'd avoided discussing. "Because I'm not so sure I'd be quite as forgiving in the same situation."

His lips curved with amusement, but his gaze held a watchful glint. "Do you need forgiveness?"

Guess it's time for that discussion.

I gave his question the serious consideration it deserved. My intentions were good, but what was that saying? *The road to hell is paved with good intentions.* I hadn't set out to hurt anyone. In fact, my decisions had been driven by a need to keep them—him—safe. That those same decisions aligned with the Council's needs was a lucky bonus, something I would admit only to myself, but never aloud. I didn't like lying, even by omission, to him or Piper, but especially him considering what was between us. But there hadn't been time to loop him in on my plans. Still, did I want absolution for my decisions?

"Yeah, I'm pretty sure I do."

"For what?"

"Lying to you. Deceiving Piper. Deceiving you." Considering how much it bothered me, it was worth mentioning twice.

He shifted his hold, cupping my face between his warm palms. "Babe, there is nothing to forgive you for."

"You were pissed."

I almost missed his wince when he nodded. "Yeah, I was, but not because of that."

I licked my lips. "Then why?"

His fingers tightened for a second then relaxed to brush absently along my cheek. "Because you deliberately put yourself in harm's way, and there was fuck all I could do to keep you safe."

As if his harsh admission were the key, his reaction suddenly made sense, and that vise that had locked around my heart for days loosened. I leaned up and pressed my lips to the scruff on his jaw. When I pulled back, it was my turn for some deep eye contact. "You know we're allowed to take turns keeping each other safe."

His lips twitched. "Yeah, I know."

My grin was small but bright. "But you don't like it, do you, Mr. Bad-Ass Protector."

"Shut up," he muttered before he covered my lips with his to ensure he made his point.

I let his kiss and his touch chase away the lingering strands of guilt, replacing them with an addicting, familiar comfort and heat. Before things could get too out of hand—well, as out of hand as possible when hampered by a sling—my phone buzzed.

We both pulled back and looked to the cell on the coffee table that now had Mari's name on the screen. That fast, the tension was back. I sat back and went to reach for it, only to hiss when that move jarred my shoulder.

Zev grabbed my free hand with his and leaned over to pick it up. I held his fingers in a death grip as he slid his thumb across the screen to answer and held the phone between us. "Mari, you've got both of us."

"Hello to you too," she said, her voice giving nothing away, but there was only one reason she would call.

"They made a decision." Nerves made my voice flat.

"They made a decision," she confirmed and didn't waste time laying it out. "You will forfeit any payment earned on this last assignment."

Ouch. Yep, saw that one coming.

"No financial penalties will be enacted."

A trickle of relief crept in, but she wasn't done.

"And your contract is on hold for a period not to exceed six months. During that time, you will not be permitted to work with Council assignments or utilize Council assets."

What, exactly, constitutes Council assets?

"At the end of your probationary period, your

professional performance will be reconsidered and your contract reevaluated for possible renewal or cancelation."

A mixed bag of reactions set in. Apprehension at losing access to seriously valuable resources that I couldn't afford on my own. A shade of resentment that the Council thought I needed to prove myself when I figured the results spoke for themselves. But the one that struck deepest? Relief that I wouldn't have to deal with the inherent danger that came with Council assignments for the next little while.

"Do you have any questions?"

I had a few, actually, but I was sure I would figure out more once everything sank in. "Not right now, but I'm sure that will change."

"You've got my number when they do," she said. "In the meantime, I'm couriering over the formal report. It requires your signature. Take your time, make sure you understand everything that's laid out, then get it back to me."

"Turnaround time?"

"Five business days."

"Will do." I wouldn't need that long. "Mari?"

"Yes?"

"Thank you." I knew she'd gone to bat for me, because with all that the Council could've done, this… this I could work with.

"You're welcome." She disconnected.

I turned to Zev, to find him watching me. "You okay?" he asked.

"Actually, yeah." I worried my lip then blurted out, "Are you considered a Council asset?"

His hold gently tightened as he dropped his head next to mine and buried his laugh in my neck. His lips brushed against my skin, setting off shivers. "Since they don't sign my paychecks on the regular, no."

"Good." It came out husky but definitely relieved.

"But the Guild…"

I winced because that meant keeping Lena and Evan clear of any jobs and going without the luxury of the Guild's menu of transport vehicles. "Yeah, that one will probably sting."

He pulled back, his gaze drifting over my face, studying me. "You good with the rest?"

I nodded. "I'll admit it's going to be a pain in my ass, but it's not going to stop me." Council resources tended to cost cake—cake it looked like I wouldn't have for a bit.

He cocked his head. "Is that relief I hear?"

I managed to stop my shrug before it happened and gave him a sheepish look. "Maybe? I mean, let's be real here. My biggest headaches have all come from Council-related jobs lately."

"True." He picked up my free hand and played with my fingers.

His touch, as innocent as it was, sent little flares of excitement through my blood. "It'd be nice to only worry about delayed packages or cleaning up magical frog spit." I loved his grin, but what I loved even more was that he was here, as a friend, as a partner, and as a lover, like he had been from the start. I wrapped my fingers around his wrist and brought his hand up so I could press a kiss against his palm.

A hint of red rode under his skin as he blinked at me. "What was that for?"

"Consider it an overdue thank-you."

His eyebrows rose. "For?"

"The alliance thing," I said, referring to his insistence back when we'd first met about the importance of cultivating alliances throughout the Families.

Understanding hit. "Ahh."

"If anything's going to keep me from going into the red, it'll be that."

"You'll probably lose a couple of them," he pointed out.

Them being families that toadied to the Council—

something the Cordova Family would never do, which was why Zev understood my decisions. "But not all."

"No, not all."

I dragged in a deep breath. "Right, I can deal with that. It just means it's going to take me longer to get to my finish line."

"You have enough to get you there?" he teased.

I hit his shoulder with a fist playfully. "Hey, now, there's enough business out there that has nothing to do with the Council, so I shouldn't starve."

"And then there's Sabella."

I gave a huff that was half amusement, half resignation, because there was no way my great-aunt would restrain herself from stepping in if needed. "There is that, but once she sees I'm fine, she'll back off."

There was a wicked glint in his eye as he drawled, "And you're determined to thumb your nose at the Council."

Determination swelled. *Oh, hell yeah, I was.* "Yeah, there's that."

"Then I guess there's only one thing left to do."

"What's that?"

"Strap in and get ready to ride."

Join Rory as seething Family hostilities and a stunning classic ride send her and Zev on a trip to Sin City in **TERMINAL DRIFT**. *Now available at your favorite bookseller!*

ARCANE TRANSPORTER

Go back to the beginning with Rory and Zev in this thrilling urban fantasy series!

Meet Rory Costas, Arcane Transporter, and strap in for a spellbinding ride through the Arcane world, where powerful magical families make the mafia look like choirboys and connections are everything.

GRAVE CARGO

When a questionable, but lucrative delivery job takes an unexpected turn, will Rory survive the collision or crash and burn?

RISKY GOODS

A dead mage, a missing friend, and an unpredictable alliance merge into a volatile package sending Rory careening through the Arcane elite's deadly secrets.

LETHAL CONTENTS

A failed assassination, a kidnapped ally, and a treasonous scheme pit Rory and Zev against a devious enemy determined to watch Arcane society crash and burn.

COLLSION COURSE

A last-minute Guild delivery, a cursed treasure, and a nefarious revenge scheme sets Rory on a collision course with one of Arcane's most wanted mages.

BLIND SPOT

A council contract, an obscure relic, and a lethal vendetta blindside Rory with dodgy ramifications and pitch her into a slippery tailspin.

TERMINAL DRIFT

Seething Family hostilities, a stunning classic car, and a last-minute trip to Sin City send Rory barreling towards a pivotal crossroad that will either put her in the driver's seat or hurtle her into oblivion.

ABOUT THE AUTHOR

"This story is an emotional roller coaster, from betrayal, anger, fear, love…" —InD'tale Magazine

Jami Gray is the coffee addicted, music junkie, Queen Nerd of her personal Geek Squad, Alpha Mom of the Fur Minxes, who writes to soothe the voices crammed in her head. Her series combine high-stakes urban fantasy and edgy paranormal romantic suspense into books you don't want to put down. Buckle up and get ready for a wild ride through the fascinating worlds of the Arcane, the Kyn, the PSY-IV Teams, and the Collapse.

Come visit Jami's website at **https://www.jamigray.com** and stay up to date on what kind of trouble she's getting into and when you can expect to join in.